The Talk of the Beau Monde

*Three unconventional sisters for
three infamous lords*

As the daughters of a famous portrait artist,
sisters Faith, Hope and Charity Brookes are
regular features at the best balls and soirees—
and in the gossip columns!

Daring to follow their dreams of being an artist,
writer and singer means scandal is never far away,
especially when they each fall for titled—
and infamous—gentlemen who set the
ton's tongues wagging!

Read Faith's story in
The Viscount's Unconventional Lady

Read Hope's story in
The Marquess Next Door

Both available now

And look for Charity's story

Coming soon!

Author Note

I never knew my father's mother.

She died before I was born at the relatively young age of sixty-five—but if the photographs were to be believed, she looked a very old lady by then. She has always fascinated me. Her four sons always spoke of her fondly but were careful in their choice of anecdotes. Her daughters-in-law would sometimes let slip in whispered conversations that she could be a difficult woman, reclusive and unpredictable. I still have no clue which version of her was the real one and suspect it was an amalgamation of both.

What I do know is that she had my father in her late forties and was ashamed to have become pregnant at that age. That when he was only a few weeks old, her home in East London was destroyed during the Blitz and she was rehoused miles away from her family. That she attempted suicide and was committed to the insane asylum. And that the stigma of her mental illness was so great nobody ever spoke of it...

VIRGINIA HEATH

—

The Marquess Next Door

HARLEQUIN®
HISTORICAL™

Recycling programs
for this product may
not exist in your area.

ISBN-13: 978-1-335-40719-1

The Marquess Next Door

Copyright © 2021 by Susan Merritt

For questions and comments about the quality of this book,
please contact us at CustomerService@Harlequin.com.

Harlequin Enterprises ULC
22 Adelaide St. West, 40th Floor
Toronto, Ontario M5H 4E3, Canada
www.Harlequin.com

Printed in U.S.A.

When **Virginia Heath** was a little girl, it took her ages to fall asleep, so she made up stories in her head to help pass the time while she was staring at the ceiling. As she got older, the stories became more complicated—sometimes taking weeks to get to their happy ending. One day she decided to embrace her insomnia and start writing them down. Virginia lives in Essex, UK, with her wonderful husband and two teenagers. It still takes her forever to fall asleep...

Books by Virginia Heath

Harlequin Historical

His Mistletoe Wager
Redeeming the Reclusive Earl
The Scoundrel's Bartered Bride
Christmas Cinderellas
"Invitation to the Duke's Ball"

The Talk of the Beau Monde

The Viscount's Unconventional Lady
The Marquess Next Door

Secrets of a Victorian Household

Lilian and the Irresistible Duke

The King's Elite

The Mysterious Lord Millcroft
The Uncompromising Lord Flint
The Disgraceful Lord Gray
The Determined Lord Hadleigh

Visit the Author Profile page
at Harlequin.com for more titles.

This book is dedicated to every inmate of
the Middlesex County Lunatic Asylum and most
especially to my grandmother Elizabeth,
who was once a patient there.

Chapter One

The most delicious rumour to find my ear this week, Gentle Reader, concerns Miss H. from Bloomsbury, a certain lieutenant who is newly returned from the Peninsula and a violet ice cream at Gunter's Tea Room. I have no idea what the handsome soldier said to the young lady in question to vex her so, suffice it to say that whatever he proposed resulted in him wearing the fiery young lady's colourful frozen dessert like a jaunty hat...

Whispers from Behind the Fan
May 1814

'Just the one dance?' The overfamiliar and persistent fool stared pointedly at the fan-shaped card dangling from Hope's wrist, which was resplendent with purposely blank spaces. Spaces he could plainly see, thanks to the stupid card's design. 'Surely, at this late hour, you can now spare me one? A cotillion perhaps...' His eyes dipped unsubtly to her cleavage again, because in the eighteen months Lord Harlington had doggedly pursued her he always struggled to focus on her face. 'Or better still, the last waltz? It hasn't escaped my notice that you haven't yet danced once.'

'What part of never in a month of Sundays do you struggle to understand, Lord Harlington?' She did not bother hiding her irritation, even though she'd worked out long ago that her dismissive and curt treatment of some men only seemed to spur them on. Not that refusing politely worked either. This one was as persistent as gangrene in a festering wound and twice as obnoxious. Being arrogant, exceedingly pompous and convinced he was God's gift to women, the hapless Harlington wrongly assumed she was playing hard to get. 'Because trust me, I would rather stick pins under my fingernails or salt my eyeballs than waste a single second waltzing with you.'

True to form and much to her irritation, her answer seemed to fire his blood further and he got that funny lascivious look in his eyes which men like him always got when she was unspeakably rude to them. Or simply when they ogled her figure. 'Would you like me to beg?'

And that was probably yet another of his perverted fantasies. Because there was something about her which always sparked this sort of nonsense from men. Whether that was down to her vivid red hair or the pale skin, the bigger than average, cumbersome bosoms she abhorred or the fact her waist was disproportionately smaller than her overly generous hips, she wasn't sure. Although, more likely, she had long been of the opinion it was a particular combination of all those obvious womanly things which life had cursed her with and which rendered her, not so much a human being in their blinkered, lustful eyes, with thoughts and feelings and opinions—but an object. A plaything. A vessel. And one they were convinced could be owned.

Which wasn't just degrading, demeaning and down-right uncalled for—it was exhausting.

'No, Lord Harlington, I would like you to go away. In a perfect world, preferably for ever.'

'You are such a tease, Mistress Vixen.' He smiled in what she assumed he thought was a sultry and seductive manner, but which was anything but, especially thanks to the dreadful nickname he had given her and always insisted upon using whenever he caught her alone. It was improper and lecherous, and she loathed it. 'I know you do not mean that.'

'If you suddenly dropped dead at my feet here in the Earl and Countess of Writtle's ballroom, I would spontaneously rejoice at my good fortune. I might even dance a jig around your corpse, my lord, because you are an irritating, nauseating, infuriating pest who gives pestilence a bad name. One who continues to labour under the gross misapprehension that when I say *no* to your unattractive offer of being your mistress, *repeatedly and vociferously*, I actually wish for you to woo me harder and that my outright and open disgust of you which is always written as plain as day on my face, is a form of flirtation. Or worse, merely a bargaining chip. Which, of course, it isn't.'

For good measure, she pointed her closed fan at him, wishing she weren't in a packed ballroom so she could smash it over his thick head. 'After a year and a half, even the stupidest of cretins would have worked out my extreme aversion to you by now. But alas, unfortunately, you are *so* cretinous, *so* thick-skinned, thick-headed and pig-ignorant, I sincerely doubt the combined efforts of a royal proclamation, an Act of Parliament and a town crier simultaneously bellowing out my complete and unwavering revulsion for you has any chance of hammering that undeniable message home.'

'If you dance with me now, I promise I shall leave you alone for the rest of the evening…' Briefly, his eyes met hers before they latched determinedly back on her breasts. 'Just grant me one dance…please. I ache for you.'

It was like talking to a wall. She rolled her eyes heavenward, praying for the strength not to kick Lord Harlington hard in the gentleman's area so that he had a proper ache to contend with. The nuisance had been following her around for the last half an hour. Instead she scanned the ballroom to see if there was any sign of anyone from her family who might save her.

Much to her chagrin, they were all too engrossed to notice she was stuck in an alcove all alone with the most nauseating of her current sorry collection of lacklustre or downright despicable suitors. Her theatrical mother, the famous soprano Roberta Brookes, was waxing lyrical in the centre of a gaggle of devoted opera fans next to the refreshment stand, while her equally famous father, the portraitist Augustus Brookes, was holding court in another crowd in the opposite corner. Both of her sisters were busy too, which was why she was left in this predicament alone. While Charity, the youngest Brookes, happily danced and flirted with everyone because she adored attention, Hope usually spent most social occasions stood with her slightly older sister Faith diligently refusing all dances because dancing with her never failed to give her dancing partners lustful ideas. Faith had always shared the same cynical view of the unworthy predators who swarmed around young ladies at social functions, or at least she had since she had foolishly allowed one past her defences.

Since then they had always protected one another and thoroughly enjoying it while they did, but things had changed of late. The dynamic had shifted, since her most reliable, formerly cynical and similar sibling had fallen hopelessly in love.

Faith was currently with Lord Eastwood, her handsome husband-to-be, hardly a surprise when this had tonight been announced as their engagement ball. And, in typical Charity fashion, the youngest of the three Brookes daughters was again the talk of the ballroom because she had, unbelievably, snared the Duke of Wellington as her current partner. No mean feat as the last time Hope had seen her, Charity had been twirling around the dance floor with none other than Lord Bryon.

Which left the floundering Hope with three choices.

Either try to lose Lord Harlington again in the crowd, which was proving difficult as he apparently had the instincts of a homing pigeon as far as she was concerned, remain stuck talking to the idiot for the duration and likely kill him before the end of the night and then face imprisonment for murdering a peer of the realm, or, most horrific and unpalatable of all, she could dance with him.

None solved the problem.

That would teach her for carrying the stupid dance card in the first place, even though she never had any intentions of using it. Her lofty plan of sneaking off to a quiet room, for the last hour, to finish writing the next chapter of her latest novel was in tatters thanks to him.

And thanks to all the words which were filling up her head and positively bursting at the seams to be let out, she'd likely have to write them all in the small hours now when they finally got home. If they ever got home before dawn—which was looking increasingly unlikely when absolutely none of the guests was leaving despite it already being a good hour past midnight.

When murdering him seemed the only viable option, another idea struck. It was sly and sneaky but undoubtedly no less than this noxious, stalking, leering libertine deserved—but it just might work.

'You can have the next country dance, Lord Harlington—but only if you leave me in peace beforehand.' Which gave her precisely one cotillion and one short quadrille to find somewhere in this unfamiliar house to hide. Ideally somewhere with a desk, a lamp and a plentiful supply of ink and paper because her mother had banned her from bringing any.

The annoying lord beamed, clearly beside himself with joy that he had finally worn her down with his superior and scintillating wooing. 'Oh, thank you, Miss Hope! You have made my night.' While he was oblivious that he made her flesh crawl.

'But only if you leave me in peace remember!' All she needed were a few undisturbed minutes to escape. 'If I see you watching me, or even as much as facing in my general direction in the next ten minutes, I shall declare my reluctant offer of a dance null and void. Do I make myself clear, Lord Harlington?'

'As crystal, my dearest vixen.' He had the gall to smile smugly at his perceived triumph. 'I knew my dogged determination would eventually pay off.' Then he tried to kiss her gloved hand and she placed it behind her back and glared at him appalled down her nose.

'I can assure you, hell would have to freeze over for me to allow *that*!' The thought of his lips anywhere near her skin made her want to gag. 'Keep your filthy hands and your slobbering lips to yourself, sir!'

'Shall I meet you back here in this alcove?'

'Yes…here would be perfect.' Because it was now the exact place where a herd of wild elephants wouldn't drag her once she had secured her freedom. As an additional incentive, she shooed him off with both hands as if he were vermin, making sure she scowled in complete disgust as she did so. 'Now go away. Leave me in peace, halfwit!'

Thwarted from touching her, he blew her a foul lingering kiss instead. 'Consider me gone…my lovely *Mistress Vixen.*'

Feeling oddly violated as well as annoyed, Hope couldn't contain the grimace as she watched him disappear into the crowd, her flesh still crawling. Perhaps one day a man would come along who surprised her? One who talked to her and not her chest. One who adored her brain and her wit and had noble intentions for once rather than entirely carnal. Every man seemed to want to skip Charity down the altar, and with the besotted Piers about to whisk Faith to the Writtle family chapel in Richmond, it seemed doubly annoying that the only place any man ever suggested taking her was to their bed.

She sighed, fed up to the back teeth with it all, but conscious there was no time to waste, she shook herself to banish all thought of Hideous Harlington, adjusted the filmy fichu she had added to her already modest gown, then swiftly searched for a suitable exit in case he realised his folly and came back. She needed a way out which wasn't obvious to escape before anyone saw her. Aside from Lord Harlington, she had already spotted another two lecherous gentlemen in the ballroom who also struggled to take no for an answer, and she didn't want to swap one plague of boils for another.

The main door was undoubtedly the quickest route, but that would take her past both the dance floor and the refreshment table, so that wouldn't do, but behind her were a line of French doors leading out to the darkened terrace.

Without a second thought, she slipped through one and dashed down the steps into the garden, fully intending to hunt for a different entrance back inside, well away from the odious Lord Harlington or any other prying and preying eyes. But the moon was full, the night air surprisingly warm and the sky so clear she could see every twinkling star.

Hope had always adored the night. She had never been an early bird and had always struggled to sleep until many hours after the rest of the household were snoring, even as a little girl. As a child she had passed the time daydreaming, creating little stories in her head to keep herself entertained and soon discovered that storytelling was her calling and her vivid imagination was always at its best when the sun, like her family, was sleeping.

Charmed and instantly at home, she ventured further into the pretty but unfamiliar garden, enjoying the dark silhouette of the fancy topiary lining the winding path. Like all such gardens in the centre of the crowded capital, this one wasn't particularly large, but it was long and narrow and its owners had created little rooms ringed with flower beds or shrubbery to give the illusion of space and the suggestion of privacy. They had achieved this so well, from only a few yards from the house, she could barely see the twinkling lights of the ballroom. She could, however, hear the alluring sounds of tinkling water, so headed straight for it.

The little white fountain trickled over a pale Grecian-style urn sat on top of a narrow pedestal, sat in a circular pond. Ringing it was a perfectly symmetrical miniature, knee high maze made up of neatly clipped box hedging, heather, and lavender.

Because she enjoyed a challenge, she followed the puzzle properly until she reached the centre, then sat on the wide brim of the pond's inviting wall—a wall clearly designed to be sat upon. It was the perfect spot to read, even by candlelight, if she had had the wherewithal to fetch a book and candle in her hurry to escape. So instead she simply sat as she supposed she was meant to and soaked it all in, consigning the opulent scenery to memory in case she ever needed it in one of her future stories.

The ghostly sounds of the orchestra wafting on the breeze.

The hoot of the solitary owl somewhere behind her.

The way a single wispy cloud floated and swirled eerily across the surface of the permanently startled face of the pearlescent moon.

The ominous crunch of gravel under a large boot…

Oh, good grief!

Her heart sank as she realised the irritant had found her, and she huffed out a frustrated groan as the undeniably male shape invaded her short-lived sanctuary.

Except this male wasn't shaped like the weedy Lord Harlington as it swayed haphazardly between the shrubs. It was tall and broad and had far too much hair. Harlington wore his fair short hair neatly plumped and pomaded *à la Brutus* like every dandy and fashionably besotted Brummell devotee in the *ton*—but this hair was a dark shoulder-length riot.

As its owner stumbled into the maze, those big boots quite oblivious of the artfully clipped intricacies of the little hedges, she noticed he also had a beard too. And an earring!

'Evening.' He raised one enormous hand in greeting, then to Hope's horror seated his bottom beside her, sending the distinctive whiff of freshly consumed alcohol her way. 'Don't mind me.' His voice was deep, the words a tad slurred. 'Pretend I'm not here.'

'You are drunk, sir!'

'That I am.' He grinned at her, the moon revealing a row of perfectly straight white teeth buried in the dense, dark thicket of his beard and two friendly but strangely compelling dark eyes. It hinted that there was a surprisingly handsome face hidden beneath all the fur. 'Just a little bit.' He held his finger and thumb an inch apart. 'But sadly, nowhere near enough as I want to be.'

With that, he produced a bottle of champagne from somewhere within his coat and idly tore off the foil. 'Are you out here hiding from all that pretentious nonsense too?' The shaggy head gestured back in the rough direction of the ballroom. 'There was so much inane wittering and preening I thought my head was going to explode.'

Hope blinked at the expensive bottle. 'Did you just steal that from the Earl of Writtle?'

'I hardly stole it. He's dishing out barrels of the stuff inside. His son's reshent…reshantly…' Two dark brows came together in consternation as his inebriated tongue failed to navigate the word.

'Do you mean *recently*?'

'Exactly.' He nodded in mock solemnity. 'Apparently the poor chap is *recently* engaged. No doubt to some witch who will make his life a living hell.'

Instantly Hope bristled. 'The witch is my sister, sir, so watch your mouth.' Nobody ever dared insult a Brookes in front of another Brookes—unless they also happened to be a Brookes.

'Is she?' He blinked and grinned again. 'Well then, that certainly calls for a shellybration.' The cork exploded from the bottle and flew in a wide arc into the trees. 'To your sister and the hapless, hopeless bastard she's marrying! Cheers!' He toasted the air and then took a long swig from the bottle before offering it to her.

She glared, affronted. 'No thank you.'

'Oh… I do apologise.' He riffled in his pocket for a surprisingly pristine handkerchief and used it to wipe the rim of the bottle, then held it out again. 'It's perfectly chilled and not too shoddy if champagne is your thing.'

'I said no thank you, sir!' She surged to her feet and he threw his messy head back and laughed.

'Oh—you're one of *those* girls.' He gulped down more of the champagne and had the gall to look at her, amused. 'The pious and sanctimonious sort.' Then he frowned as his eyes briskly swept the length of her. 'Although, if you don't mind me saying, you don't look typically like the pious sort looks. You're too…' He deposited the bottle carefully beside him and then drew an exaggerated hourglass in the air with his hands while staring her dead in the eye. 'It must be dashed inconvenient for you.'

'I'm sorry?' She wasn't sure whether she was appalled, confused or intrigued.

'To have a saucy tavern wench's body but the soul of a nun.' Hope couldn't decide which insult was worse. 'I'll bet you have to beat the men off with a stick.'

Because his gaze hadn't once dropped to her bosom despite the fact it was now level with his eyes, the truth leaked out before she could stop it. 'Sometimes I wish I carried a stick. A big one.'

'I don't doubt it.' He nodded. 'Especially when you're put together like Eve tempting Adam. Men are simple creatures, by and large, who reliably tend to be ruled by their urges and nothing fires an urge more than a woman as *womanly* as you.' He wafted his large hand to encompass her without once breaking eye contact. Then he frowned and stood, his fingers suddenly tugging one of the stray curls she had arranged to frame her face and holding it up to the moonlight to scrutinise as if it were a scientific specimen. 'Is this ginger?'

'I prefer the term red.'

'Of course you do. Because ginger is spicy and you're a prude. But whatever name you call it, I don't suppose it helps your predicament any. The face, the figure…' He tugged her curl again. 'And all this hair combined would make even the most celibate of saints pant and drool like a dog. You have my sympathies, madam, because I was cursed by the Almighty to look like trouble.' The corners of his lips twitched and his dark eyes hooded, making him look sinfully handsome as well as naughty. 'Although to be fair to him, I am more trouble than I'm not, so perhaps you can judge some books by their covers, Miss…?'

'Brookes.' She waited for recognition to dawn because everybody knew her parents, or lately her sister Faith whose engagement he was clearly attending.

It didn't. Instead he stuck out his enormous hand and used it to pump hers. 'I am very pleased to make your acquaintance, Miss Brookes.' His skin was warm and calloused, which made a very pleasant change from the sort of hands she was used to shaking. 'I am Lucius Nathaniel Elijah Duff. Which is a dreadful mouthful and all much too stuffy, so please call me Luke. I don't suppose you have a Christian name, do you, Miss Brookes?'

His mischievous dark eyes danced with amusement as they held hers. 'At least not one you'd allow any old fellow to use with impunity, what with you being one for temperance and propriety and all that.' And now he was plainly teasing her, which was new when most men simply made improper advances and stared at her chest.

'It's Hope and you are quite correct, sir, I absolutely do not give you leave to use it.'

'That is no doubt very prudent, Hope, for I am not to be trusted.' He sat back on the wall of the pond and smiled. 'So what are you hiding from?'

'Panting, drooling dogs.' She found herself smiling a little back at him before she stopped it. 'One particular hound to be more specific, who cannot take no for an answer. You?'

'Determined well-bred ladies in want of a husband. One particular well-bred lady to be more specific, who has a problem with the word no too.' He chuckled at her obvious surprise. 'I know, Hope. It's completely ridiculous and entirely unbelievable that any well-bred woman would contemplate shackling themselves to me for all eternity—but it also happens to be the absolute gospel truth. After thirty years of being considered blessedly and wholly unsuitable to all and sundry, I find myself suddenly eligible and sought after by the exact sort of woman I have always avoided and who have always avoided me back.' He took another drink from the bottle and shrugged as if he was totally baffled by it all. 'It's most disconcerting.'

For reasons she didn't understand, Hope sat back down too. He might be big, drunk and uncouth, he might also look a bit too brooding and dangerous for Mayfair, and there was no doubting he wasn't the least bit gentlemanly, but there was something about him which called to her. 'How did you suddenly become eligible, Mr Duff?'

'I have become *obscenely* rich, Hope.' His tipsy tongue tripped endearingly over the *obscenely*, making her laugh. 'I have so much money nowadays, I am practically wallowing in the stuff and I'm blowed if I know what to do with it.'

'Well that will do it. There is nothing like deep pockets filled with coin to make a debutante's heart flutter.'

He slanted her a very appealing glance. 'You're not a debutante, are you?'

'Good gracious no! I am far too old and cynical for all that. Though even if I were, I still wouldn't be tempted.' In the five years since she had first entered society, and after five years of being reduced to nought but a buxom body to be lusted over by practically every gentleman she encountered, she had been quite put off the lot of them. While other girls dreamed of snaring husbands or romance, she now dreamed of nothing of the sort. The thought of being pawed and panted over by a glassy-eyed man who only ever saw her as a pair of breasts filled her with horror. 'Nor am I aristocratic enough to be a debutante. Or at all, in fact, Mr Duff.' An aspect of her character she proudly wore like a badge of honour. 'One of my grandfathers was a mason, the other a draper.'

'And your father?'

'He's…'

'Mistress Vixen…?'

The unwelcome voice came from the direction of the terrace and Hope instantly deflated like a balloon. She buried her face in her hands and willed herself invisible. 'Oh, heaven help me!'

'Mistress Vixen?' Lord Harlington practically sang

the words as he tiptoed nearer, and she realised that if he had tracked her down into the garden, he also probably thought she had come out here on purpose to lure him for a tryst. *'I know you are out here...'*

'Mistress Vixen?' Her enormous, inebriated companion clearly found that hilarious and nudged her as he laughed. 'Is that what your drooling hound calls you? That's priceless.'

'It is not a name I have ever encouraged.'

'I should think not. It's terrible... But very funny.' He slapped his knee as he laughed. 'There's no mistaking what he's after, is there?' He playfully butted her shoulder with his. It was so solid it felt like a brick wall.

'Sadly not. I can think of many adjectives to describe Lord Hubert Harlington, but subtle isn't one of them.'

'Hubert is it?' His dark brows raised a notch. 'Were you and he once...*you know*...?'

'No!' She was horrified by the mere suggestion. 'Absolutely not! I have never done a thing to encourage him!' Or any other man for that matter. Not that that ever seemed to matter when she was cursed with red hair, big lips, wide hips and an unnecessary amount of cleavage. 'I cannot stand the sight of him. But the more I tell him off about that dreadful nickname, the more he uses it and the tenacious idiot refuses to leave me alone no matter how much I rebuff him.' As she stared indignantly, and her eyes took in the sheer size and intimidating girth of the man sat much too familiarly beside her, another idea formed.

A frankly brilliant one.

'I don't suppose I could trouble you to do something drastic to get rid of him for me, Mr Duff?' Because the slight and slender Lord Harlington would feel like a paltry sapling up against this mighty oak. He'd likely burst into tears on the spot if this brute said *boo* too, which would be marvellous.

'It would be no trouble at all, Hope. I've always fancied myself as a knight in shining armour. It would be my pleasure in fact. I'll get rid of the pest this instant.'

She only had time to smile her thanks as the hapless Harlington wandered into the clearing. A smile which quickly turned to shock a split second later as she found herself attached to her rescuer's lips.

Effortlessly, he gathered her into his arms, and bestowed upon her a kiss so gentle, yet so thorough and so decadent, she had no choice but to melt against him. And melt she certainly did, as it turned out that despite his tipsy state, Lucius Duff was irritatingly good at it. So good, to her horror, she sighed and looped her arms around his neck, completely powerless to do anything else.

'Miss Hope! How *could* you?' At Harlington's outraged squeak, Lucius Duff paused only long enough to glare at him and hold out his hand, palm out.

'Disappear, fool. Can't you see that we're busy here…?' Then his dark eyes stared deeply into hers. That palm came back to rest intimately on the curve of her hip as his lips shamelessly whispered over hers again, playing havoc with her nerve endings a bit more and doing very peculiar things to her usually level head.

When they heard the other man's outraged footsteps stomp back over the gravel from whence he'd come, he laughed again, the deep rumble vibrating seductively through his chest to hers and reminding her that she was still shamelessly plastered against him.

'He's gone.' He whispered the words against her mouth, his lips still barely millimetres from hers and his warm palm still splayed possessively across her hip.

Panicked at her own shocking behaviour as well as outraged at his, Hope immediately pushed him away and scurried to her feet, breathless, stunned and mortifyingly off-kilter.

'How dare you!'

Lucius Duff blinked at her, bemused. 'You asked me to do something drastic to get rid of him, so I did.'

'I meant by using your height...' She flapped her hands at his face. 'Or your menacing looks to intimidate him!'

'Then you might have been a bit more specific in your instructions as neither of those things sounds particularly drastic to me.' He stood too, revealing the full extent of that impressive height as he towered over her, and had the nerve to look drunkenly offended by her anger. 'Although I think my method was arguably just as effective and probably quicker.' Then offended turned to smug as he folded his arms, looking every inch the conquering hero after a bloody ancient battle. 'It worked a treat though, didn't it? Your drooling hound is gone.'

'But I got ravished in the process!'

'If you consider that a ravishing, Hope, then clearly you are more nun-like and pious than I first thought.' It was the pitying expression that fired her temper but it was his next ungentlemanly comment which unleashed the full force of it. 'But I couldn't help but notice you're not quite pious enough not to have thoroughly kissed me back.' The wolfish smile dared her to deny it.

She saw red.

Then white.

Lunged, and with one well-aimed and furious push

to the centre of his annoyingly solid, broad chest, sent him tumbling on his smug behind backwards into the pond with a hugely satisfying splash.

Chapter Two

It appears that, while deep in his cups, the newly minted Marquess of Thundersley decided to go for a midnight swim last night. Or at least that is what he told one of my sources when he was discovered dripping in the Earl of Writtle's ornamental fountain. Miss H. from Bloomsbury was also seen fleeing the garden only a few moments before, apparently in the highest of dudgeons. Coincidence, Gentle Reader? I think not...

Whispers from Behind the Fan
May 1814

'There you are, Lucius!' He winced at the sound of Abigail's voice. 'I've been looking for you all day.' Which was precisely why he had hidden himself in the music room to read his mountain of unwanted correspondence the second he had returned home, despite his inability to play any instrument. 'You missed dinner.'

On purpose.

Because he had been avoiding her like the plague and for damn good reason.

He smiled politely at his half-brother's widow, dreading what was likely destined to be one of the most toe-curling and awkward conversations of his life. 'And now you've finally found me. Did you seek me for any particular reason?'

Please let it be to apologise for your hideous suggestion from last night!

The suggestion which had left him reeling and reaching for the champagne the second he escaped the suffocating confines of the opulent Thundersley carriage, then downing half a bottle so fast he'd ended up on his arse in a pond within an hour of arriving at the damn ball.

She smiled, perching her skinny bottom on the chair opposite, and gestured towards the newspaper next to the remaining pile of unopened letters on the table. 'I see you made the gossip columns again...your poor valet spent the entire morning trying to get the algae stains out of your waistcoat.' Clearly they were going to run the gamut of painful small talk before she got to the point.

'I warned him cream silk was a bad idea.' As indeed was a valet. Luke had never had a battalion of servants. In Cornwall, they'd made do with their formidable cook-cum-housekeeper, a maid, one ancient, belligerent gardener and his mother's loyal nursemaid Clowance. 'I've never been very good at keeping clean.' Perhaps if she realised he was filthy as well as uncouth, he'd put her off him. 'I am not the least bit like Cassius—I like to get my hands as well as my clothes dirty.'

Which was just one of a thousand ways in which he differed from his dead half-brother. But then, Luke had not only been the spare and twelve years his brother's junior, but the offspring of a troublesome almost foreigner too, so it was hardly a surprise they had little in common. His mother was half-Spanish, the beautiful but fragile daughter of an ambitious count who was as ill suited to a life among the English aristocracy as Luke was. As a result, he had spent his childhood banished to his father's neglected house in Cornwall with her after her mind failed and her erratic and emotional behaviour became an embarrassment. Where, much like the house, they too were largely neglected and forgotten.

Cassius on the other hand, as the heir apparent and as English as a briar rose, stayed in the capital with their father. He'd had the finest tutors, an education fit for a future marquess and had been schooled from birth to take over the illustrious reins and the extensive responsibilities a title entailed. Whereas Luke had been left to run riot, which he had from the first moment he could run.

'I like that you are not the least bit like Cassius. You do not sound alike or look alike or share any of the same mannerisms.' Her determined tone made his toes curl inside his boots because he knew what was coming. 'And, of course, you and he were virtual strangers...' A polite way of saying they were mortal enemies. 'Which certainly makes this less awkward.'

'Not for me it doesn't.' He had tried to sidestep this discussion last night after she had ambushed him in the carriage after convincing him to attend the damn ball. When that failed, she had subjected him to a lengthy lecture on the supposed benefits of their union, and had dismissed all his objections deftly out of hand until he had reluctantly agreed to sleep on it, hoping it wouldn't just shut her up, it would make it go away. But Abigail had spent the last thirteen years as the Marchioness of Thundersley and had made up her mind it would be best for all if she continued in the role—irrespective of all his reservations. 'I simply cannot and will not marry my brother's wife. I'm sorry.'

Although he wasn't. He was horrified. So disgusted at her proposal he could barely look at her now without curling his lip in distaste.

'Can we at least have a sensible discussion about it? I should like to properly understand your reservations.' As far as he was concerned, they had already said everything which needed saying, although clearly she hadn't listened to a damn thing he had said during that dreadful, interminable carriage ride.

'Well for a start you were married to my brother.' Which did not seem to be a hurdle as far as she was concerned, but an unsurmountable one which Luke found supremely distasteful. It was true he and Cassius had been virtual strangers for the entirety of his life. They had had nothing in common except their father's unusual height and, on the rare occasion they were forced to meet, they had clashed over pretty much everything—usually his mother and the abysmal way she was treated. 'Which is morally wrong and probably against the law anyway.' If it wasn't, it certainly should be.

'It is actually not against the law of the land, I have researched it extensively, Lucius.' Of course she had. He could imagine she had been very thorough about it all too. She was the sort. From the moment he had received her letter informing him of his brother's sudden and unexpected demise in a carriage accident six months ago, she had treated widowhood as more of a great personal inconvenience than a tragedy. If she grieved anything, it seemed to be the loss of her status. Luke certainly hadn't witnessed her shed a single tear. 'Half-siblings are not explicitly mentioned in the Impediments of Affinity and so therefore there is no real legal recourse.' As he suspected, it was dubious. Not that her argument made any difference. It would be a cold day in hell before he stood at the altar with her!

'They don't need to be explicit if they are implied.'

She smiled, looking smug. 'A good lawyer can always find the devil in the detail and the house of Thundersley can well afford the best. I suppose it might be different if there were inheritances at stake and children, but obviously that will not be a problem for us because Cassius and I had no children.'

Several physicians had had to attest to the fact her womb was finally empty before they had officially granted Luke the title only a month ago because Abigail had clung to the belief she might be pregnant all that time. Whether she had believed it, or whether it had been a delaying tactic to prevent him inheriting, he had no clue but he was certain that nobody had been more devastated about the absence of an impending heir than he had been. The last thing he had wanted to do was upheave his life in Cornwall, temporarily abandon his mother and the slate business he had built from scratch, and step into his brother's ill-fitting shoes. But upheave it all he had. Four weeks into official nobility and those damned uncomfortable shoes pinched like the devil. He loathed feeling restricted and hated feeling trapped, yet trapped he was again thanks to the fresh burden of additional responsibilities he didn't fully understand which came alongside the blasted title he didn't want—and apparently Abigail was one of them.

'The lack of children was Cassius's fault by the way…not mine.' He winced at the intimacy of the confession. 'Your brother wasn't the most ardent and virile of husbands…' Luke wanted to stick his fingers in his ears, scrunch his eyes closed and run screaming from the room. 'Getting him to visit my bedchamber was like drawing blood from a stone. On the odd occasion when he did...'

He held his hand up frowning and shook his head, his entire body now so tense with awkwardness it was making all his muscles ache—including the one between his eyebrows. 'I really do not need to know any of that, Abigail.' And he certainly didn't want to have to picture it.

'No... I suppose not.' She stared down at her hands. 'But I am still young enough to bear your heirs, if that is what is bothering you.'

'It really isn't.' Heirs was probably number nine hundred and ninety-nine on his extensive list of objections.

'Good—because my physician has assured me I am in the best of health and ripe and ready to carry your children.' *Oh, good grief!* She was like a dog with a bone. 'And while the church might frown upon our union in principle, I am sure we can find a vicar who will marry us. Perhaps one in Cornwall who knows you well and would be sympathetic to our plight?'

'I don't.' And it was her plight, not his. He was tempted to shout that from the rooftops but the few scant manners which had been drilled into him meant he couldn't quite bring himself to bellow his utter disgust at a woman. 'I am not in love with you, Abigail, nor do I harbour any romantic feelings towards you whatsoever.' He couldn't say he particularly liked her much either. Like his brother and his sire, his sister-in-law was cold, disdainful and disapproving, more concerned with rank and status than substance.

She laughed at that, an annoying, tinkling, false titter which let him know in no uncertain terms she did not even consider love a consideration. 'Love rarely features in a society marriage, Lucius, at least not to begin with.' As if he hadn't witnessed that first-hand! Love hadn't featured at all in his parents' long-distance union. 'Although I am sure a mutual regard will grow if we give it time. It's not as if I am proposing we marry tomorrow. That would be outrageous.' She laughed again— part scoff, part outright dismissal as if he were the one suddenly in a great hurry to be wed. 'I still have five long months of half-mourning left before I am free.' Which beggared belief when Cassius was barely cold in the ground. Not that his brother had been particularly warm to begin with.

He had been as dictatorial and standoffish as their father had been, but significantly more callous about his familial responsibilities. At least his standoffish sire had initially tried to fix all the things that went wrong before he lost interest. Cassius had only wanted revenge for the fact his father had married Luke's unsuitable mother in the first place.

Abigail squeezed his hand, apparently oblivious that the contact made him cringe. 'Five months gives us plenty of time to get to know and *appreciate* one another properly as a husband and wife should.'

All the hairs stood up on the back of his neck at that implication. Yet that same ingrained politeness which stopped him shaking her by the shoulders and telling her she was clearly stark staring mad, also prevented him from admitting that he found absolutely nothing about her attractive either. Abigail's petite and delicate blonde prettiness did nothing for him. Her needy, clingy and manipulative character did less. He liked his women to have some fire, honesty and curves, like the delicious redhead from last night.

Now there was a woman who had heated his blood with no effort.

Even three sheets to the wind, and reeling from shock, the mere sight of the Miss Hope Brookes had been like a punch in the gut and it would likely take months for him to stop thinking about the way she had tasted. That tart mouth of hers had been plump and passionate and she had filled his arms to perfection. And felt delightfully robust in them too. He could see himself happily rolling around in the grass with Hope if he ever found the time again for a quick dalliance. If he could muster up the enthusiasm to do that with Abigail, which in itself would take a blasted miracle, he'd likely break her in the process.

Instead of saying any of that, he gently extracted his hand from her clutches and attempted to be diplomatic again, exactly as he had been last night. 'I am afraid I feel no desire for you either…and likely won't as you are and always will be my sister-in-law.' Practically incest no matter what the law had to say, when he knew he would never feel comfortable in his brother's house let alone in his blasted wife!

'I lived without desire throughout my marriage, Lucius.' Then to his horror she reached for his hand again and stroked her fingers over it in seductive invitation. 'But I suspect desire will not be a problem for us. I developed a few tricks which always worked on Cassius…'

This time, Luke pulled his hand away hard in case she finished that awful sentence. 'No, Abigail.'

Her features hardened and her lips thinned, making her look cold and mean and he couldn't help but uncharitably think that this was perhaps closer to her real nature than the façade she had been showing him. 'To what specifically?'

'To all of it. I am sorry, but my mind is made up. Whatever tenuous legal loophole you think you have unearthed, I will not marry my brother's wife.' He stood, suddenly desperate to be rid of her. 'Under any circumstances.'

'Even though I will be an asset to you?' She was relentless and, exactly as last night, worryingly determined in her quest. 'Do you know how to manage an estate and an extensive investment portfolio? Do you understand Parliament? The nuances of society? I could assist with all those things.'

It galled that she thought him an idiot, not that she would have any concept of the life he had carved out for himself in the wilds of Cornwall. Cassius had never bothered enquiring how he kept food on his mother's forgotten table or clothes on her back or paid for her medical bills or for her constant nursemaid after he had rescued her from the hellhole his brother had shoved her in. After their father had died, her meagre allowance stopped overnight. Apart from the dilapidated house and the exhausted tin mine which had been bequeathed to Luke in the will, he hadn't received a penny since the day the old man died either. Although the self-centred old curmudgeon had been reliably stingy with those pennies when he had been alive. Luke's paltry allowance, or guilt money as he preferred to call it, got swallowed up in all the other monthly household bills and any pleas for more fell on such deaf ears he had learned not to ask well before his years ran into double digits.

'You could assist with all those things without my ring on your finger!'

'But I could also make you respectable!'

'I don't give a damn about respectability!' Or about being a damn marquess either. The last thing he wanted was the obligation of an estate he had no memory of, tenants, pensions and servants on top of everything else he had to worry about. That life was *never* meant to be his.

'Then if you refuse to care about your reputation or how that sullies the good reputation of your brother, at least think about all the staff here in this house! All the uncertainty they will have to suffer with no mistress! Or worse, a new mistress who doesn't understand them.'

'Is this all about *this* house?' He almost slapped his forehead for not realising it sooner. 'Because if you are scared I will suddenly evict you to some desolate dower house somewhere in the wilds of nowhere, allow me to put your mind at rest. You can live here for ever, for all I care. I have no attachment to this place.'

Luke had always loathed it, not that he had ever spent much time here. On the rare occasions when he had been summoned, it was usually either for a carpeting or a funeral. He could count his visits here in the last decade on one hand, and two of those were to watch first his father and then his brother get lowered into the ground in a sturdy mahogany box. Every bit of this fashionable mausoleum in Mayfair felt alien and cold. Everything was swimming in gilt or marble or unnecessary and opulent tassels, and Abigail's servants seemed to watch him like a hawk in case he pocketed one of the ridiculously expensive candlesticks and pawned it.

Not to mention he could feel his dead ancestors' silent disapproval everywhere, largely because there were portraits of them all over the walls. He couldn't fathom their compulsive need to glorify themselves in perpetuity. It took a certain amount of arrogance and vanity to insist on displaying a likeness of yourself in every single room, even more to pay a small fortune to do so, however, Cassius and his father clearly had. Luke might not know much about art, but even he had heard of great masters like Gainsborough, Reynolds, Lawrence and Brookes and while the brushwork was magnificent, even those talented painters hadn't properly captured the essence of the two previous Marquesses of Thundersley properly. If you scraped back the expensive paint, all that was left were soulless blank canvases which, in his humble opinion, better exemplified them.

'I shall move out, Abigail.' The sooner now, the better. He had already taken determined steps to remove himself at the first possible convenience prior to his sister-in-law's unexpected bombshell last night. He could hardly uproot his mother to live here, even temporarily, when here had been the place where her mind had first begun to unravel. There hadn't been a significant incident in years because she was making progress in the right direction and he wouldn't allow anything to jeopardise that. She had hated this place.

So did he. But according to his new solicitor, he now apparently owned a large percentage of London because his illustrious family had always put more stock in property than people. He had houses coming out of his ears. 'Keep the house, Abigail. I do not want it.' And good riddance to her and it. He would happily never set foot here again.

She glared at him as if he were an idiot. 'You might not want it now—but you will, or your future wife will.'

'She won't.' Because he had no plans for a future wife. His particular responsibilities didn't lend themselves to marriage and all that that entailed, and likely never would. Wives expected attention he couldn't spare and likely wouldn't be particularly understanding of the fact his priorities had to lie elsewhere. And that was if they were prepared to marry a man whose blood was tainted by the curse of insanity in the first place. Not that he had ever thought for one second his mother's condition was hereditary, but as he had learned to his cost, the rest of the world weren't quite so forgiving of the condition, which was why he was always at great pains to keep it secret and protect it at all costs.

'Of course she will.' Abigail was quite agitated now. 'Addresses on Berkeley Square are few and far between and rarer than hen's teeth so if you refuse to marry me, your new Marchioness will steal it from me. Or you will realise its value and sell it for a fortune. And then what is to become of me?'

He decided not to mention the twenty thousand pounds Cassius had left her in his will alongside a house in Bruton Place not ten minutes away. Exactly like his brother and father, his sister-in-law measured her own worthiness and standing in the world by the directions written on the front of her correspondence.

But there was a simple solution to all of this nonsense. 'Then I shall transfer the deeds to you, Abigail.'

'You will?' She seemed a little placated at that and he almost sighed aloud with relief as he backed towards the door.

'I shall even talk to the solicitor about it first thing… for your own peace of mind.' Just as he would feel better as soon as he escaped. Perhaps he should do that first thing too? Take a room at an inn and put as much distance between himself and his cold, calculating and possessive sister-in-law as was humanly possible. 'It will all be sorted; I promise. And then we can forget all this awkwardness between us happened…' Not that he would ever forget it. He had never been so shocked or disgusted by anything in all his thirty years—and he had seen some dreadful things. 'Goodnight, Abigail.'

Alone in his room—or rather the innocuous guest bedroom he had taken instead of the master bedroom which both his father and brother had lain in—Luke stripped off his clothes and sluiced himself in the cold water from the jug on his nightstand. It did little to wash away the cloying layer of disgust which seemed to cling to his skin. Then he stretched out nude on top of the covers and sucked in several calming breaths in an attempt to stop his mind racing so that he could sleep.

He had never understood his family or, for that matter, the aristocracy in general. Not the way they lived, their idleness and sense of privilege, the way they thought or the things they put such great stock in, but this was a new level of strange, even for them. It was incomprehensible to him that Abigail thought it acceptable to replace one brother with another in the same dispassionate way one would replace an old pair of boots, and he suddenly felt a wave of pity for them all.

And as for her knowing a few tricks! He involuntarily shuddered at the thought.

Desire couldn't be manufactured, and even if it could he could think of nothing worse than a perfunctory coupling whose sole purpose was to beget the heirs she seemed to be obsessed with providing him. Desire should feel overwhelming and hot, as necessary as breathing, like the way Hope had left him feeling after only one stolen, drunken kiss. Even a lap full of icy pond water and frog spawn hadn't succeeded in dampening his ardour last night.

He smiled at that memory.

It might well have started as a chaste kiss but it hadn't ended that way thanks to Hope's blatant enthusiasm for kissing. The way she had buried her fingers in his hair while her tongue had tangled with his had been...quite something. And she had instigated that part of the proceedings, which alleviated some of his guilt for clumsily and erroneously kissing her in the first place. The spontaneous heat and passion of it had knocked him sideways. So much that even the champagne hadn't numbed his surprise and utter delight. She, on the other hand, had been both stunned and mortified by her distinct lack of piety and his shocking breach of propriety which he most definitely owed her a huge and grovelling apology for—hence he'd ended up in the fountain.

And rightly so.

Being drunk was no excuse for kissing her, so she was well within her rights to have torn him off a strip—and she certainly had.

After a month struggling with the fake politeness and the rigid code of behaviour in society, he'd rather enjoyed that too. Hope said what she meant and didn't suffer fools gladly. When one added those refreshing attributes to the list alongside the intelligence, the looks, the magnificent figure, the crackling hair and the hidden well of passion, she was one hell of a woman!

He grinned and closed his eyes, grateful to finally be contemplating much more pleasant things at bedtime than his woes with Abigail and all the burdens of his unwanted Marquessate. For good measure, and because he could barely remember the last time he had been with a woman, he decided to think about the delectable Miss Hope Brookes some more to help banish all those other unpleasant thoughts away.

The sultry smell of her perfume.

The perfect curve of her generous hip beneath his

palm. The soft sigh she expelled into his mouth as her lips fused with his, so real in his imagination he could almost feel it again as bone-weary tiredness tugged him gratefully into sleep.

In his dream, Hope deepened the kiss, her hand smoothing down his naked chest until it boldly wrapped itself around his erection, her triumphant chuckle at the way his body yearned for her touch.

Then he felt another whisper against his lips.

'Didn't I tell you desire wouldn't be a problem between us, Lucius?'

Chapter Three

Rumour has it that, for reasons best known to himself, the Viscount Eastwood presented his lovely new wife with a sturdy Chippendale armchair as a wedding gift...

Whispers from Behind the Fan
May 1814

'Well?' Their mother dropped her toast as a grinning Charity bustled through the door from the early morning stroll she had insisted upon taking in the middle of breakfast. 'Did you discover anything about our new next-door neighbours?' They had seen lights in the adjacent house late last night when they returned from Faith's wedding celebrations in Richmond. 'Please tell me it's a nice young family or an old lady or even a crusty and eccentric bachelor who collects butterflies and nasty bugs. I am not sure my poor nerves could take another scandalous H-U-S-S-Y right on our doorstep.'

Number Twenty-Two Bedford Place, Bloomsbury had been vacant for three months ever since the Earl of Clacton's former mistress had moved out. While she hadn't been there particularly long, four months to be exact, she had been an interesting neighbour, lacking both morals and any shame that she was a thoroughly kept woman who enjoyed the company of vigorous males far too much. But this morning, a laden cart had arrived containing an enormous bed, a couple of substantial-looking wingbacks as well as the biggest bathtub any of them had ever seen.

'It's a single gentleman according to Colonel Wigstock, who said he thinks he saw the fellow arrive some time around eight last night, although nobody else has seen him since to confirm that.'

'Old? Young?' Their father loved gossip even though he liked to pretend he was above such things.

Charity shrugged. 'You know Wigstock—he's reliably unreliable about those sorts of details. He thinks he might be a naval man.'

'Why?' As much as Hope liked to think she was above such things too, this was a new neighbour and she was more than a little intrigued. For the last hour, a succession of merchants and tradesmen had been delivering all manner of things to the house. The food alone had looked enough to feed the five thousand. If he was a sailor, he was a very hungry one.

'He's very dapper, fair and has a military bearing apparently.' Charity stole Hope's perfectly buttered slice of toast and took a huge bite out of it before she could snatch it back. 'He also has a pirate as a manservant.'

'A pirate!' Their mother was appalled. 'The C-U-T-T-H-R-O-A-T sort?'

Both sisters rolled their eyes at this because even though the youngest of them was already past one and twenty, their overprotective mother still insisted on spelling out any words she considered too unsavoury for their tender ears.

'Again, Mama, we only have Colonel Wigstock's word on that so it's hardly to be trusted. After all, he did tell the whole street Faith's new husband was a wandering gypsy simply because Piers happens to have dark hair.' Charity glided to the fireplace, no doubt to check her own hair in the big mirror over it. 'But so far, there doesn't appear to be any sign of either a wife or the sort of feminine accoutrements which go along with one, therefore I think it is fairly safe to assume our new neighbour is indeed a bachelor. Whether or not he is a crusty old one who collects insects is yet to be established.' Her sister glanced at the clock on the sideboard, then tugged on one of her perfect blonde ringlets to stare at it with disgust. 'What time is Evan bringing the carriage around again?'

Now that he was mobile again after a nasty fall which had broken his leg, their father was about to embark on another portrait commission in Mayfair and their talented mother's return to the Theatre Royal in *Così fan Tutte* had been so successful, the opera's run had been extended for another few weeks. Having secured her first singing engagement in the chorus, Charity always accompanied their mother to the theatre on rehearsal days, which would leave Hope all alone in the house for the first time in months.

'In ten minutes.' Their father gave the youngest his most stern look, as they all knew that the charmingly vain and chaotic Charity had a casual attitude towards timekeeping. 'So if you are going to have poor Lily redo your coiffure, you'd best be quick sharp about it or you'll be walking to Covent Garden!' He bashed the floor decisively with his jauntily painted new walking stick. 'I mean it this time, young lady. If you aren't down here the moment it pulls up outside, then we are leaving without you!'

'I'll be less than ten minutes, I promise, Papa.'

As Charity sauntered out as if she had all the time in the world, he turned back to Hope. 'Are you sure you don't want to come with me to Lady Bulphan's? We could have a nice late luncheon at Gunter's afterwards.'

'I'd much rather finish writing my chapter here than at Lady Bulphan's. I am so close to writing the end that my head is spinning with it all. I'd be very poor company at Gunter's today. I am too consumed.'

Which was only partially the truth.

While she really did have a head full of words and characters' voices—because she always had a head crammed full of the things—she was also quite content to avoid Mayfair, and Berkeley Square in particular, for as long as possible after the regrettable incident with Lucius Duff by the fountain last week.

She still wasn't entirely sure what had come over her that night. She wasn't usually so open with a gentleman as she had been him, or so uncharacteristically enthusiastic about kissing one either. Men, under all normal circumstances, were usually best avoided as they only ever wanted one thing. Not that she was resigned to a life of spinsterhood, or at least she hoped she wasn't, but it would certainly have to be a very special and unusual gentleman indeed to ever tempt her and he certainly wasn't that. Nor was she the sort who allowed one to dominate her thoughts for longer than was necessary. Hope was more for moving forward than looking back, except since that unfortunate but oh-so-enlightening kiss under the moonlight, even immersed in the excitement of her sister's wedding, she hadn't quite been able to shake the memory of it.

Or him.

What was it about him that scrambled her usually sound and cynical wits? He wasn't the sensible and intellectual sort of gentleman she traditionally favoured. The sort who preferred books to women. In fact, he hadn't seemed the least bit scholarly and academic and he certainly didn't look like that sort of gentleman either. Not that he resembled any sort of gentleman at all, truth be told. He was big and drunk and tactless. Too dark. Too tall. Too insightful and much too manly. Exactly as he had said, he looked like trouble—and even that hadn't stopped her from attaching herself to him like a barnacle!

It had been mortifying enough in the first place to have plastered herself breathlessly up against plain old Mr Duff—the transient stranger who would rapidly disappear out of her life—but now that she knew he also happened to be the new Marquess of Thundersley and therefore likely unavoidable in society, she was nowhere near ready to face him again yet.

Especially as he had been so gallingly smug about it all.

No indeed! When she collided with him again, she would be composed enough to glare at him in disgust, armed with an arsenal of pithy comments so that Lord *Just-Call-Me-Luke* knew in no uncertain terms that she considered him as vile and unworthy as the hideous Lord Harlington he had rescued her from.

And once she had finished giving him a piece of her mind for his ungentlemanly behaviour she would skewer him some more by lambasting his drunken efforts at kissing. The man was far too good at it and deserved being brought down a peg or two—even though she had greedily kissed him back and thoroughly enjoyed every splendid second of it.

Not that he ever needed to know that!

'If you are sure, dear.' Her father smiled affectionately.

'I am. You know I love nothing better than a silent house when the muse strikes. And no disrespect to you, Papa...'

'But I have been under your feet these past months while I have been recuperating.' He patted her hand. 'I understand completely as I too value silence as I work. Enjoy the quiet, darling. You've doubtless earned it.'

A good half an hour and a great deal of her parents hollering at the tardy Charity later, Hope finally waved them all off. Then armed with a hot cup of tea and promising herself she would not allow *that* regrettable kiss to intrude on *this* perfectly splendid day, she took herself upstairs to her bedchamber and out to her lovely little balcony overlooking the private and secluded communal garden beyond their terrace.

She had fought tooth and nail for this room when they first moved here, arguing that if Faith had her own little artist's studio downstairs and Charity had her own music room up in the attic, it was only fair she got to have the only balcony the house possessed because she loved to write outside when the weather permitted. It wasn't particularly spacious. There was only room for one wrought-iron chair and its tiny matching table, but it was private, quiet and surrounded by nature and out here she could forget she was in a big, crowded city and instead pretend to be in the blissful quiet of the countryside.

As she sipped her tea, she read over the pages she

had written the day before, adding corrections as she went as was her habit, so that by the time she reached the end of the words, she had forgotten the rest of the world, and almost forgotten the brute Lord Thundersley existed. Instead, her odd head was teaming with fresh words to add to the story.

She had a good feeling about this book. Which was staggering really after the blows her confidence had taken over the last one. From the moment the first shoots of the idea formed, it seemed to effortlessly grow and flourish, so much so, she was starting to believe *Phantasma* might finally be the book to get her published. It certainly felt different from all her previous rejected efforts. Or at least it did on the odd occasion when she allowed herself to feel proud of it, which was a vast improvement on the usual doubts she harboured about her writing talent. Doubts which had increased tenfold after her self-confidence had been eviscerated by the three respected publishing houses she had been brave enough to send her last book to—two of which hadn't bothered reading beyond the first chapter before they had rejected it out of hand.

But *Phantasma* still felt stronger. And not at all what she had seen on any bookshelf before.

She had left her intrepid heroine all alone in a derelict building on the edges of the slum. The moonlight leaking through the remnants of the long-collapsed roof picked out the cobwebs covering the cold, ancient walls as she climbed the worn wooden stairs upward towards the flapping sounds of bats beneath the creaking eaves. In her mind, the next scene was already fully formed, and the heroine would finally meet the monster. Except the villain wouldn't be the malevolent ghoul that she and everyone else expected—it would be her fiancé. A man, she would rapidly discover, so twisted by greed and devoid of all conscience he had married repeatedly for money, assuming a new identity each time in case the authorities questioned his motives, then disposed of those unfortunate wives in a shocking, gory and premediated manner once he had complete control over them.

From there, the intricate Gothic mystery she had diligently constructed over three hundred tightly packed pages would finally unravel as it reached its terrifying crescendo. After all his sickening and twisted secrets had been revealed, and as the heroine battled to free herself from his murderous clutches, the building would burn in a ferocious fire. Then, it would collapse in the inferno, taking the much-feared Phantom of St Giles and all his wicked secrets with it, as she escaped into the night towards freedom.

Hope's pen moved quickly as the story flowed and she lost all sense of place and time. The sun was already high in the sky when the nearby slosh of something which sounded like water snapped her out of her fictional world and pulled her attention to the neighbouring balcony at Number Twenty-Two.

A balcony which, to the best of her knowledge, had never been used in all the years she had lived next door to it. However today, she could hear someone moving about in the room beyond.

Intrigued, she craned over the railings to investigate further. The glass on the narrow French doors steamed and dripped with condensation. Behind the misted windows she could see a fuzzy and indiscernible human shape. It paced from one side of the room to the other, its arms constantly moving above its head. Then it stopped and stretched, the skin-coloured smudge practically filling the doors until it flung them open and the mystery occupant strode out to stare over his own railings a split second before she gasped in shock.

'Lord Thundersley!'

Hope clamped her hand over her mouth as his head whipped around, and then blinked like an idiot as she took in the full extent of the unexpected and scandalous sight of him standing practically nude in broad daylight.

He was obviously fresh from the bath. Obvious, because he was positively soaking wet and the only thing he was wearing was the towel loosely wrapped around his waist. Droplets of water fell from his shoulder-length hair, over his broad chest and dripped off his pebbled nipples. Others trickled from his short beard to the gully formed by his impressive pectoral muscles down over his abdomen, lazily following the dark dusting of hair that arrowed beneath the folds of the towel.

'Hope?' He smiled back, more water spiking his black eyelashes, clearly vastly amused to see her. 'Well as I live and breathe! What a surprise. Don't tell me you live here?' His big hands rested on his hips as he laughed, apparently oblivious of his distinct lack of clothing. 'Fate certainly has a sense of humour.'

She pushed herself upright in her hurry to escape the unexpected and shocking sight, knocking her forgotten chilled tea all over the top sheets of her precious writing as she did so. Her face burning and her eyes much too curious, she snatched the pages up and clumsily used the front of her dress to mop away the damage while the dry ones decided to flutter haphazardly in the breeze.

'You're naked!' The words came out in a mortifyingly missish squeal as she tried and very definitely failed to catch the pages.

'That I am.'

She crouched down and hastily attempted to gather

up the last six months of her work before it flew away on the breeze and entirely failing in her feeble attempts to avert her curious eyes as she did so. 'What sort of a person walks out on to a balcony in just their birthday suit?'

Their very impressive, sun-kissed and beautifully sculpted birthday suit.

'The sort who has just got out of their bath and wasn't expecting to find anyone else out here when nobody seems to get out of bed before noon in Mayfair. Clearly that isn't the case here in Bloomsbury, so...' He pointed back towards his doorway with a jerk of his thumb. 'I'll spare your blushes and go and put something on.'

Thankfully, he disappeared back inside leaving a very disconcerted Hope to briskly tidy up the mess she had made. She was frantically picking up the last of her pages when he returned, still shamelessly sporting a towel on his lower half but he had at least donned a shirt to cover the rest of him. She knew he had donned it in haste because he hadn't bothered drying himself and the soft linen was twisted as it clung to the water and was doing a very good job of translucently moulding itself to his chest like a second skin. Somehow, that effect was even more distracting because she now knew exactly what lay underneath that shirt and her vivid imagination seemed determined to picture it. He bent to pick up a single sheet from his own balcony, which in her panic she hadn't noticed had escaped, causing the damp fabric to stretch taut over his back, shoulders and muscular arms, which to her shame, flustered her further.

Good gracious he was something! She had never seen anything quite like it.

'I believe this is yours.' He stretched the few short feet between the railings to hand it back and she snatched it and clumsily stuffed it into her pile, wishing her stupid face wasn't glowing like a beacon, her mouth didn't feel quite so dry and her stupid palms weren't so moist. 'I am truly sorry for startling you. I really didn't expect to see anyone out here.' He appeared genuinely contrite.

As well as wet and sinfully and alluringly wicked.
Drat him!

'I'm a country boy, used to the privacy and solitude which comes with wide open spaces and I am still not acclimatised to the way things are done here.' Then he smiled, drat him, not in a smug or lecherous or patronising way, but in a rather shy, boyish and attractively lopsided manner as his gaze remained refreshingly locked to her face.

'And while I am apologising, I most definitely need to apologise for the other night too, Hope.' His expression was all earnest. 'Not that it is in any way a defence of my ungentlemanly behaviour, but I was a tad drunk, more than a little overwhelmed and my brain wasn't quite as sharp as it should have been. Therefore, when you asked for my help, in my inebriated and confused state I got the wrong end of the stick and stupidly thought kissing you was the best way to get rid of your unwanted admirer instead of simply telling him to leave you alone and threatening to punch the blighter on the nose if he dared bother you again.' He smiled. A wary, apologetic and slightly wincing smile. 'I am glad you pushed me in the pond, because I thoroughly deserved it.'

She wasn't entirely sure how to respond to his unexpected but rather convincing apology, or his sudden appearance on the balcony next to hers.

Nude.

'You did deserve it.' So much for skewering him with a pithy litany of well-chosen insults and knocking him down a peg or two, but at least she looked haughty, or hoped she did. 'Kindly tell me what you are doing here, *Lord Thundersley*?' She gestured more to the environs in general than the balcony because she had the horrible feeling that the pirate Colonel Wigstock had seen wasn't their new neighbour's manservant after all. 'When you have a perfectly lovely house in Berkley Square?'

'Have you been checking up on me?' He appeared delighted at the prospect, so she shot him her best withering look, determined not to be charmed by the soothing lilt of west country in his accent. 'And I swear we agreed you would just call me Luke?'

'Just answer the question, *my lord*.'

He made no attempt to hide his amusement at her snippy tone or her sudden formality, or perhaps it was her ferocious blush he found funny. Whichever it was, it made her glow redder and bristle more. 'I decided stuffy old Berkeley Square didn't agree with me, so I sought pastures new. When I discovered I owned this lovely house here, I thought Bloomsbury might be a better fit as I am reliably informed it is more eclectic and has less...'

'Aristocrats?'

'I was going to say shallowness, but I suppose they are one and the same.'

'Yet you are an aristocrat yourself, *my lord*.' A vexing, too smug and too naked one.

'That I am.' He shrugged, drawing her wayward eyes to his broad, wet shoulders. 'Though I've never had much cause to think of myself as one until recently, and even now I am not the least bit comfortable with it. I am fairly clueless about society as you can probably tell, certainly do not fit in it in any way, shape or form and, between you and me, *Hope*…' She narrowed her eyes at his continued lack of formality and he laughed. 'Would you prefer I called you Mistress Vixen instead?'

He raised his dark eyebrows so comically it took a great deal of effort not to laugh herself. 'I prefer to be called Miss Brookes, *Lord Thundersley*, as you well know.'

'That I do.' He grinned unrepentant, his perfectly straight white teeth a stark contrast to his dark beard and deep golden skin. 'But I've never been one for formality any more than I am one for rank. We don't tend to bother with all that nonsense out in the wilds of Cornwall.'

'Well this isn't Cornwall and here we have rules about wildness.'

'Daft rules. And in my humble, uncivilised and wildly Cornish opinion, unfathomable, uncompromising, unwieldy, unhelpful and unnecessary rules, which between you and me, *Hope*, I am not at all sure that I can be bothered to learn.' As a writer, she couldn't help but be impressed with his effortless and flawless use of both alliteration and clever wordplay. As an off-kilter woman who was mortifyingly too attracted to him already despite her better judgement, she was horrified to discover he was that intelligent too. She had always had a soft spot for intelligence. Intelligent men tended to be more subtle in their ogling. 'Why on earth would any sane person want to fit into society when it all seems so complicated, cloying, contradictory and so very fickle to me?'

'It is.' He was irritatingly open and honest as well. Disarmingly so. To such an extent, she had the strangest urge to lower her legendary and pessimistic guard for once while they swapped their clearly mutual opinions and observations about the ridiculousness of the *ton*— and that wouldn't do. When she knew first-hand how dangerous lowering her guard around him could be.

In case she gave in to the overwhelming temptation to linger and do exactly that, she turned towards her door and offered him one final pithy salvo before she dashed inside to compose herself. 'But all that is by the by and doesn't make me any less annoyed at you for the other night. Your unpleasant and uncivilised attempt at kissing aside…' the mere memory of it made her lips tingle '…you might have mentioned you were a marquess. It was very poor form, dishonest and exceedingly ungentlemanly that you didn't.' As that seemed the perfect way to end the conversation, she turned on her heel.

'Would my being a marquess have stopped you from dunking me in the pond, *Hope*?'

She could hear his amused grin and picture the cheeky twinkle in his eye without seeing either, yet she still felt her feet pause while she unconsciously turned to confirm it. Then, drat him, found herself lowering her legendary and pessimistic guard enough to smile the tiniest bit back at him—again against her better judgement.

'Certainly not. Marquess or no, you most definitely had that dunking coming… *Lord Trouble*.'

Chapter Four

Relieved that Clowance's letter contained no hint of bad news, Luke took his time reading it for a second time smiling. All was well in Cornwall, so that was one huge weight off his mind. Tregally Slate was apparently still thriving without his guiding hands on the tiller—he had Clowance's son to thank for that—and his mother was still coping surprisingly well with his absence. He hoped that lasted. At least until he was able to bring her here where he could watch over her himself—if he was ever able to bring her here. He was still in two minds about that, but until he understood all the complications of his inheritance and decided what to do with it, he had no choice.

He had long given up trying to predict the twists and turns of her illness. What he did know was that, despite her near three years of uninterrupted wellness she was never good with sudden change, so if moving her here for an indefinite stay proved impossible, he would have no choice but to continue to divide his already overstretched time between London and Cornwall for the foreseeable future and lose valuable weeks in the process.

But there was no point thinking about all that now. He understood she needed the constant reassurance of his presence despite her protestations that she really didn't, and the only way he could make that happen at the moment was to bring her here. And that couldn't happen until he had hired a couple more servants, a decent cook and had redecorated the master suite upstairs in readiness.

Whoever had lived here last had quite a bawdy taste in decor if the strategically placed mirrors were any gauge, and the less said about the crimson walls and jet-black plaster mouldings and skirting boards, the better.

However, finding suitable and reliable tradesmen to carry out the work was easier said than done. Back home, he knew every reputable trade, merchant and shopkeeper necessary for every conceivable eventuality. There, he could easily separate the wheat from the chaff and negotiate reasonable prices. He would solve the problem—but here, he had no contacts and nobody he knew well enough or trusted enough to recommend someone. Which meant a simple task like repainting a bedchamber was suddenly an onerous one which would take up more time. Although where he would find that time was another matter.

With a weary sigh, he glanced out of the window, the sight of pavements, buildings and carriages still an unfamiliar surprise when he was used to staring at nothing but the trees and sky. London was a different world from the one he came from and the busy city felt as alien to him as this new, sparse but gawdy sitting room. But at least the sun was shining and that made him yearn to be outside in the fresh air instead of cooped up inside.

Yet he was resigned to the fact that nowadays, even a walk was a luxury. The mountain of correspondence piled on the side table still demanded his attention, making him wince when he realised that even after two hours of diligent reading and responding he had barely made a dent in it. He swore blind the damn things multiplied whenever he turned his back. Letters of condolence from complete strangers, invitations to everything from week-long house parties to afternoon teas and speculative letters of introduction fishing for his business, or patronage or charity, arrived by the sackload every day, reminding him that he ought to hire a secretary on top of everyone else simply to avoid drowning in it.

Frustrated, he tossed the nursemaid's letter on top of them. All this additional work and the late nights spent trying to make sense of all the new responsibilities which had been thrust upon him were taking their toll. Owning a marquessate was a darn sight more convoluted and complicated than owning a slate business and selling it all—if that was indeed what he decided to do with it—wasn't going to be concluded swiftly.

To say he was swamped was an understatement.

Today, as he had for the last four weeks, Luke had spent the morning with one of his brother's overseers. Not including the crusty solicitor he had inherited alongside the myriad unwanted extra complications and responsibilities, there were three employed managers in total, each tasked with running separate aspects of the extensive investment portfolio. The personable and cheerful Mr Lessing oversaw the Thundersley ancestral estate several miles from London as well as the many farms and tenants within it. He was both approachable and helpful and, on first impressions at least, seemed to run a tight ship which Luke couldn't offload if he had wanted to because it was entailed, so he was content to leave the man in charge.

The less cheerful but still personable Mr Dent managed all the swathes of London property which were rented out for eye-watering sums but which could easily be sold on, and Mr Waterhouse, the least personable and most supercilious of the three was in charge of the stocks and shares, of which there were hundreds, and they apparently made most of the money. Those were the biggest mystery and the thing he knew the least about.

Luke's head was spinning with the scale of it all and he suspected he had barely scratched the surface. Perhaps he should do as the solicitor suggested and leave it all to the three men who had managed it all very competently for his brother while he hotfooted it back to Cornwall and forgot about it, but that didn't sit right. His own business back home might be small by comparison, but because he had built it, he understood every nut and bolt of it, and he would understand this too, damn it!

One day.

Maybe.

This place, this new life which fate had foisted upon him, was suffocating him and he already felt like an old man under the weight of it all. A very tired, very burdened and very overwhelmed old man.

He stood with all the energy of an arthritic octogenarian, feeling every single one of the unwanted and heavy burdens resting upon his shoulders, and wandered to the window intending to open it and let some of that elusive fresh air in, but as he lifted the gauzy lace curtain he saw her.

Hope was arm in arm with another young lady chatting amiably. Both were wearing pretty summer dresses and enormous straw bonnets which hid their faces, but he knew it was her by her statuesque height, the curvaceous shape of her body which filled the demure dress so perfectly it rendered it effortlessly seductive, and simply by the way that she moved. Even flustered, as she had been yesterday on the balcony, she moved with overtly feminine grace. Those generous hips undulating in a manner so sensual, she would probably work hard to alter her gait if she knew the alluring effect they created.

She was uncomfortable with her physical attractiveness. He understood enough about her already to know she would much prefer not to be a living, breathing, walking male fantasy—and who could blame her? If the behaviour of that oily, panting lecher Harlington was any gauge, she must be sick to the back teeth of being treated so superficially. Although how that idiot had missed her fascinating intelligence and dry wit was a mystery to him, as they were even more alluring than her obvious physical enticements. But then everything seemed superficial here in the capital and people only cared about the finished, polished surface of the diamond and not the clarity and purity beneath.

He watched her walk towards the little park that was Russell Square before turning back to stare mournfully at his pile of correspondence again—his never-ending pile of unwanted correspondence and ledgers and papers—and spontaneously decided that for now at least, it could all go to hell. Instead, without analysing the overwhelming and compulsive need to get to her, he grabbed his coat and shrugged it on as he dashed out of his new front door. Then skidded to an abrupt stop on the bottom step when she miraculously appeared right in front of him.

'Hello, Hope.' Instantly, the world was brighter. Especially as she appeared to have misplaced her companion and he had her all to himself. 'What a pleasant surprise.' Although she didn't seem the least bit pleased by it. Or comfortable.

'I absolutely *do not* know you!' The low hiss came through obviously gritted teeth.

'I'm sorry?'

'You—me—we've *never* met.' Her panicked eyes darted to her front door. 'At least that is what my family think.' Then she rose herself up to her full height and pasted a bland expression on her face as the door flew open and the blonde tumbled out of it doing up the ribbons of a different bonnet.

'See! I told you the blue would suit this...' The blonde paused mid-step and smiled at him, her expression instantly curious as her eyes boldly swept him up and down.

'Charity, this is our new neighbour.' Hope gestured towards him with a stiff wave of her hand. 'As you can see, we just this second collided on the steps.' An unnecessary clarification when they were both standing parallel to their own front doors. 'This, sir, is my sister Miss Charity Brookes and I am Miss Hope Brookes. We live here with our parents.'

'I am delighted to make your acquaintance, ladies.' Feeling his way and desperately trying to read the stark warning message in Hope's lovely eyes, he inclined his head politely. 'I am Lucius Nathaniel Elijah Duff.' Or at least he had been until a few months ago, but actual names here weren't as important as titles. 'The Seventh Marquess of Thundersley.' The ill-fitting addition felt awkward on his tongue. Probably because he still felt like an impostor in the role and would much rather be plain old Luke Duff again.

Miss Charity's eyes widened. It was the typical reaction he had come to expect, though he couldn't say he blamed everyone for reacting with disbelief at the news when he scarcely believed it himself. He most definitely was not marquess material and likely never would be.

'Lord *Thundersley*?' Her eyes slanted to Hope's, amused. 'What an intriguing coincidence. The same Lord Thundersley, I presume, who took a dip in the Earl of Writtle's fountain the other week?'

As there was no denying that, he nodded and offered her his best sheepish smile. 'Guilty as charged, Miss Charity... Sadly. Though in my defence, while not my finest hour, it was an accident.' At least the kissing had sort of been accidental even if his subsequent swim had been deserved. Of their own accord, his eyes wandered to Hope's lips before he ruthlessly dragged them back to the young lady he was talking to. A very pretty young lady indeed, beautiful if your taste ran to fashionable blondes, but nowhere near in her sister's league. Even suddenly mute and doing her best to blend into the railings, Hope dazzled.

'The same Lord Thundersley that the gossip columns linked to my sister?'

Hope stiffened and then quickly forced her shoulders to relax a split second before Miss Charity glanced at her, the unconvincingly baffled expression on her lovely face as hollow as the flimsy lie they were apparently constructing.

'They did?' He had to work hard not to allow his pasted smile to slide off his face under the blonde's suddenly intense scrutiny. She smelled a rat.

'Hope is the Miss *H.* from Bloomsbury. Miss *Hope* Brookes...the exact same woman they suggested was responsible for your being in that fountain in the first place, my lord. Isn't that a strange coincidence?'

'Good gracious? Is she really? Then I am doubly pleased to finally make her acquaintance as I did wonder who the notorious Miss H. was.' And now he was over-explaining things too. 'Alas, as I hail from Cornwall, Miss Charity, I am grossly unfamiliar with the capital and its inhabitants. Where I come from, gossip is so thin on the ground, the newspapers make no attempts at disguising the names of those being gossiped about with complicated secret codes. There would be no point, as everybody knows everybody anyway.'

'It is much the same here, my lord, because the code isn't that complicated any more than it is secret.' He couldn't tell if the blonde was convinced of his sincerity or not. 'Whenever the *Miss* is followed by the pertinent words *from Bloomsbury*, the entire world and his wife knows they mean one of us. My sisters and I tend to feature in them with alarming regularity.'

An interesting titbit Luke would have explored further had another, older woman not appeared at the doorway.

'Is everything all right, girls?' She eyed him dubiously as if he were some sort of pillaging marauder come to kidnap her daughters.

'Mama, this is our elusive and mysterious new neighbour... Lord *Thundersley.*'

'Oh... *Oh!*' The older woman's defensive expression instantly turned curious as she glided down her steps, as she doubtless recalled every bit of rot written about him in the last few weeks and was deciding if he were capable of it. Which clearly she did. Her eyes narrowed as they wandered to her daughter. 'I thought you had never met him, Hope?'

'Until this moment they hadn't.' It was Charity who quickly answered. 'So this bizarre coincidence has caused them both quite a shock. Poor Lord Thundersley wasn't even aware that the Miss H. from Bloomsbury was even a Brookes. Isn't that funny?' The sunny smile she shot him suggested that while she was determined to have her mother see it as coincidental, she wasn't similarly convinced.

The older woman smiled tightly. 'Then welcome to Bloomsbury, my lord. I am Mrs Roberta Brookes.' Then she stopped and posed regally as if that in itself were a great achievement.

'I am delighted to meet you, Mrs Brookes. I have been meaning to call to introduce myself properly but the last few days have been hectic as I am sure you can imagine.'

The suspicion had now been replaced by politeness. 'Indeed I can, my lord. Moving house is such an ordeal and there is always so much to do. My poor nerves were shot to smithereens when we moved in here five years ago, so you have my sympathies.' Her eyes flicked to her youngest and paused while they conveyed a silent message he couldn't begin to decipher. 'But where are my manners, my lord? You must come in and join us for tea.'

Backed some way away from the human barricade which was Mrs Brookes and Miss Charity, Hope pulled a face and shook her head, her eyes pleading before she covered it with an expression of polite blandness. 'The poor man was on his way out when I collided with him, Mama, and clearly in a rush to be somewhere.'

Luke nodded like a deranged woodpecker. 'Sadly,

that is true. I have urgent business with my solicitor this afternoon, so I must decline your kind invitation for now.' Which oddly disappointed him.

'Oh, that is a shame!' Mrs Brookes took a determined step closer. 'Another day then? Tomorrow perhaps? Which will likely be better as my husband will be home and I know he will want to meet you and welcome you to Bedford Place properly. Our cook bakes the most delicious cakes if you have a sweet tooth. Her queen cakes in particular are splendid, my lord, and she has such a way with the batter, they come out as light as a feather. I shall have her bake a batch first thing. Does around three suit?'

Behind her Hope rolled her eyes before she nodded so he bobbed his head as well. 'I shall count the hours, Mrs Brookes.' And likely would too, though worryingly not for the light-as-a-feather queen cakes.

Chapter Five

When he checked for the umpteenth time, she was finally on her balcony much later that evening. They needed to talk, not least to get their stories straight, but he also wanted to talk to her simply because he rather liked doing so.

For a few indulgent moments, Luke watched her through the glass door. She was writing again, her back to him, her quill moving briskly as she leaned her cheek heavily against her other hand. The balcony was covered in candles that picked out the fiery copper and red in her hair which hung down between her shoulder blades in a single thick plait. A few loose, messy tendrils had escaped and were curling slightly in the warm night air. She paused for a moment and stared out into the night, tapping the feathered end of her pen aimlessly against her chin before she bent back to her writing again and scribbled furiously.

It was an arresting sight. Made all the better by the way the soft fabric of the pretty summer dress she hadn't bothered changing out of perfectly silhouetted her shape. The soft muslin emphasising her small waist, the curved flare of her hips and the magnificent rounded peach of her bottom. After another never-ending dinner meeting with his crusty old solicitor, during which the fellow droned on and on about still more unfathomable stocks and bonds in his inherited portfolio, right now, she was just the distraction he needed from the strange world he had been thrust into. Where people either sycophantically kowtowed to him, imperiously looked down their nose at him or, as he had discovered with the few tradesmen he had talked to, seemed hellbent on swindling him.

But Hope was fun to talk to. Interesting. Beguiling. Intriguing.

In case he startled her again, he lit a lamp and turned it up full before he noisily opened the door. Forewarned, forearmed and much too brazen for her own good, she didn't move anything but her pen across the paper when he stepped on to his balcony.

'Good evening, Lord Trouble.'

'Hello again, Hope. Isn't it a bit late and a bit dark to be working?'

'I like the quiet of the night. I always have.'

'What are you writing this time?' He was still talking to her back.

'The same thing I was writing yesterday before you ruined my peace with your soggy and unwelcome interruption, unashamedly all in the altogether like a savage.'

'Which makes me none the wiser.' He liked that she had no respect for his new rank. 'Therefore, I must assume that you are being so cryptic and writing it so clandestinely because it is your secret diary... Filled with all your private thoughts and dreams...and deeds so shocking that you would end up being thrown out of your nunnery if anyone ever read them. In which case, it begs the obvious question...' Because he knew it would vex her, he lowered his voice to a silky whisper. 'Am *I* in it?'

Finally, she turned, feigning an irritation which did not reach her lovely eyes. 'Why on earth would I put *you* in my diary?'

'Perhaps because I am the most exciting thing that has happened of late in your dull and pious life?'

'Exciting? Not the adjective I would have chosen to describe you. Irritating perhaps…if you weren't so instantly forgettable that is.' Her plump lips curved ever so slightly, ruining her regal attempt at blandness as she put him in his place.

'Then I *am* in it. Your rehearsed disdain and disinterest prove it.' He folded his arms for good measure, making sure he looked smug so that she had to react. A woman as tart and intelligent as she wouldn't be able to allow such arrogant male superciliousness to pass unchecked.

'If you must know, it's a story.' The withering glance was a little more convincing than the blandness. 'A novel actually.' Then she looked a little unsure and embarrassed to be admitting it, so she dismissed it with a casual flick of her wrist. 'I have lofty ambitions of getting one published some day.'

He was impressed. 'I've never met a novelist before. You are officially my first.'

'I am not sure one can officially call oneself a novelist until one's words are bound in leather with one's name emblazoned on the front and sold in Hatchard's in Piccadilly—but perhaps I will be one day.' She smiled wistfully. 'Perhaps… If I ever write something deemed worthy enough by the illustrious publishers who control such things.' The way she said that sounded not so much angry as resigned. 'But alas, so far, all my endeavours to that end have proved fruitless and all my lofty ambitions are merely that.'

'What's the old adage? If at first you don't succeed, try and try again.' From the huge pile of covered pages at her feet, held down by a heavy paperweight this time, and the faded inkstains smattering her fingers, she wrote frequently and that too impressed him. They suggested she was both diligent and tenacious in her ambitions as well as hard working. Qualities of which he approved.

'That is what I try to tell myself. That and to make a dreadful pest of myself until they finally relent. Unless it is one of those days when I am so worn down by it all that I am ready to just give up all my vain ambitions of seeing my name in Hatchard's and accept somebody else's in its stead.'

'Why would you do that?'

She huffed a little as she shrugged, now clearly more annoyed than resigned. 'Because apparently Henry is a more palatable name on the front of a novel than Hope. In fact, apparently no name at all is better than the name Hope. Readers, I am frequently told in the most patronising and condescending of tones by the gentlemen in charge of such things, do not buy books written by girls.'

This was news to him. 'Why ever not?'

'Your guess is as good as mine, Lord Trouble, but I fear it is true. Can you name a female author?' She snapped her fingers as if it were a quick test.

'Mrs Radcliffe.' That he could clearly surprised her.

'And another?' He scanned his memory for a good half a minute before he shrugged, defeated. 'Exactly! That is the sort of prejudice I am dealing with.'

'I am sure there are plenty of female authors out

there.' Although for the life of him he couldn't think of any. It was hard to think straight when she was staring directly at him and looking so effortlessly seductive that his mind kept wandering. 'Perhaps it is a case of you not finding the right publisher yet who appreciates your story.'

'Yet one claimed they *would* appreciate them if Henry wrote them. I'd probably be in Hatchard's now if I relented on that petty publisher's insistence on a pseudonym.'

He had no answer for that. Unless the publishers were using that as an excuse to fob her off gently because her prose were actually awful and they didn't want to upset her. Being capable of writing copious pages did not necessarily guarantee the quality of writing and Luke was forever tossing dull books to one side because the dry plots bored him senseless. 'What is it about?' Because maybe that would enlighten him to the real cause of her rejection. 'Is it a cautionary, moral tale or does it involve knights in shining armour and damsels in distress?'

'Because obviously all women need a man to save them?' She rolled her eyes as she shook her head. 'I am disappointed you are so predictable in your assumptions, Lord Trouble.'

'It's a moral tale then. One warning of the dangers of straying from your chosen path of righteous piety. A predictably nun-like novel from a woman made of your unblemished moral fibre.'

The bookshops seemed to be stuffed with those dreadful tomes of late. They sat side by side on the shelves with the reams of nonsensical etiquette books which laid down the strange rules everybody in society seemed to put great stock in. Abigail was a huge fan of them and had been in the midst of reading one with the ludicrous title of *The Discerning Gentleman's Guide for Selecting the Perfect Bride* when he had left her. Or at least he assumed she was reading it because he kept finding it lying around everywhere. Although now, with the benefit of hindsight, he wouldn't have put it past her to have left it lying around intentionally to encourage him to heed the stupid advice on the strategically opened pages and select her as his bride before she had had to ask. That dawning realisation made him wince at his own naivety. Because of course that is what Abigail had done.

Hope folded her arms as she stared at him. It did wonderful things to her figure. 'You are the only man I have met who has ever compared me to a nun. For the life of me, I cannot fathom why.'

'When one is cursed to look like trouble, one understands that looks can be deceiving. And just because you happen to look like sin itself, doesn't necessarily mean you would act in a sinful manner.' Although despite the exceedingly modest fichu in an already modest dress, she had kissed him back, so perhaps she wasn't quite as prudish as he was making out. Before his mind aimlessly wandered down that seductive trail of thought, Luke gestured to the neat pile of paper. 'Besides, I wouldn't have to make such predictable assumptions if you simply put me out of my misery and told me what it's about.'

'I suppose it *is* a cautionary tale...' She bristled at his obvious disappointment. 'Though not in the traditional sense. It is about secrets and lies. Deceit and betrayal and greed. If there is a moral, it is that people cannot always be trusted and that you should always be wary of a man's motives until you know him well enough to

be sure of his character.' He stifled a yawn to vex her
and enjoyed the way her feline green eyes narrowed as
she pretended to look down her nose at him as she carried on undeterred. 'It's set here in the capital, in the
notorious rookery of St Giles, and centres around the
gory and seemingly senseless murders of four women.'

'Murder?'

'But not just any old murders, Lord Trouble, but murders most foul. The foulest in fact. Murders so dreadful,
so gruesome, so inhuman in their execution that the terrified residents of the slum believe that a hideous monster prowls their streets at night. One sent by the Devil
himself to punish them.' Those green eyes sparkled.

'To begin with, the gory murders seem random, but
it soon becomes apparent that they aren't. There is a
calculated method to my monster's madness and my
heroine has to unmask the killer before she becomes
his next unwitting victim.'

'Oh...' Now he really was impressed. 'That sounds...
intriguing.' And right up his alley. 'And, if you don't
mind me saying, a tad macabre for a genteel and proper
young lady such as yourself.'

'It is exceedingly macabre.'

'Like Walpole's *The Castle of Otranto* or *The Myster-
ies of Udolpho* by the aforementioned Mrs Radcliffe?'

She seemed surprised. 'You know those books?'

'Now who's making predicable assumptions? I
might look like a ne'er-do-well and a scoundrel—but I
can read, Hope. To be frank, there's not much else to
do in winter in my sleepy corner of Cornwall so I am
pretty certain I have read everything. I read *The Monk*
at twelve and it scared the death out of me. Especially
the bit where he's ripped apart by eagles and dropped
over a cliff and left to die in agony on the sharp rocks as

the tide comes in. There are a lot of cliffs in Cornwall and I live practically on the edge of one, but I deftly avoided them all for at least a year afterwards, including the one on my own doorstep.'

Her lovely face was appalled. 'Who on earth gave you that book at twelve?'

'Nobody. I found it on the dusty top shelf in the local vicar's study after he had left me there to contemplate my actions when he caught me scrumping apples from his orchard.' He smiled at the memory. 'So I only have myself to blame.'

'You really are trouble if you stole from a vicar!'

'I *borrowed* from a vicar and put the book back after dark one night while he was sleeping.' He couldn't help grinning when her eyes widened. 'We don't tend to lock doors in Cornwall and I can assure you he was none the wiser. And I prefer the term youthful high jinks than trouble. Pinching a few apples from trees groaning from the sheer weight of their plentiful fruit is hardly in the same league as murder most foul.'

'It's still appalling.' But she was amused, he could tell despite trying to pretend she wasn't. He already knew she was nowhere near as standoffish as she wanted the world to think. 'I am glad you had nightmares. It served you right for stealing *The Monk*.'

'Is your book as terrifying as that?'

Her mouth curved as she stared down her delightful nose at him. 'I sincerely hope so. Worse, in fact. It's grisly and bloodthirsty, not the least bit suitable for incorrigible twelve-year-olds or forgiving vicars. Or even irritating marquesses from the sleepy wilds of Cornwall for that matter either.'

'Then I should definitely love to read it. Despite my lifelong fear of eagles, I do enjoy a good Gothic novel.

Books should always elicit an emotional response and I haven't read anything except my brother's dusty ledgers in months.' Reading, like home and the occasional raucous night in a tavern with his old friends, was simply another joy which now had to be sacrificed.

Pity instantly swirled in her eyes. 'Forgive me... I should have offered my condolences before... I am so very sorry about your brother.'

'Not as sorry as I am.' Although more for himself than out of actual grief. It was difficult to mourn a stranger, especially such a callous, inhumane and cruel one. 'They are proving to be big shoes to fill.'

'My father only painted him last year and at that time your brother was in rude health.'

The penny dropped. 'Your father is Augustus Brookes?'

She nodded and beamed properly for the first time, leaving him once again staggered at just how beautiful she was. 'And my mother is Roberta Brookes the famous soprano, who was obviously a little put out when you didn't realise it earlier. Now even my elder sister Faith is making a name for herself in the art world, so I know all about big shoes to fill.' Her expression momentarily clouded. 'It can be daunting...particularly if you share none of their obvious talents and none of them quite understands yours.'

'I have no idea what I am doing.' The words tumbled out before he could stop them. 'I was never meant to inherit, I certainly never expected to and nobody prepared me for it. I was perfectly content running my little slate quarry and fixing my own ancient and leaky roof in the middle of nowhere, but now I have land and tenants, stocks, shares, employees and property coming out of my ears and none of it makes any sense to me at all and I have no clue what to do with it.'

'Don't you have an estate manager or something?'

'Oh, I have managers, three of them, and I am sure they would much prefer that I left them all to it like my brother did, but I am not built that way. I've never been one to rest on my laurels, I have always had to work for my living and I am used to understanding everything that is my business to know. I hate feeling so beholden and out of control.' Being out of control made him feel sick and scared and impotent again like he had when they had locked his mother away and he couldn't rescue her. But why the blazes he was telling her all this, he had no idea, other than he had the overwhelming compunction to tell someone and she was the only person he had met in London that he felt comfortable discussing it with. Something—probably extreme tiredness— told him she would understand.

'I can't even find someone decent to redecorate this house who doesn't want to swindle me. Upstairs looks like a brothel…' Should he be saying the word *brothel* in the presence of a lady? 'And downstairs looks like a tart's boudoir.' He definitely shouldn't be saying that, but he currently didn't have the capacity, the energy or the wherewithal to filter out the inappropriate.

She snorted, then laughed. It wasn't the least bit false or delicate but it was genuine. 'The decor of Lord Clacton's mistress is not to your taste then?' Curiosity then clearly got the better of her. 'Is it really *that* bad?'

'Come over…see it for yourself. On second thoughts, don't you dare. I pride myself on my strong constitution, but the colours are so shocking they make my head spin. I need to have my mother over for a visit, but I daren't invite her with it looking like this!'

'My father could help.'

'I thought he painted portraits, not walls.'

She giggled again and he found himself laughing too. It felt marvellous. 'I meant he knows lots of reputable and reliable tradesmen and will happily advise you to-morrow at tea. That's if he can get a word in edgewise, of course. My mother is beside herself with joy at the coup of being the first matron to take tea with the dis-solute new Marquess of Thundersley.' She said this un-apologetically, those cat-like eyes dancing.

'The newspapers only think I am dissolute because you pushed me in the fountain.'

She snorted at that. 'They think you are dissolute because you were found in that fountain drunk. I ac-cept no blame for that, sir.' She had him there. 'And be in no doubt, my mother only invited you to tea because she adores gossip and likes to be the first to have it so that she can spread it. You have quite the bad reputa-tion, Lord Trouble, and her mission tomorrow will be to grill you until she confirms it and then we will all have to give you a wide berth while she warns the rest of the capital of your depravity.'

'I guarantee she will adore me before the first cup is drunk. I am told I have a way with people, especially women, and I can be *very* charming. So charming it's a wonder some woman hasn't already snapped me up and rushed me down the aisle. And with my shiny new title, I am assured I am quite the catch.' Because her eyes widened at his barefaced nerve, and because she was at her loveliest and most unguarded when vexed and flustered, he couldn't resist flirting a bit simply to enjoy her reaction. 'Admit it, Hope—you are more than a little bit tempted by me yourself.'

She didn't disappoint, piercing him with a glare which was as cold and unrelenting as ice. 'What an over-inflated opinion you have of yourself. But, alas, like me, my family will see right through you. The entire Brookes clan have a nose for ne'er-do-wells.'

'Is that a challenge?'

'It's a fact, Lord Trouble, so gird your loins and prepare yourself for the Spanish Inquisition. My family are also loud, boisterous, interfering and not the least bit subtle about it. Which reminds me...' She broke eye contact to stare down at her hands. 'Thank you for not apprising them of our previous encounters. I flatly denied having anything to do with pushing you in that fountain when the papers linked me to the incident.' Her teeth worried her plump bottom lip, making him wonder if the mere mention of the fountain made her recall their splendid kiss exactly as it had him. 'It's probably best not to mention these unchaperoned little chats across the balcony either. My mother, especially, can be very protective...and I am rather fond of this room.'

'You have my word, as a man of honour, that they will be our secret.' Because he certainly didn't want them to stop. Not that he would have ever said anything to inadvertently malign her in the first place. He had been brought up to have the utmost respect for women and especially their fragile reputations. He had fiercely protected his mother's for years.

'Yes...' She smiled a little shyly this time, giving him a glimpse of the real her beneath all the tart bravado. 'That is probably best.' Then, as if she was mortified she had shown him too much vulnerability, she licked her fingers and briskly snuffed out her candles, plunging them both into virtual darkness before she gathered up her papers and stood. The only light now was the weak glow from the solitary lamp he had lit behind him by his bed which, to his still wandering mind, only served to make things feel more intimate. 'I might not be quite pious and prudish enough for a nunnery, but my mother certainly is and if she knew that…um…'

'We had shared a splendid kiss on our first meeting, you were confronted by the sight of me naked on our second and we keep having these gloriously unchaperoned and improper visits on the balcony, she'd have an apoplexy?'

'Precisely.' He could hear her amusement at his cockiness. 'And despite all that impropriety being entirely your fault, I'd be shipped off to that nunnery quicker than I could shove you in another pond for being so annoyingly smug about it all.'

'Fear not, my lips are sealed.'

'Thank you.' She exhaled in relief as she backed a little further through the doors. 'And tomorrow we shall behave as proper, polite and indifferent strangers and continue in that vein henceforth.'

'While you have my solemn pledge that I will behave in public, I absolutely refuse to do so in private. I see no reason to add propriety into our relationship at this late stage of the game. Especially as I find myself thoroughly delighted by the impropriety of it all.'

'You are incorrigible.' And he could still hear her smiling.

'That I am…but I suspect you already rather like that about me.'

'I see, my poor misguided *Lord Trouble*, that you are arrogant and deluded too.' Her affected huff lacked conviction. 'As I can assure you I have found little to like so far.'

'But a man can hope—*Hope*.'

'Oh, dear.' She rewarded his playful comment with a

saucy, exaggerated yawn. 'Arrogant, deluded, incorrigible and yet so depressingly *predictable* too. What a continued disappointment you are shaping up to be... *Luke*.' Then in a sultry swish of petticoats, she was gone.

Chapter Six

'Dorothy Philpot said she and her parents chatted to him before he went for his infamous drunken swim in Lady Writtle's pond, and they all found him perfectly amiable.' Charity's voice was nowhere near a whisper as the four of them awaited the arrival of their new neighbour in their drawing room at precisely one minute to three. 'She also said that despite the beard, she also considered him to be one of the most sinfully handsome gentlemen she had ever seen. But then Dorothy Philpot finds any man with a pulse handsome and while Lord Thundersley has a strong face, I am not entirely sure what I feel about gentlemen with beards. What did you think of his beard, Hope?'

She most certainly would not admit that she suddenly liked beards a great deal. Especially dripping wet.

And the odd earring.

'I think you should keep your voice down in case he hears.' Her little sister was as subtle as a house brick thrown through a hothouse window.

Charity shrugged, unrepentant. 'Well he's not here yet is he? So I shall continue to speculate freely about our handsome new neighbour until he arrives and I can categorically form a solid opinion of him over tea. Though I can see why Colonel Wigstock confused him with a pirate.' Purely to annoy her, her sister's voice got even louder. 'As he does look exceedingly wild and untamed with all that hair and exactly the sort you imagine grasping a helm in one hand and his rum ration in the other.'

'Please do not even mention rum!' Her mother shuddered. 'Wild and untamed is bad enough but I pray he isn't really a dissolute D-R-U-N-K-A-R-D as well. After all the scandalous shenanigans Lord Clacton's bawdy mistress subjected us to, I had rather hoped to have a more sedate neighbour this time around.'

Hope lowered her voice to a whisper on the off chance it would encourage her unsubtle womenfolk to do the same. 'As he was perfectly sober yesterday, I am not sure he is thoroughly dissolute, despite what the gossip columns have to say. You know how they exaggerate things.'

She felt honour bound to defend that slight because he was right. The only reason they had started to call him dissolute in the first place was because she had pushed him in the pond. And despite his tipsy state, he had instinctively protected her then by blaming his sudden urge to swim on the amount of alcohol he had consumed. 'And none of us witnessed the incident to fairly judge.'

That had been rather noble of him even if he had been a tad drunk. As had playing along with her lie yesterday.

But that aside, she was coming to suspect he was more noble than dissolute as a matter of course. Dissolute men didn't work for a living or want to redecorate rooms so that their mothers could visit. Nor did they read extensively. And if they did read, few had read *The Monk*, which was quite a weighty tome and which her bluestocking character approved of immensely.

Luke was, however, sinfully handsome.

Her sister and the flaky Dorothy Philpot had at least got that right. The mere sight of him in his well-fitting waistcoat and breeches last night had certainly set her pulse racing again. Largely because her vivid imagination still insisted on picturing him nude whenever they collided, and likely would the instant he arrived just to make her feel more unsettled. When her stupid heart was already beating nineteen to the dozen at the prospect of meeting him again in the first place. And for reasons she couldn't explain, his calling felt significant, even though she knew it wasn't and certainly did not want it to be. Then, to add insult to injury, her brain absolutely refused to forget that kiss. That had been the dictionary definition of *delicious* and the arrogant, eminently likeable wretch probably knew it.

'I think we should reserve judgement until we know him better.'

Charity gaped at her, slack-jawed. 'Are you suggesting Lord Thundersley might be decent? *You?* The eternal pessimist—who usually thinks the worst of everyone and everything *all* of the time?'

Hope's heartbeat sped up a little more at being called out. Because she was usually an eternal and outspoken pessimist, especially when it involved men. Then it practically bounced out of her chest when they heard the door knocker. 'I most certainly did not say that.'

Because she caught herself hissing, she affected one of her typical, cynical expressions as she continued to whisper in a more measured manner. 'I merely cautioned believing the gossips columns, when we all know, more than most, how daft most of what they print actually is.'

That earned her another disbelieving look from Charity, which with hindsight Hope realised was deserved because she never openly gave any man the benefit of the doubt as a point of principle. They were all always guilty until proven innocent, which they rarely, if ever were. The one and only recent exception to that cast-iron rule had been Piers, Faith's new husband, because he had only ever had eyes for Faith and had more than proved his mettle in the most gallant and endearing way possible. But then he was the exception rather than the rule as far as gentlemen were concerned and there likely wasn't another one anywhere close to being as worthy as him within ten thousand miles. 'As to your silly wittering on about Lord Thundersley being as handsome as sin, I would also remind you looks can be deceiving, and that easy charm and an attractive face can cover a multitude of character defects.'

'I never said he was charming.'

In case her sister handed her a shovel to dig a bigger hole for herself, Hope glossed over that damning comment. 'Regardless—despite my sensible advice warning you not to believe everything that you read in the papers, I still wouldn't trust *any* man as far as I could throw him as a matter of course, and neither should you.'

With perfect timing, the housekeeper chose that exact moment to open the door and introduce him while Luke beamed behind her, practically filling up the frame and looking effortlessly, wildly gorgeous while he did so.

'By the looks of this particular man, I doubt you could budge him, let alone throw him.' Charity's unsubtle stage whisper as her gaze boldly and appreciatively swept him up and down earned her a disapproving glare from her mother and a sharp jab in the ribs from Hope.

Typically, their father chose selective deafness and blindness as he always did when his family irked him. 'My Lord Thundersley—what a delight it is to make your acquaintance.' He rushed forward to pump Luke's hand in greeting. 'Welcome! I am Augustus Brookes and you have already met my wife Roberta and our two younger daughters. My eldest, Faith, is recently married and currently honeymooning in the West Country— your neck of the woods, my lord—and then they are to summer at one of his father's properties in Bath. Hope and Charity are to join them there in August.'

'It is a beautiful part of the country to be sure. I miss it dreadfully. I hope your daughter visits the castle of Tintagel and the coast thereabouts as that has the most stunning scenery.' He smiled with obvious affection for the place. 'Though I confess I am biased towards it as that is also my home.' Then those dark eyes sought Hope's. 'The cliffs, especially, are a sight to see. If you are brave enough to risk visiting a cliff.'

'I shall be sure to recommend them to Faith in my next letter. I am not sure if you are aware, but my eldest is also the new Viscountess Eastwood,' said her mother preening, 'and daughter-in-law to the Earl and Countess of Writtle. But listen to me gabbling on… Please— sit. The tea is already steeping and if we leave it much longer it will be stewed.'

'You are too kind, Mrs Brookes.' Then he turned towards the sofa. His easy, almost reassuring but innocuous smile as he glanced briefly Hope's way instantly relaxed her. 'And good day to you too, Miss Charity and Miss Hope.'

'Good afternoon, my lord.' Charity was using her

breathy and seductive voice, and for some inexplicable reason that galled. 'There is a space here next to me.' She shuffled to the middle of the sofa next to Hope and patted the end cushion.

'I think Lord Thundersley would prefer a bigger seat than being cramped up with you.' Her mother gestured to the wingback closest to her while shooting quiet daggers at her wayward youngest. 'Can I tempt you with some cake, my lord?'

'As I have been dining on bread, cheese and toast these past two days, cake sounds divine.'

'Why only toast, my lord?' Charity gifted him her most attractive and beguilingly interested smile.

'Because my new cook doesn't arrive till the end of the month alongside the rest of the staff and toast is one of the only culinary delights in my limited repertoire. Although I do make a rather splendid cup of tea if I do say myself, so all is not lost.'

'You are next door all alone!' Her mother was appalled. 'Oh, good heavens! You poor man.'

'At the moment, I am barely there, so it's no hardship and I rather like the peace.'

'But what about the army of servants already in your Mayfair house?' Her mother was as subtle as Charity. 'Why have none of them accompanied you here?'

'They were all so happily ensconced in Berkeley Square, it felt cruel to move them.'

'Which obviously begs the question as to what made you swap that grand house for next door in the first place?' Her sister was more shameless. 'As charming as it is, Bedford Place is no match for Berkeley Square.'

His face clouded for a split second before he masked it with a lopsided smile. 'That house felt too much like my brother's.'

'Yes… I suppose that must be difficult so soon after his passing.' Her father paused as if choosing his next words carefully before he smiled a little too innocently, clearly also fishing for more. 'And now that I have met you, I am not surprised you do not feel at home there.' Papa had not been particularly taken with the former Marquess of Thundersley and had found painting the fellow's portrait a huge chore because he had been so pompous and condescending. 'You are not at all like your brother.'

'I shall take that as a compliment, sir—even if it wasn't intentionally meant as one.' Clearly, there were no flies on the new Marquess. 'And you are quite correct. I am nothing like him.'

Poor Papa instantly backtracked. 'I meant no offence to you or him, my lord.'

'And I took none, sir, I can assure you. My brother and I are—were—as different as chalk and cheese and a veritable ocean flowed between us which neither of us made much effort to cross. I suppose that comes from having two very different mothers and vastly contrasting upbringings. I grew up with mine in a remote and ramshackle house in the countryside, a good ten miles west of the raucous excitement of sleepy Penzance and was left entirely to my own devices, while he grew up in that pristine mausoleum in Mayfair with my humourless father and all the responsibilities.'

Which threw up a million questions, none of which Hope could ask in front of her parents as they were all too personal and not at all suitable for supposed strangers.

'To tell you the truth, that imposing house is too perfect and soulless for me and I am not really snooty Mayfair's type, am I?'

Charity batted her lashes. 'Thank goodness.'

If he noticed, Luke hid it well. 'Besides, it is very much his widow's home where I am sure I got under her feet, so I was glad to leave it and give us both some space to adjust to our new situation—even if it meant swapping it for my atrocious new puce parlour.'

'Yes… I suppose it must have been difficult for both of you to adapt to such a sudden and unexpected change of circumstances.' Her father had disliked the Marchioness of Thundersley considerably more than he had her pompous husband. He thought her an unpleasant and imperious woman. Largely because she had always blatantly given the cut direct to all three of his daughters at all the social functions where they unfortunately collided. Now, despite his smile and carefully chosen words, she got the distinct impression Luke disliked her intensely too. 'Mayfair's loss is Bloomsbury's gain, my lord. You will find we are much more agreeable and less formal this side of Holborn anyway.'

'Thank the lord, for I am not used to formality.' His gaze briefly drifted back to hers. 'In fact, I loathe it as it only serves as a way for our supposed betters to put decent people in their place, when to my mind respect is something which should always be earned rather than expected as a due.' He couldn't have said anything to win her low-born parents over more and both her mother and her father nodded their approval.

'Indeed, my lord.' Papa smiled approvingly. He had always had a healthy disregard for the aristocracy despite their patronage being his bread and butter. 'I too prefer to judge a man on his merits. Yet another good reason for you to have upped sticks and deserted Mayfair. While there are several decent sorts residing there, like my son-in-law's splendid family, there are twice as many again who think themselves a notch above everyone else with no substance behind that expectation, my lord.'

'Back home, everyone calls me Luke, so I insist you do the same, sir, seeing as this is my home too now and we are neighbours.'

'Then we insist on the same, Luke, don't we, Roberta?'

Exactly as he had promised, his easy, self-effacing charm already had her parents eating out of his hand. Within minutes they all settled into the sort of polite conversation fresh acquaintances engaged in when they were on their best behaviour and keen to make a good impression. However, that only served to make Hope more uncharacteristically nervous than she already was. He clearly had no problem thinking of things to say— neither did the rest of her family—and he was effortlessly friendly and witty. Unfortunately, she seemed to have lost the power of speech and remained largely mute unless included in something specific and even then her usual powers of pithy observation and witty retort appeared to have deserted her. Fifteen minutes in, and Charity had plainly noticed her odd behaviour too and kept slipping her curious side glances which did nothing to alleviate the problem.

'Our eldest, Faith, follows her father.' Her mother was now waxing lyrical as she gave him a potted history of the family. 'And is a supremely talented artist in her own right. The picture above the mantel is one of hers, painted when she was just fourteen.'

Luke stared at the seascape and smiled as he was supposed to. 'If she was that good at fourteen, I shudder to think how brilliant her work is now.'

'When you have a free afternoon, you must visit the

Royal Academy as her magnificent *Sunset over London* is currently the shining star of their summer exhibition.' Both her mother and father beamed with pride. 'Unless you saw her stunning tableau in the Earl and Countess of Writtle's ballroom of course, as that is a triumph too and Faith's first official commission.' Her mother innocently sipped her tea and stared at him over the rim before her innate nosiness got the better of her. 'You were there weren't you, Luke? Only I am sure I saw you there…on the terrace…towards the end of the evening.'

She was so shameless. Hope willed herself invisible while focusing as hard as she could on the liquid in her cup.

'If you are referring to the unfortunate debacle with the fountain, Roberta, and my infamous dip in it, then yes, I was there.' His unoffended smile was all mischief. 'Although to be honest with you, after causing such a frightful scene and leaving with my tail dripping between my legs, I have to admit I missed your daughter's tableau. To be frank, as it was my first venture into high society, I spent most of the evening a little overawed with it all…until all that country mouse awe and wonder combined with the free-flowing champagne got the better of me. Especially after I stupidly mixed it with the fresh air I had wrongly assumed might clear my head.'

He managed to look both sincere, amused and apologetic at the same time, and so thoroughly and boyishly charming that her mother was instantly smitten by it all. 'I had never been to an affair quite so grand before and we drink plain old ale instead of heady champagne in Tregally, so *perhaps* I did not make the best first impression upon society as I could have done. I beg of you not to judge me completely on the back of it.'

'Nerves sometimes get the better of us all, Luke.

Every single time I wait in the wings before I step on the stage, they positively swamp me.'

'Me too.' Charity nodded emphatically because she knew that always made her pretty golden curls bounce in the most becoming way. 'Although the butterflies swiftly disappear as soon as I start to sing.'

'Charity follows me,' said her mother in case he missed that pertinent detail, 'and we have no doubt that one day she too will be a leading lady once she has done her apprenticeship in the chorus. Although she has done such a good job in *Così fan Tutte* at the Theatre Royal, she has now been made the understudy for the part of Despina.' A minor role at the very best, thought Hope churlishly while simultaneously wondering why she was suddenly jealous of her sister's success when she never had been before. Envious, perhaps, that she like Faith shared the same talents as their parents, but not in the competitive sense.

'Though sadly, I have yet to perform her to an audience and time is rapidly running out to do so.' Her youngest sister's eyelashes fluttered attractively. 'So nobody knows I am almost as good a soprano as my mother is.'

'I've seen you, dear.' Their mother beamed across the Persian. 'And I can confirm that you are better than me. At your age, my voice was nowhere near as powerful and your musicality is second to none. Charity is destined for great things, Luke. Greater than I could ever have dreamed of.'

'And who does Miss Hope follow?' Bless Luke for trying to include her even though it galled that he felt he had to, but he had inadvertently kicked a hornets' nest. Or a cuckoo's nest, as she was very definitely the odd Brookes out.

'Well she could have followed me on to the stage as she has a lovely singing voice, but sadly showed no interest in developing her talent.' A point of contention her mother had never understood. 'She dallied with it briefly, and was even taken on as a student of Signor Alessandro Ricci the great protégé of Bernacchi, but stopped her lessons at fifteen. Though lord only knows why. I never have fully got to the bottom of it when she was showing such promise.'

All eyes suddenly swivelled to her for a better explanation, and for a split second she almost blurted the whole mortifying truth before she stopped herself. 'There is no mystery, Mama. I just didn't enjoy it.' A statement her musical mother always found inconceivable when music was her life. 'As you are always saying, life is too short to waste your dreams on folly.' Which was the truth, in a roundabout sort of way.

Hope had never possessed either the affection or the dedication to music to want to pursue it properly. She had always preferred words over music and plays over operettas. She could sing well enough if she put her mind to it—but nowhere near as well as her brilliant mother and sister. However, the biggest reason why her lessons had come to a shuddering halt was because, at the tender age of fifteen, fate had already cursed her with the body of a woman and the fêted Signor Ricci had been the first of a long and continual line of gentlemen who were mesmerised nonsensical by the sight of her generous bosoms. Especially when they rose, fell and heaved with the exertion singing opera required and it was a constant battle to prevent him from groping them. 'My artistic talents lie elsewhere.'

'My middle daughter fancies herself an author, Luke.' Her father said this with the indulgent but ever so slightly dismissive tone both parents used when they mentioned her writing. Neither of them were great readers and did not understand how something as mundane as a book could captivate anyone in the same way as the expressive arts of painting and performing could. They were always supportive of dreams of course— the Brookes family were big on following dreams and fulfilling artistic ambitions—they just thought some dreams were more worthy than others. 'She is always scribbling away at something, and if she isn't writing her own books, she has her nose buried in somebody else's.'

'In my humble opinion, there is nothing better than a good book.' Luke's dark eyes locked with hers intently as he smiled, warming her with his approval and his unexpected support. 'Like your daughter, I enjoy nothing more than putting my feet up and losing myself in a story. I follow my mother in that. She is a great reader and spent hours sharing that passion with me as a child. That love of literature has stayed with me ever since. Our parlour in Cornwall is always scattered with our favourite novels. I shall look forward to the day it will be scattered with some of Miss Hope's too and I can have the bragging rights of knowing a famous author.' They stared at each other as he smiled, and for a moment as the rest of the room receded, she found herself smiling back.

'And speaking of parlours...' Her sister suddenly sat forward, blocking him entirely from Hope's view. Unless she craned around her. Which, of course, she would never do. Not when he apparently had the power to make her forget where she was. 'You must enlighten us about the hideous puce parlour you inherited next door, my lord.'

'I can assure you, Miss Charity, that that unsettling shade of wallpaper is merely the tip of the iceberg of the tasteless atrocities inflicted on my fine new house by its previous owner. So hideous and offensive, it makes my eyes water.' Unwittingly, Charity had thrown Luke the perfect bone, and because he needed her father's help finding suitable tradesmen to fix it quickly, he gratefully caught it, effectively killing all bookish conversation stone dead. Hope tried and failed not to feel disappointed at the abrupt change of subject which rendered her lowly artistic talents inconsequential and forgotten.

As usual.

'Lord Clacton's former mistress was a veritable paragon of bad taste, if her dreadful gaudy outfits were any gauge.' Her mother shuddered theatrically as she pulled a disgusted face. 'So I dread to think what her decor must look like.'

'It's appalling.' The way he said it made appalling sound exciting and not to be missed. 'If you would be kind enough to point me in the direction of some decent tradesmen to redecorate it, I will happily give you all a guided tour right this minute so you can experience the sheer horror for yourselves. Though I'll warn you, once it is seen, it cannot be unseen and you'll likely have nightmares for weeks.'

Chapter Seven

They almost flattened him in their haste to get to Number Twenty-Two. Like a pair of stampeding elephants, her mother and sister led the charge, leaving Hope and her still limping father trailing in their wake.

Once inside, Luke gestured to the drawing room and as her family rushed into it, he hung back so he could walk into the room last beside her, only winking at her conspiratorially when nobody else could see. 'It's a bit spartan at the moment but I fear that only makes it worse.'

'Good heavens above!' Her father's involuntary gasp said it all, as the strange shade of pink flock moiré wallpaper was rather unsettling and the floral filled Grecian urn emblazoned over it in busy stripes did peculiar things to her eyes. Above, the moulded flowers on the coving and cornices had been painted pink to match, with incongruous lime-green leaves surrounding them. Worse, the window dressings matched the offensive puce and lime-green colour scheme and gave the rest of the room a decidedly unpleasant and somewhat sinister hue. And there were tassels and fringes everywhere. Luke's unguarded description of a tart's boudoir last night was an apt one, as it certainly had the air of a bawdy house about it. Not that she'd ever been in a bawdy house of course. 'What a strange shade that is…' The more she looked at it, the more the odd colour bore a striking resemblance to raw offal. 'And I see she managed to find a Persian rug to match.' A vile monstrosity of a carpet if ever there was one.

'It's a very bold room.' For once, Charity was trying to be diplomatic. 'But it certainly doesn't suit you, my lord.'

'By that she means it's a gawdy monstrosity.' Hope laughed. She couldn't help herself because he looked ridiculous among it all. Even the chandelier and the wall lamps sprang a plethora of deep pink glass flowers among the fussy cascading crystal droplets.

'Don't be so tactless, Hope!' Her mother instantly bristled, despite undoubtedly thinking much the same. 'Monstrosity is such a damning word.'

'I am sure Lord Thundersley realises it's a garish monstrosity, else he wouldn't be so desperate to change it.'

'That I do.' His dark eyes danced as they drifted to hers over the top of her mother's significantly shorter head. 'I cannot step in here without feeling bilious, Miss Hope. Why else would I bare my soul and throw myself at the mercy of your family within minutes of meeting you all? I am a stranger in a strange land, in desperate need of a pious good Samaritan.' He was clearly enjoying over-egging things because those mischievous dark eyes were twinkling as he waited for hers to narrow, so she stared blandly back simply to thwart him.

'It's all going to need to be stripped but as long as the plaster is good underneath it shouldn't take too long.' Her father ran his fingers over one of the tasteless gold-

and-cerise tassels on the curtain tieback and grimaced. 'The only salvageable thing, as far as I can see, is the floor.'

'The parquet *is* nice.' Charity shot Luke her best come-hither smile as she oh-so-casually sauntered past him with unnecessarily undulating hips. 'And the ceiling and fireplace are quite lovely.' Then, much to Hope's complete and irrational consternation, her flirty sister's fingertips slowly caressed the back of one of the enormous wingbacks which they had witnessed being delivered with the rest of his small cartload of effects. 'And the workmanship on these chairs is exquisite.'

To her relief, he didn't flirt back or seem even remotely tempted to. If anything, he appeared oblivious of it. 'It is, though I confess I bought them more for their size than the quality of the wood turning. The furniture in the Mayfair house was so delicate and spindly, I was terrified to sit on it in case I flattened it.' Then he shrugged as he smiled at her sister before flicking Hope another amused glance which subtly let her know that he had noticed but was purposely ignoring it, and sent a distracting waft of something seductively spicy straight up her nostrils in the process. 'Back in Cornwall we prefer substance over style and make things more robust.'

'Including the gentlemen.' Charity never missed an opportunity to beguile a new victim with some well-placed flattery and likely wouldn't be happy until she had captured the heart of every breathing man in the capital, and beyond, under her seductive spell. In case he missed her overt message, she batted her eyelashes at him for good measure. 'You must enlighten me as to where you acquired that jaunty earring. I heard a rumour it was on a pirate ship...'

He laughed and tugged the gold loop as if he had long forgotten it was there. 'Sadly, nowhere near as exciting. I spent two summers on a herring boat and was goaded into the earring when I balked at the suggestion of a tattoo.'

'But still, you were a sailor. I've always thought there is something romantic about the sea…'

Hope rolled her eyes at her sister before she stepped into the breach to save him. Or at least that was how she justified her tart interruption to herself. 'What do you want done to this room, Lord Thundersley?'

'Well frankly, as you can plainly see, anything would be an improvement, but I would definitely prefer something…subtler.' Was that a veiled dig at Charity? She certainly hoped so. It would make a change to see a man not eating out of her little sister's beguiling hands. 'Something calm and soothing.'

'I cannot say I blame you. This room is a bit like a sharp slap to the face.'

Luke came up beside her and folded his arms as they both stared at the wallpaper again in mutual disgust. 'Appalling isn't it?'

'I think it's a way past appalling. I'd even go as far as to say it has boldly ventured into the darkest realms of the horrendous.' She grinned up at him, until she caught Charity watching them with interest.

Oblivious of that, Luke playfully nudged her with his elbow, causing her fascinated sibling's eyebrows to raise knowingly. 'If you think this room is horrendous, Miss Brookes, you should see upstairs. Although I am not altogether sure if I should show any of you what abominations Lord Clacton's mistress did to the master bedroom. I've certainly never seen anything quite like it before. It's enough to give anyone nightmares.'

Her father had now moved from the garish tieback to the peculiar gilt swirls painted on the door panels. 'I know a man who can fix all of this and will not charge you an arm and a leg for doing it.'

'You do?' Luke received this news like a man given a pardon on the steps to the gallows.

'I do. As I send a great deal of business his way, I shall also impress on him the urgency of the matter as he owes me a few favours and I dare say the quicker we erase this pink monstrosity from the face of the earth, the better.' Her father pulled a face as he glanced back at the curtains. 'I shall send a message to him presently and declare your case an emergency. Is it just this room or is the rest of the house as bad?'

'The master bedroom is as bad, if not worse than here. The rest, thankfully, was spared.'

'Then we must see that next!' Her mother would take no refusal and immediately started towards the door.

As he had promised, the scarlet-and-black bedchamber was worse, and after they all trailed back to Number Twenty-One suitably dumbfounded by it all, Hope was dispatched to fetch a fresh pot of tea while Luke ensconced himself with her father in his studio to discuss suitable tradesmen and realistic London prices for fixing the mess.

'What is going on?' The swift arm through her elbow stopped her short of the kitchen. 'Because I swear blind, Sister dearest, that something is.' Charity wagged an admonishing finger. 'I thought I sensed a strange atmosphere between you and Lord Thundersley yesterday, but after seeing the pair of you today, I am now utterly convinced of it.'

'And apparently I am the one with the vivid imagination?' Hope scoffed, feigning amusement as she tugged her arm away.

'There was a frisson between you.'

'There wasn't.'

'You were smiling.'

'I do smile upon occasion.'

'Not at handsome and charming gentlemen who know they are both handsome and charming, you don't.'

Hope strode towards the kitchen. 'Mama sent me for tea.'

'He kept staring at you.'

'I cannot say I noticed.'

'Probably because you were too busy sighing at him yourself.'

Hope's fingers dropped from the doorknob as she glared at her sister, her hands going defiantly to her hips while her pulse called her a liar. 'If anyone was sighing, *Sister dearest*, it was you. Shamelessly batting your eyelashes at him and seductively caressing his chair. I don't know why you don't just wear a placard stating you are ripe and ready for a flirtation and be done with it!'

'I was merely testing him to see if he was a natural flirt by nature or if it was just you who captivated him. Which it was by the way, so your jealousy is misplaced.'

'Do not judge me by your lowly standards. I have never been as easily swayed by a handsome face as you are. Nor do I practice flirting—ever—because flirting only gives men ideas and they all seem to have quite enough of those about me already without any encouragement whatsoever. And as for your ludicrous idea that I would be jealous of you for flirting with *him*, I can categorically assure you that I am not the least bit...' She found herself talking to her sister's raised palm.

'Oh, save your breath, Hope! For I am not the least bit convinced by your forceful denials to the contrary and you are an unconvincing liar. The poor man looks at you as if no other woman in the world exists for him, and you know it.' A comment which both thrilled and alarmed Hope in equal measure. 'Which begs the obvious question as to why, when one considers how fresh and new your acquaintance is…unless it isn't of course, which puts an entirely different slant on things.'

'I have no control over how Lord Thundersley does or doesn't look at me—any more than I have any sway over the way most men gawp and leer at me.'

'*You* pushed him in the fountain, didn't you?'

'Of course not!'

'Why did you push him in the fountain, Hope? What wicked and presumptuous thing did the dissolute new Marquess do?'

'I swear I never met him before yesterday.'

'Did he flirt with you at the Writtles'? Or was it worse? Did he make a saucy comment about your figure like that hapless officer at Gunter's the other week?' Charity was laughing, obviously enjoying herself while Hope squirmed. 'Or maybe he tried to steal a kiss.' Hope's spine involuntarily stiffened before she could summon the bravado to deny it, and although she covered it quickly, her canny sister saw it because her jaw slackened in shock. 'Was he successful?'

As she floundered for the correct words to express her outrage at the accusation, her younger and most annoying sibling threw her head back and roared. 'Oh, good Lord! You're as red as your hair because he *did* kiss you, didn't he? Didn't he?' She prodded her hard in the arm with her finger. 'You—*you!*—kissed our sinfully handsome, possibly dissolute pirate neighbour at

Faith's engagement ball! That's why you leapt to his defence so vociferously earlier too. *You* kissed him and *you* liked it!'

'I did nothing of the sort!' But her crimson face was confirmation enough so there was no point in denying it. Nothing ever escaped either of her sisters for long, and she was long past the point of protesting too much. 'If you must know he kissed me, quite unexpectedly and out of the blue, and got to swim in the fountain for his impertinence!'

This confession earned her a jab in the ribs this time from her sister's pointed finger. 'I knew it! I knew there was an odd air between the pair of you. It certainly explains why you are so mute around him. Both yesterday on the street and today in the drawing room, you were uncharacteristically quiet and much too polite. So much so I barely recognised you as my acerbic, acidic and cynical sister!'

'Will you keep your voice down!'

'I cannot believe you kissed Lord Thundersley over a week ago and kept it all to yourself.' Charity bounced on the spot, clearly beside herself with joy at having such a delicious faux pas to hold against her. 'It must have been a truly magnificent kiss for him to have moved to Bloomsbury on the back of it.'

That dangerous avenue of speculation needed nipping in the bud. 'It was an instantly forgettable kiss.' One that made her lips tingle just thinking about it. 'Which only came about because he was saving me from Lord Harlington's advances…'

'The plot thickens…'

'Oh, for goodness sake!' Sometimes, only the truth would do, even if it was applied sparingly. 'I went to hide in the garden because Horrid Harlington refused to leave me alone and wanted a waltz. While I was there, Lord Thundersley stumbled across me by the fountain and when we heard Harlington heading towards us, I hastily asked him if he would help me get rid of him. I was hoping he would do so by intimidating him with his height, but in his drunken state, he chose to pretend we were having a tryst instead. It was all over in seconds. Lord Harlington stormed off in a huff at being spurned and your pirate ended up in the fountain exactly as he deserved!' She would omit the naked balcony scene, and indeed balconies altogether alongside the cosy chats they had while on them. 'That would have been an end to it until coincidence moved him in next door and we collided on the pavement yesterday. Where I insisted he pretend we had no prior acquaintance as I had lied about having anything to do with the fountain and nobly he agreed.'

'Oh, he is noble now as well as charming, is he?'

'After the blistering lecture Mama and Papa gave me about my temper when that idiot soldier propositioned me at Gunter's and I covered him in ice cream, it seemed prudent to deny my hand in that within scant days of the other incident.' Hope squared her shoulders, crossed her fingers behind her back and looked her sister dead in the eye. 'That is the whole truth, and the sum total of all my dealings with Lord Thundersley to date, I swear it. Please keep it to yourself. He has since apologised for his drunken misunderstanding, but even so—can you imagine our parents' overreaction if they knew the truth? It would be blown out of all proportion by Mama as all things invariably always are, especially when the guilty party is sat in our very own drawing room.'

Charity stared at her for several moments while she forced herself to stare back unflinching. 'And there is nothing else? Only you did seem uncharacteristically quiet and occupied, and you did keep glancing at him when you thought nobody was looking.'

'Hardly a surprise when he was but feet away and a single wrong word from him could bring my flimsy lie crashing around my ears.'

'But you are never so gushing about a man. You usually loathe them before they even open their mouths.'

Usually because they had already leered at her chest before they opened them.

'Hargreaves is a good chap. Honest too…' Her father's voice suddenly drifted down the hallway from the direction of the studio, signalling they were done. 'And if you are prepared to pay a small premium to expediate things, he'll make your place presentable in no time.'

'I am in your debt, Augustus.' Luke's deep voice made her stupid lips tingle again. 'For both the sound advice and for taking pity on me and inviting me to dinner tonight. Are you sure your lovely wife will not mind the intrusion…?'

Not dinner! Please God, not dinner too!

'Dinner was Roberta's idea and she will not take no for an answer…'

She was doomed. 'Please, Charity! I am begging you, keep my secret.'

Her sister grinned. 'Of course I'll keep your secret because that is what good sisters do.'

She then spun on her heel and sauntered back towards the voices now in the drawing room, then paused to toss one final salvo over her shoulder before she turned the corner. 'But do not for one second think that I am the slightest bit convinced by your obviously abridged and edited version of events, Hope. Because I have eyes and I can see, and what I can plainly see is, frankly…*fascinating.*'

Chapter Eight

Once again, the new Marquess of T. was seen out with the B. family of Bloomsbury. However, the jury is still out as to which of Mr B.'s beautiful daughters he prefers as both were spotted on his arm at the Royal Academy Summer Exhibition yesterday. Miss C. has all the charm and congeniality, but as we well know, Gentle Reader, Miss H. has all the fire...

Whispers Behind the Fan
June 1814

'**Y**our father left you nothing?' Hope reached across the balcony railings to accept the second cup of tea he had poured her from the pot he had brought up expressly for their nightly chat.

After a week of casual unplanned but habitual clandestine conversations which seemed to last longer the more they got to know one another, he decided he might as well turn up prepared. The tea was still almost drinkable but the mound of hot buttered toast which he had also brought to share was long gone.

'Not exactly. He left me the Tregally house we live

in, although it wasn't in the best state then, the one hundred and forty acres of grazing pasture surrounding it and a tin mine without any tin in it. He left my mother—his wife—nothing. Not a single brass farthing. But he did leave instructions to my brother to deal with her exactly as he saw fit.' Which had been to have her unjustly locked in a notorious private madhouse for three years until Luke had reached the age of majority and was able to get her out of it.

But he wouldn't mention that bit.

It was a buzzing hornets' nest and much too complicated and close to his heart to lay it open for dissection. He had learned, at great cost, to be careful who he shared it with as most people judged him differently as a result, but worse, treated his poor mother like a pariah. Even back home in Cornwall, only a few trusted servants were aware of some his mother's struggles because first his father and then Luke had concealed them so well. Only Clowance was privy to the full extent of them all, and as they were ultimately his mother's struggles and she was so very ashamed of them she couldn't bring herself to even talk about them, it wasn't his place to discuss them—even with someone he trusted like Hope.

'He also made Cassius my guardian, although a fat lot of good that did me, because my dear brother wanted to immediately shove me in a uniform and dispatch me to the war.' Yet another thing they had come to blows over, because his brother knew Luke would never desert his mother and that gave him the perfect excuse to cut them both loose. 'When I refused he washed his hands of me and I was left to fend for us both.' Except it had been too late to save her from his brother's well-laid vengeful plans and by the time he had returned home to Tregally, his poor mother had been taken. Bound in a straitwaistcoat and gagged in his absence, then incarcerated in a hellhole a good hundred and fifty miles from her now completely penniless, powerless, and underage son. 'I had to earn my own living from that day forth.'

'Hence the stint as a herring fisherman.' She shook her head, appalled. 'The more I hear of Cassius, the more I dislike him. What I don't understand, what I struggle to understand when I am so close to my own sisters, is what he had against you?'

'He had it in for my mother.' An understatement. If he could have, Cassius would have had her thrown anonymously in Bedlam as a pauper and made sure they tossed away the key. A mad marchioness was an unacceptable embarrassment to the Thundersley name, ergo, they had worked hard for a good quarter of a century to erase all evidence of her. That's why his father had banished her to Cornwall in the first place after all, when Luke had still been in leading strings, and there she remained until Cassius had had her dragged kicking and screaming to the Mill House. Her unpalatable mental deficiencies were also the reason why he had also been exiled with her, because the presence of a motherless child might remind all and sundry to enquire about the mother. Not to mention the likelihood he had inherited the same weaknesses from that mother and her inferior blood, which made him as good as worthless as far as they were all concerned, and therefore best dealt with on the sly before it all became a problem too.

They were two dirty secrets brushed ruthlessly under the carpet. The family had done such a thorough job of it, he had lost count of the times he'd had to explain that he was indeed Cassius's brother and not a distant cousin out of the direct blood line who had inherited, and that his mother was still alive when they all thought her long dead. Because his father had, he had only recently discovered, told everyone that was the case.

'From the outset, Cassius refused to accept her and resented her for replacing his own mother as the mistress of the house, even though his own mother died several years before they married. He was fourteen when I came along and he didn't take to the arrival of a brother any better than he did a new stepmother.'

It was likely then that his only sibling's relentless campaign of vitriol had begun, and as the heir and because his father wasn't particularly bothered about mending the rift when Luke was just the spare, it slowly undermined their status within the family until they were unceremoniously pushed out of it. Not all his brother's doing, of course, because his father had always been stubbornly cut from the same cloth, but he had certainly fanned the flames before he had poured lamp oil on them later on. 'The best word I can think of to encompass our sibling relationship was hostile.' If they hadn't been already dead, Luke would certainly have enjoyed strangling both men with his bare hands.

'That is so sad—for you and your mother. To have no family...'

Luke nodded, because he supposed it was, although he had never known any different. 'Sadder for my mother than me I think because her own family were so far away she had no one. Although her mother was English, her father was Spanish and she grew up in Andalucía, so she was basically a foreigner in my brother's eyes. And because my father married her solely because she was beautiful and had a very distant and tenuous family link to the monarch of Spain—perhaps not the best criteria for choosing a wife—they had nothing in common. It was an arranged marriage which never worked. She was too young and a fish out of water. He was too old and set in his ways and saw no earthly reason why he should have to change them. Their temperaments clashed, their cultures and customs clashed, and they never ever really even liked one another.'

Talking about it all so openly over tea, when it was never discussed at all, was churning up all manner of forgotten memories, most of which wholly unsuitable for a discussion. 'In fact, now that I think upon it, when either mentioned the other, even in the most general and innocuous sense, it was always with pursed lips. That they lasted two years living under the same roof was a miracle.'

It was only later, as an adult, that he learned she had basically been little more than a prisoner in the Berkeley Square house for the last year she lived there.

She could, he conceded, have been deemed too ill to go out on physician's orders, which might well have been the case, and be misremembering what happened. Thanks to her illness, his mother's memory of certain periods was unreliable and she had none at all of huge swathes of time. Luke had certainly been too young to remember the truth. All he recalled were her constant tears during those early years in Cornwall and days when she never seemed to leave her bedchamber. A familiar pattern which had repeated itself after he had liberated her from Mill House and the main reason he was plagued with guilt now at having been gone so long from her side. When news of Cassius's untimely death reached Cornwall, his mother had insisted he head to London, urging him to use the opportunity to have an adventure. But every day he feared hearing her health had declined again and worried about not being there for her and by default, her recovery going rapidly backwards. Clowance was a godsend, but when she was in the grip of her demons, his mother had always needed him more.

Another buzzing hornets' nest.

Hope's auburn brows were furrowed in anger on his behalf. 'Still, it was your father's responsibility to have made proper provisions. It was thanks to his negligence that you were both allowed to be abandoned by your nasty brother.'

'That it was. But...' Luke shrugged. He had spent years feeling angry and bitter about it until he had realised all that vengeful negativity really only harmed him. His father hadn't cared two hoots either way and in his self-righteous hatred, Cassius thoroughly enjoyed having the upper hand but fate had certainly punished him by taking him so early. That he had been taken before he could ensure his hated half-brother couldn't inherit a penny would also ensure the bastard couldn't rest in peace, and that petty knowledge made Luke's unwanted inheritance slightly more bearable. He hoped the snake spun in his grave for eternity. He deserved nothing less. 'That neglect also made me the man that I am. I wouldn't be half as resourceful, resilient and utterly irresistible otherwise.'

'Or quite so arrogant.' She stared at him blandly over the rim of her cup. 'How did you get from herring to slate?'

All her curiosity told him that she liked him. At least in private when they were alone. In the week since her parents had taken him under their wing, Hope had been careful to be either uninterested or dismissive of his company during the two dinners he had attended. Even when he had been dragged to the Royal Academy by Augustus to see his eldest daughter's painting, she had kept her distance. But out here, when it was just the two of them beneath the moonlight and Charity wasn't watching them like a hawk, she lowered those defences and they talked.

And talked and talked.

'It's an ironic twist of fate, I owe my stingy father for that too. Because the useless tin mine might not have had any tin left in it, but the land around it and the caverns it left below were all slate. I figured people always need roofs, so I started chiselling the stuff out to sell locally and it grew from there.'

'*You* chiselled it out?' Clearly that prospect astonished her. 'On your own?'

'I'll have you know I'm a dab hand with a pickaxe.' To get a rise out of her, because sparring with Hope was now his most favourite pastime, he flexed his bicep. 'Did you think these impressive muscles, that I cannot help but notice you admire so very much, came from barking orders?'

Her features remained as flat as the precisely cut roof shingles Tregally Slate was now renowned for. 'If you are going to be tiresome, I'm going to bed.'

'Then hand over the first couple of chapters of your precious *magnum opus* so I can read them while you are gone, as I'm not the least bit ready to sleep yet and am in dire need of something exciting to read.' He had tried all manner of ways to get a glimpse of her story, but so far, she had batted each back. Yet her secrecy, and her reluctance to even hint at the main crux of the plot, only intrigued him more. He held out his hand across the three-foot void of empty space between their adjoining balconies, daring her to put them in it. 'Yesterday you said it was practically finished and promised faithfully that I could read it once it was done.'

Instantly, she was defensive. 'I am still pondering over the exact wording of the final scenes. I need to get those right.'

He wiggled his outstretched fingers. 'Just the first chapter will do for now.'

'Thanks to all the incessant hammering and distractions from your army of workmen again today, it still isn't ready.'

'Yet two days ago you faithfully promised me that you were deliberating about copying the first few chapters out and taking them to that publishing fellow in Paternoster Row...' Only because he was diligently cajoling her into chasing her dreams because she seemed so reluctant to. 'What's his name? The one who said he really liked the first book but wouldn't publish it unless you changed your name to Henry...' He snapped his fingers trying to remember. With all the Thundersley invoices, ledgers, stocks and bonds he had been wading through of late, his mind was stuffed with random names which meant nothing. 'Crocker and Co.?'

'Cooper and Son.' She was staring down at her hands, which was odd for Hope, when she normally stared him dead in the eye. Even when she was being aloof in front of her family, she did so boldly. More unusual was the fact that her hands were suddenly busy in her lap, when Hope wasn't a fiddler. The only times he had ever seen her not as physically calm as a swan on a millpond was when he had flustered her.

She was uncomfortable about something and not just his request.

'Hope?'

Her spine stiffened as she winced. 'I sort of took your advice on that.'

'Which means you didn't take it at all, did you?'

'I thought I would try an experiment…and I sent it to him via messenger instead of visiting…only I didn't send it as me…not after last time. Though I am in two minds about the hasty decision now.' She stood and began to nervously pace the tiny confines of her balcony. 'You see, in a moment of temper, I made a name up to see if that made a difference to the way it was received.' She stopped pacing to glance at him, then quickly away. 'I sent those chapters as H. B. Rooke and gave him my grandparents' postal address in Whitstable instead of here.'

'A very smart move.' Even though he was put out that she would allow that faceless Cooper fellow to read it before him, he couldn't help but admire her industry and the clever subtlety of the name she had chosen.

She huffed out a relieved breath. 'Do you think so?'

'Of course! That way, when he raves about it, as he undoubtedly will, and begs you to allow him to be your publisher and offers a king's ransom for the privilege, you will be able to prove to him categorically that a girl can write a book that people want to buy. That's presuming you are going to reveal that you are the genius behind it, as I'd hate to see the fictional and androgynous H. B. Rooke on the bookshelves when it is Hope who deserves to be there.'

'Precisely!' She beamed at him across the railings and it made his heart stutter. 'You see right through my fiendish plan.' Then the smile wavered. 'Only now I

have to go through the unmitigated torture of waiting…
perhaps for the axe to fall yet again…and it will be an
interminable wait thanks to the detour it will take via
Whitstable.'

Of its own accord, his hand reached over to cover
hers on the railings and something odd happened because he felt it everywhere. Even the night air around
them seemed charged with something extraordinary.
'Good things come to those who wait, Hope. Mark my
words, Mr Cooper will love *Phantasma* and so will the
world once they get to read it.'

'How can you know that when I haven't even let you
read it yet?'

'Because you wrote it, Hope, and you are brilliant.'
She was too. Brilliant, unique and dazzling. 'And before you argue that inescapable fact and accuse me of
being kind, in the short time I have known you, I know
without a shadow of a doubt that you are the most brilliant and clever young lady I have ever met.'

'Sometimes, Lord Trouble, you say the nicest things…'
She gazed intently at the spot where their bodies joined
and swallowed, making him wonder if the simple, innocent touch was having the same spellbinding effect on her
as it was on him, until she gently tugged her hand away
and retreated back a step as if she needed to put some
uncharged air between them. Then her eyes locked with
his—part wary, part bemused. 'If you carry on being so
charming, and despite my better judgement, I might even
have to start considering you a friend.'

From a woman who had good reason to have scant
regard of men, that honour felt special and humbling—
though worryingly nowhere near enough. And by the
way she instantly straightened as soon as the tender

words were spoken, and briskly turned her back to him to pick up the pile of her precious handwritten pages on her table, clearly intent on rushing inside, she was mortified to have shown him that she cared.

He almost reached out to twist her back to see exactly what she was feeling for himself, but realised that if her need mirrored his he would be left undone and there was a very real chance he might kill whatever it was that tenuously was building by acting upon it.

Which, of course, he was in no position to do.

To cover the sudden veil of awkwardness which now hung between them as well as preserve the genuine friendship which was blossoming between them, Luke attempted a flirty grin as he leaned nonchalantly on the railings and churned out the sort of words she would expect and which would set them back on their almost but not quite even keel.

'I knew my boyish charm would eventually win you over.'

Whatever was going on between them wasn't something either of them were in any hurry to explore just yet and, with his life more complicated and burdened than it ever had been before, that was probably just as well. He needed a friend now more than he needed the responsibility of being more than one, when he could barely walk under the weight of all his myriad responsibilities as it was. A short dalliance was one thing, but he knew already he wouldn't be able to settle for a dalliance with her.

'If we are friends, Hope, does that mean I can finally read your first chapter now?'

She turned, hugging the papers to her chest, her familiar bored mask fastened firmly in place again.

'*If* and *when* we are friends, Luke, and only when the book is finished…maybe.' The ghost of a smile and something else still lingered in her eyes. 'But thank you for the tea and the toast. Unlike your company, they were excellent.'

Chapter Nine

*The new Marquess of Thundersley made his debut
in the House of Lords today and stunned everyone
present with his eloquence during a debate on
the state of England's roads. His arguments for
improving them were apparently so convincing he
swayed several committed naysayers into voting
for the bill. Could it be, Dear Reader, that we have
misjudged him...?*

Whispers Behind the Fan
June 1814

It had been the first time Luke had set eyes on Abigail
in a fortnight and as they were in plain sight of at least
a hundred excited opera goers crowded in the foyer during the interval, there was no polite way to avoid her
without causing a scene. His own fault. If he had stayed
with Augustus who was still holding court in the corner, and not wandered off to see what, or more likely
who, was keeping Hope, this harpy would never have
had the opportunity to catch him alone.

'Good evening, Lucius.' She proffered her glove-cov-
ered hand so that he could kiss it and he found himself

strangely grateful for the reassuring layer of dark satin
which spared him from touching her skin. 'You have
proved to be a difficult man to pin down now that you
have become quite the gentleman about town.'

'Abigail.'

Even that single, tart greeting took all his effort to
muster. He stared wistfully over at Hope now on her
way back from the retiring room and, in typically Hope
fashion, she had inadvertently dragged along some
bothersome flotsam and jetsam in her wake.

Two well-heeled and besotted young gentlemen were
doing their best to charm her, entirely ignorant of the
fact that their wide-eyed fascination with her fiery hair
and voluptuous figure was guaranteed to have the opposite reaction. Already she wore that apathetic and unsubtle irked expression which she always wore around
such irritants and he could only imagine the insulting
and tart answers she would have for whatever honeyed
twaddle they were spouting in their quest to seduce
her. As he thought it, she speared one of them with a
blatant poison verbal dart and the idiot blinked as if he
must have heard it incorrectly, then brayed like a don-
key when he wrongly assumed she was being droll.
Her plump lips flattened in instant irritation, then, as
if she sensed Luke watching from afar, their eyes met
across the crowded foyer and she rolled hers heavenward, knowing he would understand exactly what that
meant.

They had solidified their unlikely friendship in the
past two weeks, yet already he valued it above everything else he had here. They flirted—or rather he flirted
to vex her while she playfully glared—but mostly they
talked. About everything and nothing. She listened to
all his woes concerning solicitors and the superficial-

ity of London, while she bemoaned the idiot men who thought her dim-witted fair game and, once the moaning was done they discussed books and politics, disappointment and dreams. Everything really.

Or almost everything.

She was reticent about sharing anything detailed about her writing and he never volunteered the truth about his mother or the real reasons why he had moved to Bloomsbury in such a hurry.

Abigail noticed him staring at Hope and frowned, then immediately smiled her brittle, ever so wounded smile which he now saw right through. 'I am glad I ran into you... I have been desperate to speak to you since you left. I sent another note to that effect last week. Did you not get it?'

She knew he had because she had instructed the messenger to wait for his response and Luke had tossed the boy a sixpence and told him to tell Her Ladyship that he had no response and likely wouldn't for at least the next few months. Exactly what was there left to discuss?

'As I assumed you only wanted to flog the dead horse of your unsavoury marriage proposal or attempt another wholly inappropriate and unwelcome seduction, I decided to ignore it.'

Almost a month since and he still couldn't quite believe the bare-faced nerve of the woman or not feel disgusted by what she had done. Thankfully, he had awoken before anything regrettable happened, the last remnants of his rampant desire for Hope shrivelling like a salted slug on a wet path as he had screamed his outrage from the rooftops.

He folded his arms, letting his irritation show. If they were going to flog dead horses, he had his own rotting nag to flay. And politeness be damned, for once he would not pull his verbal punches with a woman or care about their feelings.

'To be frank, I find myself strangely grateful you showed your true colours in all their manipulative glory when you did, because I had been desperate for a decent excuse to leave you for months. It was only ingrained politeness and my foolish belief that I needed to look out for my half-brother's grieving widow which kept me there. Thankfully, I have purged myself of both misconceptions and am nothing but relieved to finally be shot of *you*.'

He intended to stride off then, even started to, but she grabbed his sleeve as her face crumpled with hurt. 'Wait…please.' Fat tears instantly swam in her eyes which made him feel bad for speaking plainly even though she had had it coming. They were enough to make him follow when she tugged him into a secluded alcove. 'Please hear me out. Please allow me to apologise, Lucius… I beg of you.'

Luke folded his arms, making no attempt to hide either his disgust or his suspicion until the first tear fell and he instantly felt a cad.

'I am so sorry… It was so wrong of me. Desperate even…b-but…' As her bottom lip trembled she spared them both the embarrassment of a scene by turning so that her back was to the crowd before she buried her face in her hands. 'I am s-so l-lost.' Fresh tears hovered on her bottom lashes threatening to spill at any moment and she impatiently swiped them away. 'Just know that I wasn't myself that night… I am still not to be honest. I really do not know what has got into me of late. I am so confused.' She touched her forehead. 'And so very sad all the time.'

Luke's ready pity annoyed him because he didn't

trust her or this uncharacteristic display of emotion. Unbeknownst to her—or perhaps with brutal intent—she was jabbing at his most exposed nerve with her tragic behaviour. His Achille's heel.

Surely that wasn't coincidence?

He had learned to trust his gut, as it had not failed him once in all his life, and his gut called foul. Yet it wasn't in his nature to be callous and unsympathetic of another's pain either—especially when he had caused it. He stood awkwardly for several uncomfortable moments while she composed herself and he tried to figure out if her pain was genuine.

When she finally looked up at him, her eyes were red-rimmed and her features pale. 'Do you ever feel like your world is spiralling out of your control, Lucius?'

Often. Almost daily of late and he loathed it. 'Sometimes.'

'These last few months since Cassius passed have been so awful that some days I feel as if I am losing my mind.'

And there they were. The magic words. Not that his mother had ever uttered them when her illness held her in its unrelenting grip, but which he had learned to understand were the truth whenever she had lost the capacity to see the wood for the trees.

'I know it is no excuse, but nowadays I barely recognise myself. Not what I think or how I behave. The dead and numb way I feel inside…some days all the misery just becomes a blur, yet I haven't even cried yet.' Then she hiccoughed out a bitter laugh as her fingertip wiped away the solitary tear trailing down her cheek. 'At least not until now… Isn't that strange?'

'Grief affects us all in different ways.' Although he sincerely hoped that six months of pent-up grief weren't all about to come tumbling out right here in this Covent Garden theatre. His gaze drifted helplessly towards Hope who had managed to shake off her unwelcome suitors and had re-joined her father, willing her to turn and notice he was trapped so that she could extricate him from his needy sister-in-law's clutches, but she didn't. For future reference and for the sake of himself, he should probably appraise her of his situation with Abigail so she could come to the rescue in the future.

And while he was appraising her of Abigail, maybe it was time he entrusted her with the whole truth about his situation?

He almost had, once or twice, especially now that his mother's visit loomed, and he was worried sick about how that would affect her. The travelling alone was daunting enough because he had no idea how she would react to it, but as his mother was, understandably, an intensely private person and London, with all its bad memories and nosy people, could well prove to be her nemesis. But even so, there was no putting her visit off either. He got the sense from her letters that she was desperate to see him and absorb his strength. No outright alarm bells, not yet at least, but enough niggles to make him uneasy about how the next few months would unravel and to wish he had someone to share it with. At least if Hope was aware of the issues, she could be an extra pair of trustworthy eyes in Bloomsbury when he had to be elsewhere.

And then, of course, there was the niggling need to confess it all to her anyway to see if they could be more than friends. He had never entertained that possibility before, but every night after he left her and he couldn't stop thinking about her, a growing part of him wished she would always be beside him. An extra pair of trustworthy eyes and a soulmate in every sense of the word…

'I never expected to become a widow at thirty-three, Lucius.' Abigail's voice pulled him reluctantly back and uncharitably, he was surprised she was that young. He had always assumed she was nearer his elder brother's age than his. 'I assumed I would be a mother by now, surrounded by children to love and busy raising my family…but your brother was…' She glanced away, her breath coming out in staccato bursts as if she were determined to ruthlessly hold back all her emotions. 'I apologise.' She flapped her hand this time as she shook her head. 'It is wrong to speak ill of the dead and though he might well have been my sorry excuse for a husband, he also was your brother.'

'There was no love lost between Cassius and me. You know that.'

'I do. And I worried about the chasm in your relationship and tried to convince Cassius to mend it.' Had she? He had seen no evidence. 'I even tried talking him out of what he did to your mother, but he would not be swayed.' Luke instantly stiffened, not wanting to hear any excuses for that travesty and certainly not in the packed foyer of a theatre. 'Even though I thought his actions were unchristian.'

'Unchristian!' The anger came swift and hot. 'It was criminal, Abigail.' To put it mildly. 'She had been doing well for years.' He remembered that halcyon decade with bittersweet fondness because he had believed she was finally cured. She laughed. She went out and she had embraced and enjoyed life, until the cruelty of his brother had sent her to the fetid inner circle of damnation of Mill House. 'There was no moral justification

for him to have done what he did. There was barely a
legal justification either!'

His brother too, had found a loophole in the law, and
had got one of her original London physicians, a man
who hadn't treated her in fifteen years, to sign the certificate condemning her. And with a certificate from
one of the most respected doctors in Harley Street at-
testing to her madness, he had then legally hired people to use brute force to have her committed within
hours of their father's funeral and while Luke was con-
veniently two hundred miles from home attending it.
The location had been deliberate too, when he could
have found any number of similar cesspits in Devon
or Cornwall, Cassius had chosen one on the plains of
Wiltshire, over a hundred and fifty miles inland from
Tregally, and had given them strict instructions not to
allow her any visitors. A cruel stipulation, but because
it was his money which paid them, Cassius's hired gaolers stuck to it like glue.

'I sincerely hope he rots in hell for it!' The senseless, brutal damage of those three hideous years still
lingered and likely always would.

Abigail wiped a fat tear away, nodding. 'I cannot
say that I blame you. In your shoes I would hate him
too, though there was no love lost between him and me
either...by the end.'

Behind them, the five-minute call rang out, reminding everyone to return to their seats and he sensed Hope
was watching before he saw that she was hanging back
waiting for him and wished he were callous enough to
abandon his sister-in-law to her tears. Instead, while
she wept and blew her nose, he reluctantly shook his
head, mouthing the words '*two minutes*' to his friend
and praying this wouldn't take that long. Hope smiled

in sympathy and followed the crowd and he wished with all his heart he could have gone with her.

Lord, she looked lovely tonight.

Green was certainly her colour and the conservative drape of her plain silk gown did splendid things for her figure, turning the demure garment into a temptress's gown which set off her fiery hair to perfection and unintentionally rendering her the most striking woman in the room. Luke would have complimented her when he first saw her this evening, because she fair stole his breath away with her unique beauty but knew she wouldn't appreciate it. Hope didn't trust flattery, and as he had repeatedly watched gentleman after gentleman turn to stare covetously tonight, he understood why.

Most of those gentlemen only saw the sinful face and figure, but only the truly privileged ever got to peek at the complex and alluring woman who inhabited it. Luke was obviously beguiled by her fine figure, to be frank what hot-blooded male wouldn't be? But he was thoroughly seduced by her mind more. She was sharp. She was smart, she was tough and she made him smile. Especially when they were alone on the balcony and they dissected their day.

'I am so alone, Lucius. Husbandless. Childless... Rudderless.' He had to stifle the groan which threatened to escape, reminding himself that, like it or not, Abigail was still his responsibility. 'I have spent the last decade being every inch the Marchioness of Thundersley, trying to please him. I ran his household. Planned meticulous meals which he frequently missed. Organised all the endless parties and dinners at his behest purely so that Cassius could impress his associates. Answered all his correspondence. Dealt with all the unsavoury issues he created as best I could. Kept his secrets. Protected his reputation. And now I do not even have that purpose to keep me sane.'

She stared down at the ruined handkerchief twisted in her fingers. 'I am mortified by the awful things I did last week. But I wasn't quite myself that day and the world seemed...a very dark place indeed...' The raw nerve vibrated as she plucked it again. 'And look at me now. Blubbering in a theatre. Sometimes, I think I would make a ripe candidate for the lunatic asylum.' He had always loathed both of those words—lunatic and asylum—so filled with condemnation and hopelessness. 'Because my rash behaviour lately is so out of character and irrational that it scares me, especially as now I have managed to drive you away with it too.'

'Things will get better.'

She risked peeking up at him again and he was sure he saw genuine fear in her eyes, even though his head cautioned it was all a little too convenient.

'Will they?'

He knew better than most how change could play with the mind. His mother's illness sometimes swung wildly, negatively and irrationally at the smallest deviation from her routine and until he had understood that, responding with forbearance rather than frustration, she had made slow progress—or none. Abigail had no one in that soulless mausoleum to show her the same care, except the servants now that he had abandoned her.

'Time heals all wounds Abigail.' Not strictly true as it was time, combined with patience, compassion and a great deal of money which had eventually helped his mother. She would likely never fully heal. He knew that now and accepted it. The damage done to her by first his neglectful father and then after his vengeful brother had broken her spirit had been too great.

'Will you help me?'

More storm clouds gathered ominously around his head. 'As much as I am able.'

'Thank you. You have no idea how much that means. You are the only family I have left here in London. That is if I still have a place here in London...' She forced a smile and something about her wide-eyed and innocent expression instantly seemed fake. 'Do I still have my beloved home which Cassius never thought to leave me?'

In his haste to escape her that fateful night, Luke had completely forgotten about his offer. While he was glad to leave Berkeley Square and all its bad memories behind, that she had reminded him he had gifted it, so soon after apparently bearing her tortured soul to him, reminded him that leopards rarely changed their spots and that his gut was rarely wrong. 'It is still yours.'

'Oh, thank goodness.' She squeezed his hand. 'I was dreading you would have me shipped back to my father in Wiltshire a hundred miles away from everything I hold dear, like your brother did your poor mother.'

'I am not Cassius. That house is yours for as long as you choose to live in it, Abigail.'

'I should like it if you weren't a stranger to it... *Brother*.'

His canny gut clenched in warning some more, while his mind whirred. She was desperately lonely and lost. He knew how that felt and, whether he liked it or not, they *were* family and she was still his responsibility.

Dear god, he hoped that wouldn't be for ever.

'I won't be.'

She smiled, her bottom lip still dangerously quivering a little. 'Then how about dinner tomorrow? Nothing formal. Just a nice, cosy *family* supper? It would give me something to look forward to...'

Chapter Ten

The Theatre Royal saw Mrs Roberta Brookes
accept, not one, but five standing ovations for her
final performance in Così fan Tutte last night.
However, while nobody doubts her virtuosa performance was a triumph, it was her daughter
Miss Charity Brookes who stole the show after
she hastily stepped into the role of Despina at the
last moment when the original actress was indis-
posed. The audience sat transfixed at the sheer
beauty of her voice, many declaring she sang like
an angel—which, regular readers of this column
will doubtless appreciate, is gloriously ironic,
considering her less than angelic reputation...

Whispers from Behind the Fan
June 1814

Twenty-One Bedford Place was packed to the rafters
and she had lost sight of Luke in the melee over an hour
ago. Obviously, with Charity watching the pair of them
like a hawk for any signs of partiality, and because Hope
was supremely conscious of the fact that she was rather
partial to him despite her legendary pessimism regard-

ing men, she had made no effort to seek him out even though she wanted to.

She had barely seen hide nor hair of him for three days since the opera, and in the brief exchanges they had managed when they had twice collided in the street, she had not had the opportunity to ask him what his sister-in-law had said to sour his mood. Because there had been no denying that during the second half, after he finally returned to his seat a full ten minutes after the performance had started, the newly minted Marquess of Thundersley had had a face like thunder itself and, for reasons she wasn't prepared to decipher, that had worried her.

It wasn't like Luke to be so dour and occupied, and with him imminently leaving Bloomsbury for at least the next two weeks, she was eager to get to the bottom of it before he left for Cornwall to fetch his mother and she worried the entire time he was gone.

'Are you sure you would not appreciate the fresh air on the terrace?' Lord Ealing was like an irritating insect. Or perhaps, with his lipless mouth and short, stick-thin body, an eel lurking in the reeds waiting to pounce on an insect. 'Only it is rather stuffy in here and you do look a bit flushed, Miss Hope.' The darting eyes flicked back and forth between her apparently hot face and her décolleté as if he had no control over them. If she had had the common sense to grab a shawl before the party started, she would be making a point of tightening it around her to let him know she found his gawping both rude and offensive.

'If I look anything, my lord, it is bored.' She never should have listened to Charity and worn this particular gown or allowed herself to be talked into eschewing the gauzy fichu she had laid out to pair with it. The single inch and a half of cleavage it revealed was proving to be problematic as it drew male stares like a magnet. Before Lord Ealing's bulbous eyeballs had latched on to her, it had been Horace Strickland the renowned painter of horses and purveyor of profusive perspiration, and before him it had been the husband of a well-known actress who had now sunk so irredeemably in her estimation that she would never be able to be civil to him again.

And they were only an hour in.

'Haven't you got someone else you can bother?'

'You know my tender heart only beats for you, my flame-haired and fulsome Aphrodite.' Those eyes fixed to her chest as the tip of his tongue moistened his non-existent lips, making her feel dirty and exposed.

As usual, she covered those unpleasant internal sensations with outward disdain. 'Then I fear your tender heart is doomed for ever to be disappointed, my lord, as mine barely notices you exist.' To prove that inescapable fact, Hope glanced wistfully towards the hallway, wondering if anybody would notice if she slipped upstairs to continue meticulously copying out her finally finished manuscript. Or change her stupid gown. She most definitely had to change this gown. 'In fact, at this precise moment, I wish with all my heart that you didn't.'

Like the idiot he was, Lord Ealing was delighted by her insult. 'If your continued uninterest is a calculated feminine tactic to pique my interest further, you should know it is working for I am charmed completely by you, Miss Hope. Utterly and *hope*lessly charmed.'

'Oh, good grief! How unoriginal and tedious.' Luke suddenly appeared out of nowhere at her elbow like a giant henchman, the seams of his coat straining across the pickaxe-honed muscles of his belligerently folded arms. 'You have my solemn pledge I will never make a pun out of your name again, Hope.' Then he seemed to increase in height as he loomed menacingly over Lord Ealing, pinning him with his icy glare as he forced him to look up at him. 'Why are you still stood here when the lady clearly told you to go and bother somebody else?'

'Well... I... Um...'

Her wild-looking knight swatted the intimidated gnat away with a dismissive brush of both hands. 'Be gone, fool, before you annoy me too and then you will be sorry.'

And miraculously, just like that, he was.

Luke smugly watched the odious lord scurry across the drawing room as if his breeches were on fire, then grinned, thoroughly pleased with himself. 'Well who knew? Intimidation *is* as effective a deterrent to an unwanted suitor as a romantic tryst is? Although I still prefer my method and, I suspect, so do you.' He winked then, making no attempt to stifle his amusement at bringing up that kiss again simply because he enjoyed reminding her of it as often as possible to vex her.

Not that she needed his reminder. Her wayward thoughts revisited the dratted thing much too often of their own accord.

'I can assure you there was nothing romantic about your drunken slobbering, Lord Trouble.' As she shuddered in mock disgust, because the wretch hadn't slobbered in the slightest and knew it, she fought the urge to smile back at him. She allowed only the corners of her mouth to curve upward because she was pleased with her quick response now that she had finally conquered the flustered blush which always accompanied his con-

stant reminders. 'But I thank you for your timely interference in my predicament all the same. Lord Ealing's
pitiful attempts at seduction were starting to grate and
I promised my parents faithfully that I wouldn't make
a scene. They still haven't forgiven me for tipping an
entire decanter of port over Lord Ogilvy's head in the
middle of their last soirée, though to be fair more because they had the devil of a job getting the stain out
of the Persian than because I punished Lord Ogilvy for
excessive ogling.'

'Sadly, I suspect I have only granted you a temporary reprieve from the ogling tonight.' He inclined his
head to where the eel-like Ealing sulked as he glared at
them. 'As your sunny, welcoming character has clearly
made a lasting impression on him. Alongside a few others, I notice.'

If he had noticed, he should have rescued her sooner.

'We both know it isn't my character which attracts
them like flies to the dung heap.' Curse this stupid
gown! She had only donned it because she had wanted
to look pretty, and she had only wanted to look pretty
because of... Instinctively she narrowed her eyes at
Luke, peeved that this was actually all his fault and
more peeved that it really wasn't. 'Why are men so reliably shallow?'

'To be fair to my sex, it is a base animal instinct
we have no control over and, as much as it might pain
you to be so, you are rather...*beautiful*. Exceptionally
so tonight.' It galled her that she was thrilled with the
compliment, when such nonsense from other gentlemen
was usually met with short shrift. But Luke wasn't most
men and he had never stared at her in the lascivious way
most men did. He frowned as his dark eyes swept her up
and down then focused resolutely on her face. 'Perhaps

a sack might disguise the problem? Something baggy enough and thick enough that it conceals all that overt and striking femininity you were cursed with.'

'Are you suggesting *their* ungentlemanly behaviour is somehow *my* fault?'

He laughed as she bristled, holding his palms up in surrender. 'Not in the slightest, I wouldn't dare say anything of the sort, so don't you dare reach for the port and douse me with it. Those men are crass, ill-mannered brutes, ruled entirely by their urges and who should be heartily ashamed of themselves for their unseemly leering and panting. I am merely suggesting a way that you might mitigate against all the unwanted attention which *you* so obviously loathe as that gown is, frankly, temptation personified and it requires a strong male constitution to admire it with restraint.'

His fingers dispassionately tugged at the lace of her short, capped sleeve. 'And the damnedest thing is that I know on any other woman, this same frock would look positively demure, plain even, as it is neither too low nor too tight and not the least bit showy. Yet…' He sighed as he let go and shook his head as if it was all an unfathomable conundrum. 'On you, it is a deadly weapon. So much so, you outshine every other woman in this room. And without even trying to.'

He did compliments so well and that one in particular warmed her, so she schooled her features into her blandest mask in case it showed. He was much too self-assured already, he really didn't need any more encouragement. Not that she had any plans of encouraging him. 'Sackcloth is notoriously itchy.'

'It is and it's bound to chafe. But if sackcloth is not to your taste, a nun's habit would likely have a similar effect on all the collective lusty males in the vicinity.

Or then again, maybe it wouldn't, as there is something devilishly attractive about the forbidden and you are bound to look positively sinful in a habit too. Because you look positively sinful in everything without trying to too, don't you—my flame-haired and fulsome *Aphrodite*.'

He was insufferable. 'Clearly you could have rescued me ten minutes earlier, couldn't you? But you were having too much fun at my expense.'

'That I was.'

'And you wonder why no woman has rushed you up the aisle?'

'It's a mystery to be sure.' He raised his arm. 'Care to take a turn around the terrace for some fresh air with me instead, and we can discuss it further?'

'Only on the understanding that I am taking a turn purely for the fresh air and most definitely not your dull company.'

'I assumed that was a given, Aphrodite.'

After a quick check to confirm Charity was nowhere in sight, Hope happily threaded her hand through his elbow and allowed him to lead her to the open French doors on to the terrace and freedom. They weren't the only people escaping the crush inside, so when they couldn't find any peace to discuss anything properly beyond small talk, in silent tacit agreement they edged towards the gate in the back hedge and escaped out into the communal garden beyond when nobody was looking. Unsurprisingly, for ten o'clock in the evening, it was deserted. Certainly quiet enough that she could finally ask about his sister-in-law.

'What got your dander up the other night at the theatre?'

'Nothing…' He huffed out a groan. 'Everything.'

'Did the Marchioness put a flea in your ear?' Because Hope hadn't been able to stop herself watching the pair of them tucked away in that alcove. The strange intimacy between them had bothered her. She wasn't prepared to call it jealousy, though suspected it might well be as she had experienced a pang of something akin to it when she watched him touch the woman affectionately. 'She seemed upset.' Or at least the vile woman had done a very good job of looking suitably tragic once she had cornered him alone, though those tears had dried remarkably fast in Hope's humble opinion. Doubtless because she had got her way.

'She did more than put a flea in my ear. She deposited another ton of unwanted responsibilities on my shoulders.' For a moment his eyes were bleak before he shook it away with a theatrical shiver. 'But as you know, I have attractively broad shoulders.' Like her, Luke was the master of changing the subject when the topic wasn't to his liking. 'In other exciting news, not only have the decorators finally gone but I have almost managed to dig my way to the bottom of the never-ending mountain of papers I inherited.'

'Do you understand it all?' Because she knew it bothered him that he didn't. After his brother's shoddy treatment of him, he was a man who had to be in control of his own destiny, even if that meant burning the candle at both ends, though he preferred to make light of that diligent aspect of his character too.

'I have a solid grasp on the estate matters as they aren't too different from running my house in Cornwall—just on a grander scale. And I am pretty sure I finally understand the property aspect.' Of course he did, because as well as wading into Parliament as if he had always been part of it, he had spent the last fortnight visiting every street in the city that he owned bricks on so he could familiarise himself with each one. 'But the stocks and shares still baffle me. The Thundersley finger seems to be dipped in all manner of pies but I am yet to ascertain their fillings to decide if I want to keep them. I blame the names. They should be more explicit and give clues to the nature of the business rather than rely on pointless surnames which ultimately mean nothing to the consumer. If everybody used something sensible like Tregally Slate I wouldn't be so confused.'

But they both knew he wouldn't remain that way for long. As if he read her mind, he shrugged.

'I've set the supercilious and condescending Mr Waterhouse the herculean task of writing me a detailed summary of each and every company I hold a share in as I won't be party to any unsavoury money-making ventures or any that think they can get away with not paying their workers a decent wage for an honest day's work.' She liked that about him. He never settled for anything he didn't want and fought tooth and nail for what he believed was right. She almost pitied Mr Waterhouse, who was clearly a fool if he did not realise that his new master was a formidable, driven and principled man not an arrogant, abdicating fop like his brother.

'How did he take that?'

'Surprisingly well, as he is currently bending over backwards to impress me. It is amazing how agreeable even the most disagreeable individuals can be when they are subjected to the legendary Duff charm...your good self included.'

As he was now subjecting her to the seductive power of his most wolfish expression, those naughty dark brown eyes twinkling, she refused to take the bait. 'He is falling all over himself purely because you pay his

wages. Deep down he dislikes you as much as everyone else does—my good self included.'

'And believe me, he gets paid handsomely too. Can
you fathom that he gets five times what I pay my best
manager at Tregally? I swear the cost of everything
here is so extortionate it's criminal. Did I tell you I had
to pay fifty pounds and eight shillings for a sofa! And
I knocked the swindler down! He originally wanted
sixty.' He looked quite ferocious when outraged, even
though she knew without a doubt Luke didn't truly
have a ferocious bone in his body. He would have made
an atrocious pirate. Although, to be fair, he probably
wouldn't have had to plunder and pillage because he
would have thoroughly charmed his unwitting targets
out of their booty instead. He had a talent for disarm-
ing people. 'But at least the room is finally finished.
Would you like to see it?'

'What? Just me and you? All alone in the dark. In
a bachelor's house! Unchaperoned? Do you want my
mother to kill you?'

'In case you haven't noticed, we are all alone in the
dark unchaperoned already and as we never have a
chaperon on the balcony, I fail to see what difference
it makes.' But from the suddenly wicked glint in his eye,
he was well aware why she wouldn't dare take him up
on the offer. Here, with the sounds of her mother's soirée invading the silence, they weren't really alone in the
truest sense of the word and on the balcony, the double
sets of railings were their strict chaperons.

'You are incorrigible.'

'That I am, Hope—but you like me for it.'

'In your dreams perhaps.'

He smiled, unoffended. 'Enough about my woes.
How go things with your monster?'

She considered lying, but knew it wouldn't wash. 'The jig is up, he has received his well-deserved come-uppance and the book is finally done.'

He stopped walking and beamed at her. 'That's splendid news! Are you happy with it?'

'I have come to the conclusion that I am too much of a nit-picking perfectionist to ever be truly happy with it, but I am happy enough that I've spent the last few days making copies to send out to other publishers.'

His face clouded with instant sympathy. 'Crocker and Co. rejected it?'

'Cooper and Son have remained depressingly silent.'

'It has only been a few weeks. I'll wager they'll have made an offer by the time I get back from Cornwall, but you are wise to spread your net wider. It is never advisable to have all your eggs in one basket.' Then his feet paused again. 'And speaking of Cornwall and the jig being up, does this mean I can finally read it? I am going to need something to keep me sane during my interminable and solitary journey to the south west.'

Flapping butterflies instantly invaded her stomach and swiftly turned into gulls. 'I am afraid I still need the original to make the copies.'

'But you promised.' Two dark brows kissed in con-sternation a split second before he crossed his solid arms and glared. 'And if I know you, madam, like I know I do, you have already made at least one full copy and are merely making excuses to fob me off again.'

Hope tried not to wince at the accuracy of the charge but it was too late. She wasn't bland enough, quick enough, and he saw it.

'I knew it! You have a copy raring to go and have probably already earmarked it for the next publisher on your list.'

Also true. She had made a list of all the people who would receive the elusive H. B. Rooke's macabre manuscript.

'How come you are prepared to allow two faceless publishers to read the damn thing, yet you refuse to trust me with your work even though you know I love a good Gothic novel and cannot wait to read yours? I thought we were friends, Hope. Friends trust one another.'

'It is because we are friends that I am reluctant to share it with you.' *Phantasma* meant so much to her— what if he hated it?

'Yet I share everything with you unreservedly, Hope, because that is what good friends do. All my trials and tribulations, all my many failures, fears and each of my tiny successes.'

'You never have any failures, only successes so you have no concept of what failure or rejection feels like.'

He dismissed that with a roll of his eyes. 'If your ultimate goal is to see your story on the shelves of Hatchard's where anyone can read it, I fail to understand why you keep putting up pathetic barriers to keep me from doing so.'

He made a good point, an entirely logical and sound one, but her writing was just too personal. So personal, logic didn't come into it.

'Because this book is me, Luke. My thoughts. My demons. My essence. Sharing it feels too much like bearing my soul and I...well...am not sure I am ready to bear it to you in its entirety yet. No matter how many times you throw that gauntlet down and dare me to do it.'

'Asking you to trust me is hardly throwing a gauntlet down.' He was hurt by her defensiveness. 'If I have made you feel pressured rather than encouraged, then I am truly sorry for that was never my intention.'

'You haven't...' As her friend, he at least deserved the whole truth. 'I have never trusted easily and men least of all.'

'That is a shame.' His face fell further and she could tell her clumsy words had wounded. Hardly a surprise when she had effectively just lumped him in the same boat as the Ealings and Harlingtons of the world when he shared none of their abhorrent traits. 'I cannot help being male but despite that unfortunate birth defect, I have always trusted you, Hope. And unreservedly too.'

And heaven help her, she was sorely tempted to trust all of him, and that alone was too momentous to contemplate when the eternal and often justified pessimist in her feared she was bound to be making a mistake.

'Have I not proved my mettle as a decent and reliable friend to you yet?'

Of course he had and that was part of the problem. Luke never did anything by halves. Whether that be supporting her in a lie in front of her family or saving her from amorous men.

He was too decent. Too reliable. Too thoughtful and way too tempting. He also listened to her, encouraged her and believed in her. Too perfect a man, all things considered, for her guarded, wary heart to believe could possibly be true.

She turned away while she tried to put her unsettling, warring feelings into words, hugging herself unconsciously until she was brave enough to face him again. 'If you must know, your honest opinion terrifies me.'

She trusted him enough to confess that at least.

His eyes seemed to look into the same soul she was so desperately trying to keep hidden. 'Why?'

It was the sympathy which undid her and the understanding, lop-sided smile, as if he saw it all anyway but respected her dreams too much to trample all over them.

'What if I cannot write, Luke? What if all the publishers I approached last time were right and Mr Cooper was merely fobbing me off gently when he said they couldn't make money printing anything written by a woman? What if I have been fooling myself all these years, working towards nothing and I really don't have the same level of talent for something as my brilliant parents and sisters do?'

As delighted as she was for Charity for her well-deserved success, the odd one out, cuckoo-in-the-nest middle sister inside of her wished it hadn't come before hers. Having all the newspapers singing the youngest Brookes's praises so soon after they had done exactly the same for Faith, had completely shredded the last of Hope's confidence and left her feeling inadequate and panicked about her future.

'What if all I really am is this?' She gestured to her body and the stupid, feminine gown she shouldn't have worn expressly for him. 'All show and no real substance. The only Brookes with no real talent for anything beyond attracting shallow men without trying and sending them cross-eyed with lust.' Why was she suddenly confessing her deepest, darkest fears when she had never once confessed them to anyone before? Not even her sisters knew the confident bravado she wore like a shield hid a seething pit of insecurities which ran the gamut of everything from her fear of being an impostor as a writer to her ingrained self-consciousness about her overly womanly body. 'What do I do then?'

She expected him to laugh at her foolishness. Instead, he simply sighed as he took her hand and squeezed it, giving her the ridiculous urge to lace her fingers in his and hold on for dear life. 'Trust me with your book, Hope, and if it is truly a reflection of everything that you are, I have no doubt it is destined to be brilliant.'

'And if it isn't and you hate it?'

'Then as your friend I shall be honest enough to tell you, so that you can fix it. Because if you want it bad enough you *will* fix it, Hope. I know this because we are kindred spirits, you and I. Both too stubborn and determined not to succeed no matter what the odds.'

She dithered, wanting to entrust him with her precious manuscript, while fearing the fact that she wanted to. She was used to being self-sufficient. She had never had a mentor to guide her in her dreams in the same way her sisters had with their parents. They encouraged her, of course they did, but not in quite the same way as they did Faith with her art and Charity with her music. She had never had anyone who valued the sublime power of the written word with the same ferocity as she did. That alone deemed him worthy. So why was she still scared?

Perhaps because no matter what, Luke always knew the way and landed on his feet when he arrived while she always stumbled, never quite knowing where she was going. She released her hand from his.

'You think we are kindred spirits?' If only they were. 'I envy you your innate self-confidence and ability to master and then conquer every challenge life throws at you. You glide effortlessly over every hurdle with a big, lopsided grin on your face, knowing exactly what needs to be done and charming everyone to your way of thinking to make it so, completely unhampered by all the insecurities, barriers and disappointments we mere mortals are saddled with.' How wonderful it must be to be him. 'You are fearless, Luke, not fearful. Whereas I am all bravado.'

He reached for her hand again and wrapped it in his. 'Then pick up the gauntlet, Hope, and be fearless. It really is as simple as that.'

Chapter Eleven

*And speaking of the talented B. family of Blooms-
bury and the Theatre Royal, the least accomplished
daughter Miss H. was seen once again last night
hanging on the arm of the erudite new Marquess
of T. Could it be, Gentle Reader, that with both
her talented sisters' stars rapidly rising and with
nothing as impressive on her limited horizon, the
temperamental Miss H. is trying to compete by
seducing the inexperienced peer into making her
his Marchioness...?*

Whispers from Behind the Fan
June 1814

Luke stared at the damning pile of papers on his mattress and sighed. Two chapters into Hope's novel and he
felt both humbled and guilty that she had put her trust
in him and heartily ashamed of himself for bullying
her into submission.

Perhaps bully was too strong a word, because he
hadn't forced her to hand it over, but he had certainly
cajoled, charmed and manipulated her into surrender-

ing her manuscript by ruthlessly using their friendship as a lever.

As he had anticipated, the writing was good. Excellent in fact. What he hadn't expected was the profound effect it would have on him. He could hear her voice in every sentence. Her prose was as rich and vivid as her hair, the mystery she was quietly weaving as complex and subtly layered as the woman that she was. Already, only twenty pages in, he was immersed in the cruel world she had created, driven by greed and avarice, poverty and desperation. She painted the rookery of St Giles as a wretched, insular and hopeless place where the need to survive drove every inhabitant to think only for themselves. Lost, forgotten and abandoned to their fate. The dregs of an unfeeling society who blamed them for the crime of being born.

Having suffered from both desperation and poverty, as well as being born wrong, Luke appreciated her insight and her sympathy for the unfairness of their circumstances. He now had to add compassionate to the growing list of qualities he admired in her, and that both called to him and niggled.

She had said *Phantasma* was her essence. Her thoughts. Her demons. And because he already knew her so well, she was right—he could see into her soul. That rare and precious privilege now overwhelmed him because the heroine on the page was, to all intents and purposes, Hope laid bare. A woman who struggled with her worth and her place. Who dared to dream and wanted more, but who thought deeply, cared passionately but trusted sparingly, hiding it all beneath a thick veneer in case her vulnerabilities were ruthlessly exploited by those who always want something that isn't theirs to take.

Exactly as he had exploited them to get his own way.

Luke had used every trick up his persuasive sleeve to get his clumsy fingers on her manuscript and he had flatly refused to take no for an answer even though it had pained her to hand it over.

And he'd lied to her.

Not with any intended malice or forethought, but certainly intentionally as well as by omission. She thought him fearless and undefeatable, and because he worked damn hard to give off that impression to keep the secrets he guarded hidden, and he liked that she, of all people, viewed him that way, he hadn't corrected her in her assumption. He had also lectured her on trust, claiming she had his implicitly, when she hadn't and that his life was an open book when nothing could be further from the truth.

At the time, he had been quite comfortable with his behaviour because deflection and misdirection were such an intrinsic part of his everyday armour, it hadn't occurred to him to remove them, but now that he had read a mere fraction of her work he knew he owed her more. Real trust had to be earned not demanded and true friendship worked both ways.

Annoyed with himself, he strode towards his balcony to see if there was any sign she was still up. He had heard the last revellers leave her mother's soirée only an hour or so ago and she was, by nature, a reliable night owl. But her bedchamber was as depressingly dark as common sense reasoned it would be at four in the morning, the only signs of movement coming from the edge of lace curtain softly billowing in the warm night air from the cracked door.

'Hope…' His whisper echoed too loud in the silence. 'Hope, are you awake?'

He waited.

Nothing.

Luke didn't dare raise his voice. In deference to the season, practically every single window on the long terrace of houses was laid open to the breeze and the last thing he wanted to do was raise one of her family and alert them to the fact he shared a bedchamber wall and adjoining balcony with her. Instead, he searched around his own for something suitable to scatter at her glass, and when he found nothing he sighed.

They had said their goodbyes tonight because his carriage would arrive at dawn. After such a late night it wouldn't be right to call on the family before the sun came up, and even if he did, that wouldn't guarantee him enough privacy with Hope to tell her all the things he should have told her before now. Closely guarded, intensely private and personal secrets which he would have to tell her in a fortnight upon his return rather than trust her with now, as she deserved.

He stared at the open door again, trying to talk himself out of the inappropriate solution which had popped into his head, then winced as he considered her likely and justifiable overreaction.

It couldn't be helped.

He had urgent things he needed to tell her that wouldn't wait two weeks. Before he thought better of it, he threw one leg over the railings, then quickly straddled the three-foot gap which separated his niggling conscience from his best friend who deserved nothing less than his complete and utter trust.

'Hope…' He inched her door open gradually and poked his head inside, trying to spare her from the understandable terror she would inevitably experience at having an intruder break into her bedchamber while she slept in it, and spare himself from any hard projectiles she aimed at him as a result. 'Hope…wake up.'

Still nothing.

As his eyes adjusted, he could just about make out the Hope-shaped lump in the bed, clearly sound asleep if her deep breathing was any gauge. 'Hope!' As he was half inside, he made sure he was louder this time and was rewarded by the sound of a belligerent moan a split second before the lump shot bolt upright.

'Argh!'

'Shh…' He rushed forward, his finger to his lips. 'Don't scream. It's only me.'

'Luke?' He could see the startled whites of her eyes now as they focused beneath the tangled curtain of hair. Her bleached knuckles clutching the bedcovers to her chin for dear life. '*Luke!* What the hell do you think you are doing?'

'I climbed over the railings.'

'I worked that part out, cretin!'

'I wanted to talk to you.'

'What? *Now?*' She shuffled backwards towards the headboard where the moonlight hit to see him better, unaware it allowed him to see her face completely and her expression of startled concern rather than fear. 'And it couldn't wait?'

'Not two weeks it couldn't.' He bounced awkwardly from foot to foot, supremely aware that he could have handled this all so much better, if only he had been thinking straight and wasn't always so blasted guarded about his life. 'Can you spare me a few minutes?' Because something inside, something different was germinating and if he was going to allow it to grow as he suspected he wanted to, he needed to let her in.

She frowned and stared at him as if he had lost his

wits, which he supposed, given the circumstances, was entirely fair. 'Do I have a choice?'

'You see, the thing is…' It was probably best to get it over with. 'I haven't been entirely honest with you and after going on and on about trust and friendship earlier, I realised that I have failed you on both counts.' Because standing felt too awkward, he went to sit on the bed only to have her swat him hard on the arm.

'Stay well away from me, if you please.' She reached out and grabbed the brass candlestick on her nightstand and wielded it in front of her like a weapon.

'I've not come to ravish you.'

'And I'll not be accountable for my actions if you are within arm's reach and be in no doubt I will bludgeon you to pulp if you come any closer.' Knowing her legendary temper, Luke didn't doubt it for a second. 'Just say what you need to say and get out!'

'I am not fearless, Hope. Not even slightly.' His wary heart was hammering against his ribs at that admission. 'In fact, I spend a good deal of my life worried sick and the rest contemplating the inevitability of the next betrayal or catastrophe. If I seem to effortlessly jump over hurdles, it's only because I am in a hurry to get over them before I slam into the next one which will defeat me, and I do know what failure feels like as it is my constant companion and I am fairly certain I shall have to live with that awful, helpless feeling for the rest of my life no matter how hard I try to succeed.' His knees seemed to give way then, but thankfully she didn't carry out her threat to bludgeon him as he sank slumped and dejected on to the furthest end of her mattress. 'I wanted you to know…thought you should know…that my mother is ill and despite my very best efforts, I've failed miserably for a quarter of a century to cure her.'

'Oh, Luke... I am so sorry.' The mattress shifted as she brushed his shoulder. 'Is it...is her condition... fatal?'

'It's not that sort of illness, more's the pity. Not that I wish her dead, of course, I love her to distraction... but if there were visible physical symptoms her malaise would be easier to understand and treat. But it's here.' He tapped his temple, feeling strangely emotional to be admitting it aloud because he feared her reaction so very much. 'Her mind is...fragile. And sometimes she's...' Because there was a strange knot in his throat threatening to choke him he huffed it out. 'Well, to be frank, to a layman I am sure that sometimes she would seem to be as mad as a hatter.'

She blinked back at him in the darkness, the sliver of moonlight rendering some of the copper strands in her hair silver. It was completely loose, he now realised, tumbling wildly over her shoulders and down her back and thanks to the ribbon ties of her nightgown being undone and the neckline all awry, one of those shoulders was practically bare.

'Is she always...?'

He shook his head. 'It comes and goes. Sometimes it lasts hours, other times days, but thankfully nowadays it doesn't last months.' Or years and years. Of staring tearfully out at nothing and keeping him at arm's length. 'It's the reason my father shipped her off to Cornwall to be treated out of the sight of the precious and judgemental *ton* he put such great stock in. He considered her illness a distinct character weakness and very poor form, as if it were all her fault. A self-indulgence which was an entirely unacceptable trait in a wife.' He paused, trying to gauge the full extent of her horror and when he saw only concern for him, instantly felt better.

'It's also the reason my brother and I hated one another. Cassius couldn't see the point in continuing to pay for the physicians once my father died. So instead, and even though she was perfectly well, had her locked in a filthy and inhumane lunatic asylum where he doubtless prayed she would catch something nasty and die out of sight and out of mind before I could legally get her out.'

'Legally?'

'You have to be over the age of majority to take over the care of a dependant. I was only eighteen when dear old Papa snuffed it. Cassius arranged it all behind my back while I was with him at the funeral.' Bitterness at that cruelty spoken aloud made the bile rise and burn his throat. 'By the time I got home it was too late. She was gone and I couldn't defend her.' That single failing, although not his fault, ate away at him like a cancer. 'And as she was a tidy and regular income for them, Mill House was never going to make her better when it was in their interests for her to be at her absolute worst.'

Hope's hand had covered her mouth. 'He left her there for three years.'

Luke nodded, the guilt choking him. 'He also did all in his power to prevent me from visiting. You should have seen the state of her when I finally got her out, Hope.' He baulked at the memory. 'Emaciated, terrified, nonsensical, addicted to the laudanum they'd pumped into her to keep her quiet. You wouldn't keep a dog in such conditions. It took a year to nurse it out of her, and another year after that to get her on the road back to the way she was before they crushed her spirit.'

Then, like an erupting volcano, it all spewed out.

Everything he knew about his mother's illness but had never confided in anyone before.

The first months of her marriage when the melancholy had started after she had been separated from her family and her homeland, then had been forbidden to attend to her dying mother in Spain or return to her funeral. Her isolation and eventual banishment to Cornwall. The early years of his childhood when his father engaged all manner of quack cures from afar in the vain hope one might work but which all only served to make it all worse. The water therapies. The bloodletting. The hours spun at speed in the rotary chair until she was so dizzy she was sick for days afterwards. All designed to wrench the badness out of her as if she had been inhabited by some parasite which could be physically removed.

Then, when nothing alleviated her symptoms, they were abandoned again, although this time for the best. It was during those quiet years she eventually emerged from the fog thanks to a friendly local physician who prescribed gentle herbal tisanes, fresh air, exercise and calmness. He taught Luke to read and as soon as he could, encouraged him to read to her. It had been then that he had finally got to know his mother and come to realise that she could be witty and clever, thoughtful and reasoned as they had finally bonded over a shared love of books, blissfully forgotten and ignored at last by his father who had washed his hands of it all.

Hope held his hand as the story turned more sinister after his neglectful sire had passed, and Cassius had wreaked havoc on their lives, and he recounted the inhuman treatments Mill House deemed appropriate. There, punishment disguised itself as care. Restraints, beatings, purgatives, isolation and starvation. The exact opposite of all the things which had allowed her to flourish. When her mind faltered under the brutality of it all, and unbeknownst to Luke who had been twice arrested and banned from setting foot on their lands again by that time, they drugged her until the drug became her master and she had no clue who he was when he was finally able to liberate her. And only then because Cassius refused to pay another shilling to her gaolers from the day Luke reached his majority.

At his wits' end, working his fingers to the bone cutting slate and with every available penny at his disposal, Luke had then put her in the hands of the pioneering Quaker physician, Dr Edward Long Fox, at his newly established and humane asylum, Brislington House, in Bristol. Where, in the lush, tranquil grounds and in the comfort of her own private room, his mother's healing finally recommenced, taking a further three years of toing and froing before she was well enough for him to be able to bring her back under his care and home to Cornwall permanently.

Finally, his voice hoarse and with the faint promise of dawn whispering on the horizon, he confessed his fears for now and the reasons why he was risking that recovery to fetch her to Bloomsbury.

'She's been so well now for so long, I am terrified my prolonged absence from Tregally and the enforced separation will send her backwards. She needs me, Hope. I've already been away too long yet I still have so much to do here, so many fresh burdens and responsibilities to decide what to do with, I cannot spare the time to be in Cornwall. I am so torn, Hope, caught between the devil and the deep blue sea. I just pray I am doing the right thing in bringing her. Or that I am not too late and fresh damage hasn't already been done while I wasn't there to stop it.'

She squeezed his hand as she stroked his hair, drawing his eyes to their tightly intertwined fingers, reminding him that at some point during his confessional, he had been so desperate for the contact that he had laid his head on her shoulder while he poured out his entire heart.

Everything.

And most definitely far more than he had originally intended. Leaving him feeling raw and exposed and decidedly off-kilter.

The awkwardness of baring all his soul so out of the blue and irrationally now threatened to suffocate him, so he extricated his fingers and he stood before the tears ominously prickling his eyes actually fell and he disgraced himself completely.

'Anyway... I just wanted to trust you with my darkest secret seeing as you entrusted me with your book. Fair's fair and all that...' He backed towards the door, hating the fact he had put tears in her lovely eyes too with his depressing, uninvited tale of woe. 'It's wonderful by the way...the book.' He forced a smile, hoping it would lighten the sombre mood and leave her with a more familiar memory of him before he left. 'I am only two chapters in, but I am already hooked. I cannot wait to dive into the rest of it...but...but obviously, if you'd rather I didn't because I did rather bully you into handing it over, I can give it back.'

Clearly stunned at the bizarreness of it all, Hope blinked up at him from the crumpled pile of covers on the bed and then she shook her head.

'Oh, Luke...'

Then all at once, she launched herself at him, wrapping her arms around him and hugging him for all she was worth.

Apparently, it was just what he needed and he clung back, gratefully absorbing her strength as he buried his face in her hair.

He had no earthly clue how long they stood there. All he knew without any doubt was that he didn't want to let go and she seemed in no hurry to make him. He could feel her nakedness beneath the diaphanous layer of her nightgown, the womanly curve of her hips where his palms rested on them, the soft imprint of her full breasts pressed against his chest, and though his body revelled in those things, the embrace wasn't carnal. It was tender and honest. Cathartic. She seemed to sense he was undone and gave him all the time and the affection he needed to repair himself.

Somewhere in the distance, a clock struck five, the chimes dragging him to the present and forcing him to step away. 'The Thundersley carriage will be here at six.' And soon her house and the outside would wake, and he would be discovered or seen and ruin more than her night's sleep if he didn't make haste. 'I should go.'

'You should.' She smiled in the doorway as he backed on to the balcony. 'Unless you really do want my father to shoot you.' She had apparently forgotten she was only in her nightgown, and despite the yards of delicate fabric which had gone into making it, the weak light of the predawn was enough to render parts of it translucent. The silhouette of her lush shape was his parting gift, reminding him of what it felt like to desire without warning. It hit him like a punch in the gut and stole his breath.

All curves.

Unrestrained full breasts round and heavy, the peaks

of her nipples clearly defined in the drape of the material, the dusky shape of them trying to tempt his eyes from her lovely face. Fiery hair a tousled silken curtain his fingers suddenly itched to touch. The sultry narrowing of her waist. The seductive voluptuousness of her bottom. Things he should have been aware of when he had held her in his arms, but hadn't, but that he was supremely aware of now.

He smiled back and meant it, feeling strangely lighter and younger than he had for months. 'Thank you…for listening and for not bludgeoning me to pulp.'

'You are very welcome.' A little self-consciously, but too late to reverse the effect her womanly body was having on his, she folded her arms and leaned on the doorframe. 'Safe travels, Lord Trouble.'

'I should be back in two weeks.' Or less if he could manage it now that two weeks was too long. 'Keep an eye on the house for me.' And now he was procrastinating, lingering and indecisive.

'I will.'

She watched him throw both legs over the railings, but a second before he bridged the short but perilous distance between their two balconies, she called him back and as he turned, gripping the rail for all he was worth, she pressed her mouth to his, her kiss poignant, heartfelt but much too short before she jumped back and blushed scarlet.

Stunned, he touched his lips. 'What did that mean?' Because he desperately needed to know.

'Nothing…' Still blushing she strapped on her dismissive mask. Only it appeared more defensive than dismissive. 'At least, beyond a friendly farewell.'

'It didn't feel like nothing.' Because it certainly felt

like something. Something huge and daunting and, frankly, wonderful. 'Or friendly.'

'You are tired and upset and overawed and clearly reading more into it than it warrants.' And she was flustered. 'Don't you dare confuse a friendly gesture with anything else.' Gloriously flustered.

'Why not? Would it be so terrible? I mean, we voluntarily spend all our spare time together, get on like a house on fire, trust one another implicitly and there is a palpable...*something* between us which surely even you cannot deny. To all intents and purposes, we are practically courting already...'

His heart was racing at the admission, though bizarrely not with panic. If he had to hazard a guess at what was going on inside him, it was excitement, which was astonishing when he had just put himself through an emotional mangle and didn't think he had the capacity to experience any more emotion, let alone such an uplifting one. He had assumed that his life would always be much too complicated to consider tossing any thoughts of a permanent romance into the mix. That he didn't need any more responsibilities and burdens as he had quite enough already. Yet it all suddenly felt reassuringly right as Hope was neither of these things. In fact, right now, she was the balm which eased them. The one thing he needed to fix all his current problems and ills in one fell swoop.

'We most definitely are not courting!' She had passed the point of flustered and replaced it with outraged panic. He decided to take that as a very good sign because she had lost the wherewithal to don her trusty mask of indifference which was her most constant companion.

'Perhaps not in the traditional sense with bouquets

and love poetry and flowery declarations, but when do we ever do anything in the proper way, Hope?' The more the idea took root, the more it appealed.

Him and her.

Her and him.

It just worked.

'Will you stop spouting nonsense and go away before someone sees you!' True to form, she was now trying to brush away her discomfort by deflection. 'Can't you see the sun is coming up?' She uncrossed her arms and flicked an impatient hand in the direction of his balcony with such force that her unbound breasts moved beneath her nightgown until she hastily folded her arms over them again, horrified. 'Go! Before you fall to your death, you stupid man!'

'You care at least. Surely that's a start?' Now that he had voiced what he hadn't realised was in his heart, he wasn't going to let her ignore it. Instead, he would find a way to make it happen exactly as he always did when he encountered an obstacle. He knew already, no other outcome would satisfy him.

She rolled her eyes and glared imperious, the very picture of unimpressed which was ruined entirely by the twitching fingers at the end of her still firmly crossed arms. 'If I presently care for anything, I can assure you, it is only for the safety of my mother's rose bed on the terrace. I've always been particularly partial to the yellow ones because they smell so lovely and I would be distraught if your ungainly Cornish corpse flattened them.' And with that, she strode inside with her nose in the air and loudly bolted her door.

Chapter Twelve

*Rumours abound, Gentle Reader, that the unlikely
romance between the charming new Marquess
of T. and the feisty Miss H. from Bloomsbury has
definitely cooled as nobody has seen them out and
about together in weeks. I am reliably informed,
however, that this popular young lady has been
more than adequately entertained in the meantime
by the smitten but very married Lord J. instead...*
Whispers from Behind the Fan
July 1814

The brisk walk around Bloomsbury Square had done
nothing to improve her odd mood. The wretch had said
two weeks, which in Hope's book was fourteen days—
fifteen at a push if one allowed for leeway—but as he
had been gone for twenty days already with not so much
as a letter of explanation, her poor nerves were shot to
pieces.

There were urgent things which she needed to discuss with him which she couldn't confide in anybody
else. Like the gushing request from Mr Cooper himself,
from Cooper and Son, to have the rest of *Phantasma*

sent to him by express because the three chapters H. B. Rooke had sent from Whitstable were, according to him, the best and most intriguing opening of a novel he had read in years.

Or how his mother had coped with his absence and how he had coped with the potential aftermath. Were things dire or were they on an even keel and she was being unnecessarily anxious? His awful rendition of his mother's illness, the neglect she had suffered by his father and the atrocities the poor woman had endured at his brother's hand, and then the struggles they had both had to get her well again had played on her mind for the duration of his absence, to such an extent it now seemed like her burden too. Emotionally invested yet a frustratingly impotent bystander who could do nothing but wait for news. That Luke had had to deal with it all alone for so many years, had had to work and struggle to pay for it all when the Thundersleys had so much, and had done so stalwartly, with such love and compassion had done something odd to the way she felt about him.

After much soul searching, and twenty interminable restless nights, she was now prepared to concede that, despite his vexing and smug manner and his charming overconfidence, she had had some affection for the dratted man before he had bared his soul. Undeniably, there had been some unfortunate attraction too which she had done her best to ignore, even though that had proved to be impossible. Now that he had entrusted her with everything and exposed himself in all his flawed but noble glory, the ground had shifted. And because she couldn't stop thinking about him, and because most of those thoughts weren't all occupied with friendly concern but superficial nonsense like the way he smiled or the way he looked at her or the way that he tasted, she was also prepared to concede there was something else at play.

She missed him dreadfully, worried about him incessantly, lusted after him constantly and was frantically counting the minutes until he returned. There was also a strange stirring in the vicinity of her heart which simply would not shift, no matter what she did.

All unsettling signs that platonic friendly affection had covertly grown into something else.

Something which frankly petrified her pessimistic and wary heart.

Something which she might have ruthlessly buried out of principle, and sheer self-preservation, had she not done the unthinkable and kissed him like she meant it. And certainly something she wouldn't be so preoccupied with had the dratted man not left her a hand-picked posy of dew-covered yellow roses and left them on her little table on the balcony for her to find straight after he had left.

Exactly as a thoughtful suitor would do to a woman he was courting.

Which wouldn't have been a problem at all if she hadn't put all but one of the thoughtful flowers in a vase on her nightstand where she had sighed over them much too often until there had been nothing living left to sigh over. Or if she hadn't diligently pressed the most perfect bud in a heavy pile of books straight away so that she could always keep the damning thing for ever in the little musical box in which she kept all her most precious things.

She huffed out an annoyed sigh as she left the park,

then immediately beamed with joy at the sight of a carriage pulling up outside Number Twenty-Two—one comfortingly emblazoned with the Thundersley crest in gold leaf on the door.

Hope quickened her pace, aiming for nonchalance but likely failing miserably, coming within spitting distance of the thing as the footman opened the door. But instead of Luke's huge booted foot, it was a delicate feminine one which emerged, closely followed by the rest of the Marchioness.

His sister-in-law took one look at Hope and frowned as she usually did when they collided, before she covered it with a brittle smile. 'Miss Brookes.'

'My lady.'

The obligatory curtsy pained her because she had no respect for this woman and resented having to pay it. Especially when the Marchioness had never been anything but atrociously rude to all three Brookes sisters at every possible occasion. That Hope had garnered a begrudging *Miss Brookes* this morning was an achievement when on at least the last six occasions where they had collided, the woman had given her the cut. She would have cheerfully left the awkward conversation at that too, had the woman not simultaneously started up the steps to Number Twenty-Two as she went to her own front door.

The Marchioness eyed her suspiciously. 'What are you doing here?'

'I live here.'

Her eyes widened at that. 'You live next door to Lucius? *Here?* On Bedford Place?'

'I do.'

The cold, ice-blue eyes narrowed as they scathingly

looked her up and down. 'Was he aware you lived here before he moved in?'

The insulting implication was explicit. That somehow Hope must have lured him here with her ample charms intent on seducing him to better herself, as all the scandal rags suggested.

'Not to my knowledge.' And not that it was any of this woman's business anyway. 'But you would have to ask him to be sure.'

'I most certainly will. He has a reputation to protect.'

'And living next door to me will somehow damage it?'

'You would know the answer to that better than I, Miss Brookes, seeing as you are no stranger to the scandal sheets yourself.' The Marchioness's gloved hand rapped impatiently on his door. 'But men will always be men, won't they? And I console myself that the Duff men bore quickly then swiftly move on. Once he has entertained himself enough with the *limited* delights of Bloomsbury, of course.' She cast a critical eye over his neat, terraced town house, which identically matched every other on Bedford Place. 'As surely even you have to concede that this is hardly a fitting address for a marquess, no matter what the initial allurement.'

'Or repellent.' Hope smiled innocently, making a mental note to ask Luke the real reasons why he had left Berkeley Square while suspecting this sort of puffed-up and pompous behaviour was entirely to blame.

With a brittle smile, the mean-spirited Marchioness rapped on his door a second time while Hope rifled in her reticule for her key, sorely tempted to give the rude woman a proper piece of her mind but not wanting to cause Luke trouble by doing it. As the awkward silence stretched and the key refused to be found, she decided to hasten the woman's departure instead despite the overwhelming urge to leave her stood on the doorstep.

'You should probably know that Luke is not yet returned from Cornwall and it is his housekeeper's day off.'

The Marchioness blinked as if that inescapable fact could not possibly be the truth. 'But he is due at mine for dinner tomorrow.'

'He is?' This was news to her.

'We dine together every Friday, and he always tells me it is the highlight of his week, so I am sure he will be back in time.' He had never mentioned a regular Friday dinner with his brother's widow either. The Marchioness turned and sailed back down the steps, clearly put out beneath the regal smile. 'Dear Lucius was devasted to have to miss the last two as he so looks forward to our intimate and cosy little suppers. But alas, his dull business in Cornwall couldn't be delayed no matter how much he was desperate to delay it, though I sincerely hope for his sake it doesn't inconvenience him still further as we are having lamb and lamb is his favourite.'

There was a strange undercurrent to her sudden chattiness which grated, almost as if she had a point to prove and wanted to put Hope in her place for some reason. Or perhaps it was merely the woman's supercilious attitude which grated.

'I hardly think Luke views fetching his mother as an inconvenience.'

The well-shod foot paused on the carriage steps, but when she turned around this time, she seemed more stunned than regal. 'He is bringing his mother back with him?'

'It was the sole purpose of his trip to Cornwall.' Some devil inside her couldn't help but stir the pot more by putting the Marchioness firmly in her place too. A little competition would do her inflated ego good. 'He's been making preparations to receive the Dowager for weeks. He's even had the house redecorated for her visit. Surely he mentioned that momentous news during one of your many intimate and cosy little Friday night suppers?'

It was late afternoon when the other Thundersley carriage finally rattled up Bedford Place. Being reliably nosy and shamelessly tactless about being so, both Charity and her mother hurried out to greet it, leaving Hope to trail in their wake. Though for once, she was grateful they were so unsubtle because she needed to see Luke for herself to ascertain the lie of the land and she was more than a little curious to meet his mother. Before his heartfelt confession on the night of his departure, he had mentioned her often in conversation and always with the slightly put-upon affection which close families used when their beloved nearest and dearest exasperated them. However, now that she knew about the woman's long battle with illness, she had no earthly idea what to expect. She pictured a frail and gaunt woman with tortured eyes, though that was certainly not what he was helping out of the carriage. Instead, she was robust, grinning and had the same dark colouring as her son but with a smattering of white at the temples. An insider's peak at how well he would age.

After her came another smiling woman, perhaps a little older, significantly plumper, hair more salt than pepper and a kindly look about her. That had to be Clowance, his mother's companion-cum-nursemaid, whom, Luke had confided, had been with them since his mother had been well enough to return home.

As if he sensed her, Luke's eyes lifted to Hope's, where she had hung back on the steps, and he slowly smiled, and in that moment she realised that everything was all right.

'You are back, Luke!' Her own mother had a talent for stating the obvious. 'And this must be the Dowager.' She beamed at her. 'You are so like your son, my lady. The resemblance is uncanny.'

With his customary good humour, and despite the fact that he had been travelling for days and doubtless just wanted to stare at his own drawing room walls with a restorative cup of tea in his hand, Luke stepped forward to make the introductions. 'Mama, this is Mrs Roberta Brookes, not only my good neighbour but also the famous soprano.' Her mother preened at the perfect compliment. 'And this is her youngest daughter, Miss Charity Brookes, who is also a supremely talented soprano…ladies, this is my nagging mother, Lady Maria Duff, and her long-suffering and sainted companion, Clowance.' His mother jabbed him in the ribs with her elbow.

'Please ignore my idiot son. He thinks he is amusing though heaven only knows why.' She took both of her mother's and Hope's hands in hers. 'I am so delighted to meet you, Mrs Brookes. Luke gushes about you and your family and I am humbled by the generosity you have all shown him. He says you have practically adopted him since he moved here and have even fed him, which was very brave of you considering he eats like a horse.' She turned to her sister. 'Miss Charity, you are as pretty as a picture, just as Luke described.'

Then those dark eyes turned to her with undisguised interest. 'And *you* must be Hope. I have been especially looking forward to meeting you. My son speaks of you most fondly…'

A statement which did odd things to Hope's insides and made both her mother and Charity exchange a very telling look, before her instantly grinning sister decided to have some more meddlesome fun at her expense. 'Can we offer you some tea after your long journey while your baggage is unloaded? You must be parched.'

'I am sure the Dowager is exhausted after her journey. I am sure they all are.' Hope looked to Luke for reassurance. 'And would prefer to orientate themselves at home this afternoon.'

'Not at all, my dear. We stopped for a delightful luncheon and a walk not two hours ago which quite revived us all, so some tea would be lovely.' His mother threaded her arm through Hope's. 'And please, as you are already such dear friends of my son and because Dowager sounds so old and decrepit, I absolutely insist you all call me Maria.'

Chapter Thirteen

Luke barely managed to snatch two minutes alone with Hope that same evening before his mother hunted him down and demanded he play cards with her. Before she caught the pair of them smiling and skirting around each other tentatively on their scandalously adjoining balconies, and promptly informed her overprotective family of that fact, he'd had no choice but to bid Hope a hasty goodnight and rapidly close the French doors. The rest of the next day wasn't any better because they hadn't collided at all. So he was pinning all his hopes on stealing a moment with her tonight after his mother had readily agreed they should accompany the Brookes family to Vauxhall Gardens to watch the fireworks despite the prospect of crowds.

As much as he was concerned for her potential reaction to being confronted with more people in a single park than probably inhabited the whole of Cornwall, he was also encouraged she was prepared to give it a go. Since the moment they had left Tregally, his mother seemed to be on a mission to try and do things which she hadn't done in years. Pushing and testing herself and surprising them both in the process. On their con-

voluted journey back to London, and at her insistence
and without any words of caution from Clowance, they
had stopped for a few days at both Exmouth and Bristol, where she shopped, took in the sights and for the
most part seemed to enjoy herself.

There had been a couple of incidents where it all
got on top of her. Once in Exmouth only a day or two
in when she lost sight of him and Clowance and she
briefly panicked. Then she became a little teary and
anxious after she had visited Brislington House to pay
her respects to Dr Long Fox to show him how far she
had come in her recovery. He put the latter down to all
the bad memories which had forced her to need that
kind and forgiving sanctuary in the first place. Awful
memories which must be constantly close to the surface now that she was confronting London again after
nearly a thirty-year absence—but at least Bloomsbury
wasn't Mayfair. He couldn't imagine her coping with
those demons quite so well.

He stared at her across the carriage and saw none of
the obvious signs she was overawed. If anything, there
was an encouraging glint of anticipation in her eyes.
Still, it was better to be safe than sorry.

'If it all gets too much, I shall plead exhaustion and
we will leave.'

'Oh, do stop fussing, dear.' She said that a lot to him
of late. 'I wouldn't have accepted Roberta's invitation
if I did not feel I could cope. Some fresh air, pleasant
company, an evening picnic and some fireworks sound
delightful after a long week of travelling. I am tired of
living like a hermit and now that your life has changed,
so must mine. What if you decide to make your permanent home here in London? And you get married and

have children here? I want to be part of that, Luke, and not from afar.'

He nodded, not wanting to acknowledge her casual comment about grandchildren because she had mentioned those rather a lot of late too. Besides, it was kicking another buzzing hornets' nest which he also didn't want to discuss with her in a carriage—or anywhere just yet—and that was Hope. The woman he had alternately fantasied about, lusted over, pondered and pined for constantly, for three long weeks.

Damn he had missed her!

Her presence, her conversation, her clever mind and her companionship, yet he had no earthly idea if she had decided to batten down the hatches after he'd brought up the subject of courting or if her drawbridge was down in welcome. He supposed he was about to find out and found himself on unfamiliar tenterhooks for her decision. He had never courted a woman before. He had dallied. Sometimes for weeks. But never with more permanent and daunting intentions. Was she even amiable? Was it even feasible with his life so complicated and his responsibilities so complex? All he knew, was he was prepared to give it a try if she was.

'You smell very nice tonight, doesn't he, Clowance? Are you wearing cologne?'

She knew very well he had never owned a bottle of the stuff in his life before. 'Everybody wears it here, Mama.'

'I like it.' She smiled exactly as she did when she was up to no good. 'I like that new waistcoat too. It's very smart. If it wasn't for your customary dishevelled hair and scruffy beard, I'd barely recognise you. You have become quite the dashing gentleman.' She stared at his head and frowned. 'As you are a marquess now, haven't you considered getting it cut?'

'No.'

Of course he hadn't and nor would he even though she always nagged him about it. The wayward hair had always annoyed his father, then later his brother, and in a world where the younger version of himself had had so little control over anything in his life, for years, that one minuscule bit of rebellion had been the only thing he could do.

She sighed. 'I didn't think you would have but I suppose some ladies like the craggy, rough-and-ready look in a man.' He offered her his best teasing smile as confirmation, expecting her to roll her eyes and tell him off for being vulgar like she always did. Instead she grinned and raised her eyebrows as the carriage slowed at the gates of the park. 'I suspect Miss Hope Brookes is one of those women, isn't she? Just as I suspect that she is the reason why you purchased cologne.'

While he carefully considered how to respond to that, Clowance patted his leg in sympathy. 'I told you you'd regret bringing her here. She has a bee in her bonnet about you settling down, young man, and I fear she'll be insufferable until she gets her way.'

With perfect timing, Augustus Brookes's grinning face appeared at their window and nipped the awkward conversation firmly in the bud. 'In a miracle of biblical proportions, the Writtles have secured us all a supper box which is practically on top of the bandstand so we shall have the very best view of all the entertainments tonight. However, I am told the crowds on the Grand Walk are already horrendous, so if we all get separated among the thronging masses, aim for the Turkish Saloon.'

As they alighted, Hope was mere feet away and looking so lovely she fair took his breath away, but he didn't dare leave his mother who was holding on to his arm far more tightly than a woman who was completely relaxed in such boisterous surroundings ever would. But she managed the long stroll to the supper box without any issue, and even managed to coo and sigh at all the thousands of pretty coloured lights which twinkled in the trees and illuminated the pathways.

Once seated, and separated from all the chaos around them by three sturdy walls, she settled down quickly and threw herself into conversation with the other matrons in their party—Roberta, the delightful Countess of Writtle, mother-in-law to the eldest Brookes daughter Faith who he still hadn't met, and a very pleasant lady called Mrs Philpot who was apparently the family's oldest and dearest friend as well as the mother of Charity's wide-eyed best friend Dorothy. A young lady who seemed to have a great deal of trouble not staring at him and giggled and blushed like a beetroot whenever he spoke to her. As was expected at such gatherings, Luke placed himself among the gentlemen where Augustus typically held court. The Earl of Writtle proved to be good company and Mr Philpot, Dorothy's jolly father, seemed to have a never-ending supply of jokes to keep everyone entertained. His serious son Griffith, however, seemed to find the whole thing a chore and had appointed himself his sister's chaperon instead, which was likely a very good thing considering she was constantly being waylaid by Charity.

However, in all the jollity, and for the entire duration of the meal and while the orchestra played, it proved to be impossible to have any sort of meaningful conversation with Hope. All they managed were a few shared looks across the vast expanse of the table. Finally, as the palpable buzz of excitement signalled the fireworks were about to begin and he resigned himself to being thwarted from speaking to her properly yet again, Charity piped up.

'Surely we are not staying here to watch them?'

'Of course we are, dear.' Full of ham and too much tart, Roberta had clearly taken root for the night and was horrified by the suggestion. 'If we leave this box we shall lose it and have to stand with all the hundreds of people who couldn't find a supper box for the orchestra's final performance.' She shuddered as if such a thing were, not so much an inconvenience, but entirely unacceptable. 'Which would make us all a target for P-I-C-K-P-O-C-K-E-T-S.'

'But the best views are at the other end of the gardens, nearest the firework tower.' Charity pouted. 'I should like to see them in all their glory without any obstructions.'

Her mother pointed up to clear night sky. 'As the only obstructions are clouds and there aren't any, why suffer the long walk when we only have to come back this way afterwards?'

'Can Dorothy and I at least go? There is so much light here that it spoils the brilliance of the display. It's less bright at the opposite end.'

'By that she means it's pitch black at the other end,' muttered Griffith beside him through gritted teeth. 'The Dark Walk is a notorious place for trysts and assignations.'

Which all sounded utterly perfect to Luke's ears. 'I would be happy to escort all the young ladies if the rest of you prefer to stay here.' His gaze flicked to Hope's briefly in case he had inadvertently announced his intentions to the entire party.

The younger Mr Philpot glared at him. 'As would I.' Although it was patently obvious he would much rather boil his own head than accompany him and was only doing so in case Luke had any designs on his little sister's virtue.

'Then it's settled.' In case it wasn't, he stood and made sure to solicitously help both Charity and the giggling Miss Philpot to stand before he held out his hand to Hope who had yet to show any inclination to do so. 'Will you be joining us?'

'If I must.' Her fingers touched his, awakening every single one of his nerve endings all in one go.

They set off in one close bundle, all three of the ladies in the middle and the two gentlemen flanking them at either end, but had hardly gone more than a hundred yards when Charity declared that the main route through the arches was too busy to manoeuvre swiftly and decided they should take the quieter Lover's Walk instead. The name felt significant, and as Charity rushed ahead, dragging Giggling Dorothy and by default Grouchy Griffith as well, he and Hope trailed behind.

She seemed in no hurry to compete with the others, but if the several feet she put between them was any gauge, she was also in no hurry to be more intimate.

'How is your mother?'

'Surprisingly well, all things considered, and apparently determined to grab life by the horns.'

'That's good.'

'It is.'

As there weren't usually silences between them, this one hung heavy. Almost as if they were both suddenly timid of one another and awkwardly feeling their way on decidedly unchartered ground. Their eyes met, and ridiculously they both instantly looked away and his toes curled inside his boots as he racked his brains for a way to start the conversation he had been desperate to have since at least the last week.

'Thank you for the roses.'

'You are very welcome.' Apparently his legendary gift of the gab and scintillating Duff charm had deserted him, and Hope now seemed determined not to look his way at all and was staring resolutely at the path ahead as if her life depended on it.

'What did they mean?'

'Nothing…' *Coward!* 'At least, beyond a friendly farewell.' And now he was mirroring her dismissive words from their last night on the balcony, when he didn't mean them at all.

'Oh…good.' She almost smiled, but not quite in relief. 'It was a thoughtful gesture—even if you did decimate my mother's prize rosebush to get them.'

More silence.

This one so painful it made his teeth ache.

All his fault too. She had given him the perfect excuse to say all the things he had no idea how to say when she had brought up the stupid flowers, and he had ruined the opportunity with meaningless drivel. And if he didn't step up soon, then this whole evening was doomed to be a litany of meaningless drivel.

Annoyed with himself, he stopped dead. 'This is ridiculous!'

She had paused too, and was now watching him warily. Behind her, the other three were still too close for comfort. Whatever he said, and whatever her reaction, it was too personal and private to do it in front of an audience. But as he couldn't put it off any longer, Luke grabbed her hand and tugged her from the dimly lit path into the dark privacy of the trees. It was time to take a leaf out of his mother's book and grab life by the horns.

'Hope, I...' He had no earthly idea what to say, knowing only that something needed to be said so that they both knew exactly where they stood. 'The thing is...'

I missed you.

I need you.

I want you.

I think... I think I might be in love with you.

'The thing is...' God she was beautiful stood gazing up at him. And she wasn't wearing her usual mask, he realised. There was no bravado. No affected disdain. No bold stare. Her eyes were serious. Her focus intent, as if searching for the truth in his, while anxiously waiting for him to find it. They were both wary and expectant. Hopeful and scared.

Well, at least he was hopeful and perhaps she looked scared. He was past the point of feeling rational.

In the end, he didn't wait for the right words to miraculously materialise, because there were no right words to describe what he felt. So he did what his body was telling him to do, what his whole being needed to do at that precise moment, and just kissed her instead. Dragging her into his arms and pouring his heart and soul into it so that she would be in no doubt how hopelessly undone he was.

How much she had undone him.

His foolish heart soared when she sighed against his mouth and her body instantly melted against his. Luke needed no further encouragement to deepen the kiss, losing himself completely in the moment. She tasted of the strawberries she had eaten for dessert. Of sweetness and passion. Of comfort and rightness. Of everything he had spent two months dreaming of.

In case he was going too fast or misinterpreting her signals, he tore his lips away and tried to give them both the chance to come up for air and re-evaluate, but Hope was having none of it. Unceremoniously, she dragged him back, looping her arms tight around his neck to anchor him firmly in place in case he had any foolish ideas about being gentlemanly again.

Not that being gentlemanly was possible when his body was on fire.

He had no idea if it had been he who had staggered forward or if she had dragged him further into the trees with her, but somehow her back rested against the wide trunk of an ancient oak and his desire was flush against her belly. She ran impatient fingers through his hair, her questing tongue tangling with his, her full breasts flattened against his chest, rising and falling in time with her erratic breathing.

Somewhere, disjointed in the distance, were the sounds and smells of fireworks but neither of them could have cared less. He filled his hands with her bottom, traced the shape of her lush curves with his palms, overwhelmed by her perfume. Her beauty. Her passion.

Just her.

When his greedy hands finally cupped her breasts over the fabric of her dress, she moaned and arched against them, her own fingers boldly exploring his bare skin beneath his shirt, and he was lost.

And likely would have blissfully remained so if the impatient sounds of Griffith Philpot searching for them hadn't dragged them both, with the utmost and belligerent reluctance, crashing back to earth.

Chapter Fourteen

To say it felt odd to be having a perfectly normal conversation over their balconies less than two hours after her hands had shamelessly caressed his buttocks was an understatement. It felt odd because it felt normal, and it felt odd that she still thrummed from the after-effects of their thwarted passion. And it most certainly felt odd that she wasn't the least bit sorry for being so shamelessly wanton, though Hope did wish her stupid, much too cumbersome bosoms would desist feeling quite so…needy. That they did, when she would much rather never think about the wretched things at all, was most distracting.

'It is an amazing book, Hope. Gripping, insightful,

filled with suspense and double bluff. You certainly had me fooled to the very end at the true identity of the phantom. I knew Mr Crocker would bite your hand off for it!' Luke was delighted with her news. 'Did he give any indication how long it would take for him to get back to you with an answer?'

'Mr *Cooper* has asked for a meeting at his offices a week Tuesday.'

His palm slapped his forehead as he grinned. 'Cooper! Why the blazes do I keep calling him Crocker?' It was beyond her. 'But that is fantastic, Hope. He must want it, else he wouldn't waste your time with a meeting otherwise.' He eyes were alight with delight for her. 'You did it, Hope! You are going to see your book in Hatchard's.'

And there was the rub. The thing which had been the cause of much hand-wringing since Mr Cooper's letter arrived via her grandparents in Whitstable this morning. 'Technically, at this point, it is still H. B. Rooke's book, not mine, and after last time...'

'How could he possibly reject it? It's a masterpiece, Hope, and I am not just saying that because I am rather partial to you. I am saying it as a reader of probably thousands of books. *Phantasma* is one of the best novels I have ever read. I couldn't put it down and when I did, I raved about it for days. Ask my mother. I drove her mad with my incessant gushing, especially as I flatly refused to allow her to read it even though she begged me to hand your precious pages over and even threatened my person at one point—but I was resolute.' His dark eyes were suddenly tender. 'I told her that you had entrusted it to me and that the only way she could get her grasping hands on it was if she had your permission.'

'I am not sure it is suitable for your mother...not after

all she has been through.' *Phantasma* was dark to its core. 'I fear it would unsettle her.'

His bark of laughter was a surprise. 'She's had to deal with real monsters, Hope, your fictional one won't faze her. She's always adored the macabre, ever since she read that copy of *The Monk* I liberated from the vicar, she cannot get enough of it.'

She was horrified. 'You gave your mother *The Monk*? What if it had brought upon one of her nervous panics?'

He shrugged as if he hadn't even considered it. 'She loves to read. And she devoured it in a day. We have always swapped books. Besides, I was twelve then and she had enjoyed a long run of good health at that point which lasted for several years.' His face clouded as he remembered the turning point. 'To be frank, Hope, I think she was cured by then and likely would have remained so if it hadn't been for Cassius.' Then he shook his head impatiently. 'But enough of that. You are going to be published, Hope! I couldn't be more proud that my intended is going to be famous!'

His declaration momentarily threw her. *'Intended?'*

'Well that's where this is going, isn't it?' He feigned some smugness. 'Now that we are officially courting.'

She took a few moments to roll that idea around in her mind, waiting for the inevitable pessimistic warnings to urge her to back away from it, and when none came nerves flooded her. Things were moving fast. Too fast. And while they might well be going in the right direction, the perfect direction, prudence dictated the need for caution. A little more time to get to know him fully before she jumped in with both feet as he seemed quite content to do. 'Does it have to be official?'

He frowned. 'What does that mean?'

Unthinking, she fiddled with her fichu. 'Just that official suggests we are shouting it out from the rooftops, and among our families, that will likely put a lot of expectation and undue pressure on us to rush into things which shouldn't be rushed into.'

He folded his arms and stared at her pityingly. 'Coward.'

'It is not cowardice...' Although it probably was. Her heart was certainly now racing and not from residual passion. *Intended* sounded serious—unexpected, exciting and utterly lovely as far as her heart was concerned—but serious enough that her pessimistic head didn't quite believe it. 'It is common sense. We barely know one another really and we might...'

'By *we* might you mean *me*.'

'I mean nothing of the sort.' Although she did. Yes, he was charming and noble and seemingly decent to his core and, yes, he didn't treat her like an object like most men did, but things were all moving too fast. So fast since tonight's incendiary kiss, she could barely think straight, when she knew a kiss was no measure of a man's sincerity.

'If you are going to be a coward, Hope, at least be an honest one. I might have only known you a matter of months...'

'Less than two!' Which was the crux of the problem. Or at least one of the cruxes.

Those vexing dark eyes rolled skyward. 'I might have only known you *less* than two months, but I'll wager I already know everything about you that it is possible to know—including how your suspicious and pessimistic mind works. You fear that I am too good to be true and that given enough time and opportunity, I will soon prove myself to be as unworthy and shallow as all those drooling hounds who only ever see your breasts instead of you. You suspect that I am putting on a façade of noble decency and pretending our relationship means more to me than it does simply because I want to bed you.'

He had managed to succinctly reduce all her fears, built up over a lifetime of experience and disappointment, into a few sentences. It was galling that he actually did know her that well. Galling too, when she had never once mentioned to him or anyone how self-conscious she was about her cumbersome bosoms, yet the clever wretch had worked that out all for himself too. As she glared and tried to think of a suitable answer which wouldn't make him smug, while simultaneously not allowing him to realise that she didn't trust him fully yet because her suspicious and pessimistic mind did require more proof, he smiled his customary cocky, lopsided smile. 'Guess what? I *do* want to bed you!'

He grinned at her affront. 'I cannot wait to bed you. You are the most beddable woman I have ever met, Hope, as well as the most vexing, and I shall spend all of tonight tossing and turning and yearning, thanks to that splendid kiss earlier, because it wasn't anywhere near enough to sate the rampant lust that I have for you. Lust which is still coursing through my veins and has pretty much since the first moment I clapped eyes on you sat by that fountain. However...'

The wolfish smile slowly changed into a different sort, the sort which was all Luke beneath the bravado.

'Unlike those idiots who only ever see your breasts and who assume that because you were given them you must have been created by the Almighty solely as a vessel for man's passions—I don't want to just bed *them*.' He pointed directly at her chest while still managing to look her directly in the eyes. 'Because my ardour and affection is for all of you, Hope. Your tempting body is but a fraction of what I want to possess and having you in the carnal and physical sense would feel hollow without having your heart and soul too.'

She had no earthly idea how to respond to that or even how she felt about it, but conscious that her jaw now hung slack at his hugely improper but strangely thrilling words, she forced herself to close it as he jabbed the night air with his finger.

'And I'll tell you another thing, my seductive sceptic, I have selflessly decided to deny myself the pleasure of bedding you until you entrust me with all those things unreservedly. In fact, I shall go one further. I shan't make any attempt to have my wicked way with you until you declare your overwhelming love for me and expressly invite me to. How is that for noble and worthy?'

He was exasperating with his perfect compliments and annoying respect for her fears. But words were words and he had always had a way with them, but actions spoke louder. She wasn't entirely sure what sort of action she expected from him on top of all those notable things he had already done to make her wary heart waver, but decided she would know it when she saw it. Until then it was better to be safe than sorry.

'I still see no hurry to make our courtship official.'

He rolled his dratted eyes again. 'That is because you are a coward and I am fearless—but at least you concede we are courting at least.' Doubtless before she could argue that point too, he took himself back inside, closed his stupid French doors on her and pulled his curtains closed.

Chapter Fifteen

Rumours abound, Dear Reader, that the charming new Marquess of T. is about to announce his engagement! And if the sudden arrival of his reclusive mother is any gauge, we anticipate a very hasty wedding indeed. Could it be that the bountiful Miss H. from Bloomsbury, who I am reliably informed appeared intriguingly more bountiful than usual at the theatre last week, is in a hurry to wed...? Or are we all labouring under a misapprehension?

Whispers from Behind the Fan
July 1814

'It is an excellent story, Miss Brookes. Suspenseful, chilling and yet still filled with humanity.' Mr Cooper steepled his fingers on his imposing ebony desk and smiled as he glanced down at the thick manuscript piled symbolically between them. 'And despite your convoluted ruse to get me to read it...' A ruse he had not taken well when she had first arrived for their appointment. 'I would be delighted to publish it. There is a strong market for the Gothic at the moment and your story is without a doubt one of the best examples of the genre I have ever read.'

She beamed at him in elation, suddenly overwhelmed with emotion to have been deemed worthy enough for such an honour and relieved that she did indeed have a modicum of talent for something, and something she loved to boot. 'Thank you, Mr Cooper!' She couldn't wait to tell Luke she was finally going to be in Hatchard's. He had insisted on accompanying her here and was likely wearing away the pavement outside because she had refused him entry into the publisher's office because she needed to do this for herself.

'I'll give you twenty guineas for the copyright.' That knocked the wind out of her sails, as it took her precious manuscript completely out of her hands and then prevented her from earning any more money on it if the book became a success.

'The copyright isn't for sale, Mr Cooper.' As tempting as it was to settle for thrilled that her work was finally going to be published, she had done her research. Years and years of research while she waited for this opportunity to finally knock. It was the main reason why she had been so determined to court Cooper and Sons in the first place. They were the biggest and best publishing house around, with a brilliant reputation, so they could afford to be choosy.

She knew that and he knew that, but only moments ago she had promised Luke faithfully she would hold firm. Do not sell yourself short, he had said repeatedly over the last week as he schooled her in the dark art of the business transaction, and never accept the first offer. In business, being able to look a man in the eye and negotiate as if you truly have something they want is the key to getting them to do exactly what you want.

And as Luke seemed to be the master of getting people to bend over backwards to do exactly as he wanted, she was prepared to stick to his sage advice like glue. He wanted what was best for her and *Phantasma*. Mr Cooper wanted what was best for Cooper and Son.

'While twenty guineas is a generous offer, and I am pleased to hear it, Mr Cooper, I am seeking a profit-sharing arrangement. I need no advance.' *Phantasma* would stand on its own two feet. Deep down inside she believed the story had what it took. So did Luke who never stopped raving about it to anyone who would listen, so much so, even her parents were taking the time to read it and they never read. And clearly so did Mr Cooper else he wouldn't be offering twenty guineas to own it lock, stock and barrel.

The publisher pondered this for several moments, his finger tapping his chin as he stared at her, no doubt waiting, exactly as Luke had cautioned, for her to crumble first. Then, when she didn't, he begrudgingly nodded.

'I would consider that. Your story is certainly appealing enough and fits the current appetite for the macabre perfectly. What sort of terms are you looking for?'

'A tenth of each book sold.' He didn't baulk at that because she had done her research and knew that was within the realms of the going rate. It was reasonable but not outlandish. When he took out her share and the cost of printing, distribution and the bookseller's cut, he would still earn a tidy profit. And profit, as Luke had also rightly pointed out, was every businessman's true paramour. 'And I want my name on the cover.'

Instantly his face changed. 'As H. B. Rooke—yes. That pseudonym, it is a nod to your true identity but suitably vague not to raise undue alarm. As you doubtless already know, the general public find literature more palatable if they think it has come from a man's pen.'

'As most readers are female, I struggle to believe that, Mr Cooper.' What he actually meant was that he found it more palatable. He and likely every other male publisher out there.

'Yet there it is.' He smiled, unapologetic. 'If you're desirous of seeing your name on the front, Miss Brookes, then perhaps one of the vanity presses are a better option for you to consider than Cooper and Son.' Even though they both knew that it was also the least profitable route because not only would Hope have to pay all the costs herself, she would then also have to distribute it. Whereas, Cooper and Son were the most successful publishing house in the country and sold their books to hundreds of booksellers from Land's End to John o' Groats. If *Phantasma* was going to be a success, and if she was ever going to see it on the shelves in Hatchard's, she needed a proper, experienced publisher behind her. 'H. B. Rooke is practically your name anyway give or take a few handy spaces in the text, it seems petty to split hairs over a trifle.'

A trifle!

It was hardly a trifle when it meant the world to her!

She wanted to scream her frustration at the man and if she had had a real trifle handy, he would soon be wearing it.

'Hold your fiery redhead's temper, harridan! No matter what the provocation.'

Luke's final words before she entered this office echoed in her ears.

'Call his bluff instead. Business is a game, play it like

*you are a master. Show him you are prepared to walk
away—and do it if you have to. N-E-G-O-T-I-A-T-E!'*

The wretch had even spelled that last bit exactly like
her mother purely to vex her.

*'Believe in yourself and your story, Hope, because
I do.'*

With her heart in her throat, and bravado firmly
strapped in place, she shrugged in what she prayed appeared an unperturbed manner. 'I think I shall wait
to see what Longman's offer is first before I take that
route.' It was a gamble choosing Mr Cooper's biggest
rival only two doors down on Paternoster Row, especially because she hadn't heard a squeak out of them
since she had sent them a copy of her book two weeks
ago, one she hoped paid off as she gathered up the manuscript. She would certainly strangle Luke if it didn't.
'Thank you for your time, Mr Cooper.'

She stood, turned and with a cold trickle of sweat
dripping down her spine, walked with purpose to the
door.

'A hundred guineas for the copyright or a fifteenth
of the profits.' It was a staggering amount for a debut
author and he knew it. 'And that is my final offer, Miss
Brookes. I really want that book.'

'But I still do not get my name on the front, do I?'
She could see that as clear as crystal in his wily old
eyes.

'Correct...but...' He sat back in his chair and stared
at her levelly as if weighing her up. Then exhaled
slowly. 'I am confident enough in it that I will meet
you halfway.'

'What does that mean?'

'It means that you agree to be H. B. Rooke in the
first instance, and in return I shall give you my word

that if this book does as well as we both suspect it will, then Hope Brookes will be emblazoned across the second edition and upon every edition of any subsequent book you write for me.'

According to Luke, *the best compromise should hurt you both equally.* And at least this was a compromise. It still hurt, but she hadn't lost and Mr Cooper was throwing her a bone. 'Will that offer be written in the contract?' She wouldn't settle for an empty promise.

'There are no flies on you, are there, Miss Brookes?' He smiled as he nodded, clearly impressed. 'Yes. I will have it all put in writing too.'

'Can I think upon it?' It wasn't quite her dream come true but it could be, and that was surely a gamble worth considering?

'Of course—as long as you do not expect me to wait for ever while you court my competition. There are no flies on me either, Miss Brookes, and I won't be used as leverage.'

'Only until tomorrow.' She needed to consult with Luke first, even though her gut told her this was likely to be the best offer she could expect when she had never had anything published before. And the cold hard truth was that she'd have bitten his hand off for a mere tenth without quibble if that offer had come with her name attached.

'Well?' Luke dashed towards her the moment she stepped into the churchyard of St Paul's where he had been pacing for the last half an hour. 'Has he made you an offer?'

She nodded, looking at little stunned by it. 'Fifteen per cent.'

More than she had hoped for. 'I knew it!' He picked

her up and spun her in a giddy circle. 'And you negotiated! I am so proud of you!' He couldn't resist giving her a quick kiss as he lowered her to the ground. 'You did it, Hope. You are going to be in Hatchard's!'

'I am.' But she wasn't beaming from ear to ear at the prospect as he expected. If anything, she seemed deflated. 'Or at least *Phantasma* will be.'

Luke almost kicked a gravestone, he was so furious. 'The fool won't allow you to use your real name, will he?'

'Not to begin with. For the first edition I must be H. B. Rooke, which is my name I suppose, give or take a few pertinent spaces in the text.' He forced himself to remain tight-lipped while she regaled all the terms where she tried to put a brave face on things and his heart bled for her. It was all so unfair. Such a dilemma wouldn't even be a dilemma if she were Mr Henry Brookes and not Miss Hope.

'What utter nonsense!' Luke was sorely tempted to head directly to Paternoster Row and give the blinkered fool a stern piece of his mind. 'Your book isn't a gamble, it's a dead cert and he knows it! Else he wouldn't have sweetened the deal with a fifteenth. Please tell me you haven't accepted.'

'Not yet.' He huffed in relief. 'But I think I have to, don't you?'

'Of course you don't! There are other publishers! Better publishers.' And by Jove he would march into each and every one of them on her behalf this very afternoon and make them read her brilliant work. 'We shall approach them all forthwith. Mark my words—old Crocker will rue the day he tried to hoodwink us.'

'Oh, for goodness sake it's Cooper! *Cooper* and Son. And there are no better publishers of Gothic fiction than

Cooper's. Or any other sort of fiction for that matter. They are and will always be my preferred choice, even if I have to swallow being H. B. Rooke for ever!'

She was selling herself short and it was killing him. 'Then let me go and speak to the esteemed Mr Cooper now and help him see reason.'

'Do you seriously think intimidating him is going to glean a better result? He'll likely rescind his offer and I will have burned my single biggest bridge.'

'I wasn't planning on intimidating the idiot. I am not that daft. I was merely suggesting that I take over the negotiations on your behalf.' Clearly the man had a problem with women if the fear of having the name of one of them on a book gave him palpitations. 'He'll listen to me. I'll dazzle him with the Duff charm and by the time I'm done, you'll have a proper deal on the table, not the outrage he's trying to palm you off with.'

That was obviously the wrong thing to say because she went from frustrated to incandescent in the blink of an eye. 'This is a proper deal and I am not an idiot, Luke!'

'I didn't mean to imply that you were. But you have to concede that publishing is obviously a man's world. Therefore, it stands to reason he'll be more agreeable to dealing with a man. He probably took one look at you.' He flapped his hand to encompass the flower-shaped buttons on her emerald-green pelisse and jaunty feminine bonnet. 'Didn't take you the least bit seriously and typically thought he could take advantage as all men do when confronted by a beautiful young woman.'

The funny thing was, even as he said the words, he realised they weren't the right ones. Not only were they poorly chosen, they were *bad* words. Reducing Hope to a physical mass of attractive constituent parts which entirely lacked any substance, reason or agency of her own. Reducing her to the very thing she abhorred the most. He flapped his hand again, intending to make it right, then realised he was wafting it not just in the vicinity of her silly hat and prettily braided bodice which had formed the basis for his clumsy argument—but to her breasts. The exact same breasts most men couldn't seem to tear their eyes from.

Her tone was clipped. Her expression haughtier than he had ever seen it but her eyes radiated such disappointment he got the distinct impression, if she had had a weapon, she would have used it on him in a heartbeat. Coldly and precisely. 'Thank you for that resounding vote of confidence in my abilities, Luke. I do so enjoy being underestimated and patronised by a member of the superior sex.' She spun on a self-righteous heel and he grabbed her arm. She glared at his hand in utter disgust until he dropped it.

'I didn't mean any of that how it sounded.' This time he would choose his blasted words more carefully. 'I can see how it could be taken as patronising, demeaning even, but I was genuinely trying to be supportive when I...'

'And to do that, you needed to remind me that to most men, a woman who looks like me is only good for one thing? Because I can assure you, I need no reminders of that. Helpful gentlemen have been reminding me of that unfortunate fact near daily since I was fifteen.'

Now she was being unfair! 'I have never...'

'Not never, Luke, for you just did.' She swept her arm up and down his body from ribs to chin in the exact same flippant manner which he had likely just done to her, making him wince to have the mirror held up to his face. Then she mimicked his voice, perfectly capturing the hint of west country in his accent but making him sound like a stupid and insincere oaf as she parroted some of his ill-chosen words back to him with her own acidic take on them.

'*Obviously he didn't take you seriously, Hope. How could he possibly take you seriously when you look like you do?*'

Then she shook her head, her lip curling in disgust. 'And I thought you were different.'

She couldn't have wounded him more if she had had a weapon.

'Hope…' He held out his hands beseechingly. 'I'm sorry. Sincerely sorry. Why are we fighting when we are on the same side? When I offered my well-intentioned assistance just now, I certainly never meant to offend you, although clearly I have. Neither did I mean to imply that…'

She held up her gloved hand. 'I am going home, Luke. I have important things to think about which concern *my* future, and would much rather think about them without feeling any more furious at men in general, and *you* in particular, than I already am.' She marched towards the neat row of hackneys lined up outside the cathedral and he followed, desperately trying to work out how to make it right after he sent it all wrong, until she suddenly turned and skewered him with her glare.

'If you have any respect left for me whatsoever, or indeed if you had any real respect for me in the first place, kindly leave me to do my thinking in peace as what *I* decide to do about *my* book is, frankly, none of your business. And if you set one of your clumsy big feet anywhere near Mr Cooper's office to offer your well-intentioned and superior manly assistance to *my* negotiation, I swear I shall never speak to you again.'

Chapter Sixteen

Hope went out with her family that night to celebrate and he wasn't invited. Which was a shame for so many reasons, not least of them that a prior engagement would have spared him the painful chore of another one of Abigail's cosy family suppers. Now, instead of toasting the woman of his dreams for her well-deserved success among people whose company he enjoyed, he would have to listen to his sister-in-law prattle on about her woes across his father's imperious dining table instead.

His own stupid fault and doubtless no less a punishment than he deserved for charging in like a bull at a gate, trying to take over and running roughshod over all her feelings. Even Charity, who loved to stir the pot, had cautioned him to keep a wide berth when he had attempted to call on Hope earlier, so he knew things were serious. He was resigned to the fact he would have to issue his grovelling apology later when he saw her on the balcony.

If he saw her on the balcony.

He climbed the front steps of the Berkeley Square mausoleum like a condemned man on the way to the gallows, hoping against hope that this dinner wouldn't be as tedious as the last one and already counting the minutes until he could leave.

'Lucius!' Since their reconciliation at the opera, Abigail always insisted on kissing his cheek which meant he had to kiss hers, then made a great show of straining to look behind him. 'Is your dear mama not joining us?'

The invitation had included his mother, not that he had told her that. She had been doing such a good job of coping with being in London, he was in no hurry to spoil things by dragging her back here to the place where all her troubles started. He had also been keeping her well clear of high society too—just in case that triggered something.

'Sadly no. She is still settling in.' A flagrant lie when she had already made herself quite at home, and thanks to her fast friendship with Roberta, already had a better social life than he did and he had been here months, not a week. She was blossoming in Bloomsbury and long might that continue.

'Oh…such a shame as I was so looking forward to meeting her. Maybe I should call on her one day instead. A nice afternoon tea next week?'

'Yes. I am sure she would be thrilled.' She wouldn't. His mother took an automatic dislike to anything pertaining to his half-brother and had taken to calling Abigail the Bride of Beelzebub whenever he mentioned her in conversation.

She threaded her arm through his possessively, her small breasts squashed much too familiarly against his bicep as she hung on him like a limpet while they walked towards the dining toom. As usual, she insisted he sat at the head of the formal table and sat beside him. He hated that chair as it had previously held the bottoms of his brother and his father, and the spectre of them still seemed to linger on the upholstery.

'So how are you, Abigail?' As much as he didn't care, it was always best to get that question over with first as it usually took at least the first two courses for her to tell him.

'Frustrated by our mutual solicitor still—but what else is new?' He might have known her first complaints would be material. 'I swear he's shilly-shallying over the transfer of deeds unnecessarily to fleece you of more money for the task. I fail to understand why he cannot simply swap your name for mine as the owner of this house, despite all his protestations that it is not that simple.'

'It would be that simple if my name were on the deeds, but alas, he was in the process of legally transferring all of the Thundersley estate over to me, which I am led to believe is always a lengthy process even with a will in place.'

Not that Luke had been included on that will as his brother hadn't mentioned his name once on that unwieldy document. Clearly he had still been of the opinion he would beget some heirs before he had the thing drawn up and would be horrified to learn that because he had driven his phaeton at speed into a wall before getting around to that chore, the law automatically passed it to the next blood recipient in the male line. Which had meant Luke had unexpectedly got it all— and not just the entailed part which Cassius would have had no control over—before his sibling could mitigate against it. Pettily, that was the one aspect of his new fortune Luke took the most pleasure in.

'However, the solicitor assures me that once all that

paperwork is done, it will be a simple enough task to transfer ownership of this house from me to you.'

She groaned, as if it was all a dreadful inconvenience to her. 'I do not suppose he has given you an estimate as to when he believes the paperwork will be finalised? My husband has been dead almost eight months and my entire life is still up in the air while all this drags on. It is not good for my nerves, Lucius.' A statement which inevitably led to a long diatribe about the current state of those nerves, complete with more tears which left him more cold than sympathetic. The dessert arrived before the topic changed, and rather abruptly it changed to him. 'I see you are still a regular fixture in the gossip columns.'

'They do seem to like me disproportionately at the moment.'

'Doubtless that will be because of all the time you are spending with your new neighbours.' Her lips thinned even though she smiled. 'As sadly the surname Brookes is synonymous with scandal.'

'I suppose while they are writing rot about us, it gives some other poor blighter a reprieve from it all.'

'From that, I take it that you and the middle Miss Brookes are not engaged?'

'Of course we aren't.' Yet. But he wasn't as averse to the idea of marriage now as he had been a few months ago.

'And there is no child due?'

'No.' Not without an immaculate conception.

'Good…' She sliced the apple tart with more force than was necessary and slid it on to his plate. 'I am relieved to hear it. As I wouldn't put it past a Brookes to use something like that to entrap you.'

That comment instantly raised his hackles. 'She wouldn't and I resent the implication.'

Instead of bristling at the rebuke, she sighed and appeared concerned. 'Oh, Lucius…as much as it pains me to meddle, on this occasion, and as we are family, I fear that I must. Please be careful…for that entire family are not quite what they seem.'

'I will not allow the Brookes family to be maligned, when they have been nothing but good to me.' Luke immediately pushed the dessert plate away, not that he had had much appetite for it anyway. 'And would much prefer we changed the subject.' Preferably to one which didn't make him want to howl at the moon.

Her hand covered his on the table, instantly leaving him cold. 'You are still new here, Lucius. New to the capital and to this life, so perhaps you are a bit more green around the gills than most peers about the way of things…but please, for your sake, be in possession of all the facts before you do something you might bitterly regret.'

He pulled his hand away, bitterly regretting coming here in the first place. 'By facts, you mean rumours when I can assure you I have no time for silly gossip.'

'There wouldn't be so much gossip about the family if there wasn't a grain of truth in it, Lucius. You know that.'

'Do I? This week alone I have apparently become both engaged and become an expectant father simply by going to the theatre.'

'Some of my friends have already expressed their concerns over the acquaintance. Concerns which I share, by the way, for what do you really know of them—of her—beyond that which they want you to believe?'

'I know all I need to know about Hope and her family to come to my own conclusions, thank you very much.' And he wouldn't sit here and hear either her or them slandered. 'And I fail to understand why I should care what *your* friends think of mine?'

'If we ignore, for one moment, the poor connections and dubious lineage of the parents…'

'I have no interest in either of those things.'

'Well you should, Lucius, and not because anyone thinks it would be unseemly for you to marry beneath yourself, but because the Marquessate is an attractive proposition and lesser people will take advantage of that fact.'

'Lesser people?' He scoffed because she was being ridiculous. 'The Brookes family have no need of my rank and title, as they are doing quite well enough on their own.' To prove it, he pointed to the enormous Augustus Brookes portrait of his pompous brother looking imperious on the wall. 'How much did you have to pay for that monstrosity, because I know for a fact Augustus doesn't get out of bed nowadays for less than a hundred guineas!'

'Perhaps, but the coup of rising in the ranks is not to be ignored. Money alone will not get them accepted here.'

'Yet the Brookes family seem to be on the exact same guest lists as you and I.'

'Not on every guest list, Lucius.' Her expression of disdain suddenly matched his disapproving brother's on the wall. 'There are still many esteemed houses which exclude them, thank goodness. Nor have they ever been allowed into Almack's, which speaks volumes hereabouts.'

'To you maybe, but not to me.' He pushed his chair

from the table and was about to stand and make his excuses, when she grabbed his sleeve.

'Are you aware the eldest recently snared herself a wealthy viscount? She took advantage of the gentleman at a very difficult time in his personal life and then, once she had thoroughly seduced him, she marched him down the aisle in case he had a change of heart?'

'Lord and Lady Eastwood seemed perfectly happy with their situation at the Writtle Ball.' He hadn't properly met Faith and her husband Piers, as he had been drunk and reeling at their engagement ball before Hope had dunked him in the fountain, but from what he had briefly witnessed, it didn't take a genius to see the pair of them had been besotted.

'Don't be naive, Lucius. Those Brookes girls are predators and always have been. The youngest is a shameless flirt who goes out of her way to flatter and bewitch the most eligible gentlemen at every entertainment, and from what I have heard, is quite overt about it too. The way she pursues Lord Denby, the heir to the Duke of Loughton is quite shameless. What is that if it is not predatory?'

There was no denying Charity did enjoy the effect she had on men and did seem to have a *tendre* for Lord Denby, though heaven only knew why as the man was a dreadful dullard, but she was young and her interest in a future duke was likely more harmless than predatory. He had a great deal of time for the girl and considered her one of his staunchest allies in his own pursuit of Hope even though she had flirted shamelessly with him the first time they had met too. But once Charity realised he only had eyes for her sister, she did everything in her power to encourage that—including giving them space at Vauxhall by chasing that future Duke.

'Flirting isn't a crime, Abigail. If it was, I'd be locked in Newgate by now.'

'There is no smoke without fire, Lucius, and she is very indiscreet. The mother is worse. She adores gossip and has the reputation for spreading it.' That he couldn't deny, as Hope had said as much herself, though Roberta was never malicious. Not really. 'Is it wise to align yourself with such a family when you have quite *particular* secrets to keep which could destroy the Thundersley reputation in one fell swoop?'

He resented that implication!

'If you are referring to my mother, then the only aspect of what happened to her which could destroy the Thundersley reputation is the appalling way they treated her!'

Abigail's lips pursed. 'My point was merely that your poor mother would be devastated to have all her dirty laundry washed in public, especially now that she has returned to London. Whatever happened to her, whether by Cassius's hand or your father's, she has thus far been spared the shame of it. I am sure it is a secret she would wish to keep to her grave, and therefore, we must be careful whom we share it with. I certainly wouldn't trust the youngest or the opera singer with it as far as I could throw them...' Abigail shuddered as she clutched her heart. 'And do not get me started on the middle daughter. Now there is a shameless harlot if there ever is one!'

Luke tossed down his napkin and stood. 'You go too far, Abigail! There is only so much of your vitriol I will humour.' He had reached his limit long before the witch had brought Hope into it.

'Oh, Lucius...' Feigned concern again rather than defensiveness or contriteness, the fluttering hand now

hovering by her trembling lips. 'You already have feelings for her, don't you?'

While he debated how to answer, she sighed again, more pitying this time. 'I can see why you have been seduced. That redhead has the sort of allurements which strip a man of all sense...and she uses them with such deadly precision. But be sensible... Please.'

'Goodnight, Abigail.'

She caught his arm at the door. 'I am not telling you to completely avoid the association, Lucius. Men will be men and it is only natural that you should wish to indulge your passions. But be pragmatic about it. You do not have to marry the wench to have her as she will likely accept a lesser arrangement if the deal you offer is favourable enough...exactly as she has done before without the promise of a ring on her finger.'

He pulled himself roughly from her grip, refusing to believe that vitriol. 'Enough, Abigail! Or so help me!' He had always been brought up to be respectful of all women, yet he had never felt so violently angry towards one. Had she been male, he would have knocked her out by now for maligning Hope so, when he knew her well enough to know it couldn't possibly be true. If you delved beneath the surface, Hope was more prude than seductress. More saint than sinner.

'If you do not believe me, ask around. I know of at least three gentlemen who have sampled her delights...' She followed him as he stalked to the front door, unrepentant for her vindictive slander. 'So sample them too if that is what your whim dictates—just don't be a fool about it. A man in your position has to think pragmatically, Lucius, especially when he needs to avoid a scandal at all costs.'

He flung open the door. 'Hope is not a whim, Abigail.' She was everything. 'And if you ever speak of her with such flagrant disrespect again, I promise you, I will not be responsible for my actions!'

Luke was too angry to confine himself to the carriage, and instead walked the two miles home to Bloomsbury, all the while thinking of Hope and how unfair it was that she was so underestimated and unfairly judged by everyone. He would hold his own hands up to that today too, for he had misjudged her in assuming she wouldn't be able to properly negotiate on her own behalf when she was one of the most canny and intelligent people he had ever met.

As if she would intentionally sell herself short with *Phantasma*…when her heart and soul was on every single page. Instead of being delighted that the most significant publisher in the country had wanted her book, offered a compromise and had paid dearly for it, he had been disparaging. Unintentionally, because it had come from a good place—but the road to hell was paved with good intentions and he hated himself for upsetting her.

By the time he reached his house, hers was pitch black. All of Twenty-One Bedford Place was sleeping, including Hope. Or at least he assumed she was sleeping as no light bled on to her balcony and the door which was usually ajar to let in the crisp summer air of the night was, unsurprisingly, very clearly shut and likely bolted too in case he was tempted to wander. She wanted him to spend the night in purgatory and he couldn't blame her. He deserved to be there. If nothing else, it gave him some time to work on a proper apology. Something which would mend the breach and warm her heart too. And obviously, something which told her in no uncertain terms what a ham-fisted idiot he was.

He took himself off to his study to ponder it, and for some reason started to jot his jumbled thoughts down to make sure he left nothing out when he prostrated himself at her feet in the morning and begged for her forgiveness. Once that deed was done, and because he knew he wouldn't sleep anyway, he decided to tackle the ever-replenished and growing mountain of paperwork on his desk.

On the top of the pile was another thick report from Mr Waterhouse. His half-yearly summary of share dividends which likely added significantly to his already obscene fortune he still had no clue what to do with beyond give them away. He picked it up and scanned the pages, all tightly but neatly organised in his portfolio manager's rigid handwriting. Alphabetised and arranged in simple columns—company, amount of shares and dividend paid. The *A*s alone took up half a page and made him a tidy two thousand. Staggering really. To think that his brother must have opened a similar statement every six months, earned that much money with absolutely no work or effort from himself, and still slept at night knowing his younger brother toiled on a herring boat to make ends meet while his stepmother languished in Mill House in the most stark and rancid conditions.

It honestly beggared belief when all this money simply brought him guilt because there was more of it than he could possibly ever spend, and yet there were so many in the land who had so little. For a long time, he had been one of them, so he knew how soul-destroying poverty could be and while his brother had never felt compelled to share his good fortune around, Luke wasn't made like that. Thank goodness! Despite his current ridiculous workload, lofty plans were already formulating to put some of this tainted money to good use. A free school in Tregally, to help all the children of all the impoverished miners better themselves and escape the cycle they were born into. Perhaps a few here in London too, as lord only knew the hordes of shoeless ragamuffins needed some hope for their futures. And, and this one was the closest to his heart, a proper hospital to care for the tortured people like his mother. One nothing like the horrific and harsh places like Mill House and Bedlam, but instead one run along similar lines to Brislington House where the patients would be treated with dignity and compassion. One that would likely cost a fortune so it was just as well he had one.

Feeling slightly better about his inheritance, especially because his plans for it would have both his callous brother and indifferent father spinning in their graves, he ran his finger down the *B*s, taking in the company names and trying to recall what they all did.

Bright & Knowles £100
Broughton Imports £750 10s
Burstead Shipping £423 9s 6d...

Luke flipped to the next page.

Crocker & Co...

He laughed without humour.

So that was where he had got that blasted name from! He apparently owned a quarter-share in the company. Who knew? Not that he had any clue what the blighters did still.

Crudgeley, Whippet and Runt...

A ridiculous name for a company if there ever was one.

Davis Lamp Oil...

Finally, one whose name made perfect sense. His eyes took in the huge chunk of *D*s and he frowned. So many *D*s but only two *C*s? How peculiar.

Assuming he had missed a page, he flicked backwards and huffed because he had.

Caledonian Canal Company...

That was a company name he fully approved of.

Cattons £40 2s 6d
Century Holdings...

It was anybody's guess what they held on to.

Charteris Insurance...
Citizen Bank...

And then he saw it.
Slap bang in the middle of the page.

Cooper and Son £624 4s 9d

Chapter Seventeen

It was shortly after breakfast that Mr Cooper's note arrived saying that he had had a change of heart. As much as it delighted her to know *Phantasma* would now be published with the name Hope Brookes on the front, her heart was too full already to care quite as much about this achievement as she thought she would. While her parents crowed and congratulated her, her fingers kept touching the precious letter she had stowed in her pocket and her thoughts kept drifting to the man who had left it on her balcony with another bunch of hand-picked yellow roses.

Because Lucius Nathaniel Elijah Duff, the Seventh Marquess of Thundersley, had quite a talent for prose himself, albeit not the most romantic sort by any standard. But more so to her because they lacked the flowery and poetic sentiment she had always distrusted. Luke's words had, either intentionally or not, touched the most soft and guarded part of her heart, and she was most definitely going to treat it as her first official love letter which she would treasure for ever.

On the pretext of chasing more tea, she escaped to the quiet of the hallway and read it one more time, just to be certain she hadn't imagined the wonderful implications she had gleaned from the text.

My darling Hope,
Sometimes I am a ham-fisted clod with straw for brains.

> *Yesterday was one of those times.*
> *I am still kicking myself for unintentionally demeaning your achievements and spoiling what should have been a celebration by charging in and assuming I knew best when clearly I do not.*
> *Know that I am sorry and that I am inordinately proud of you. I wish I could promise faithfully that I will never behave with such supercilious cloddishness again but, alas, I fear that we both know such a miracle is unlikely to happen.*
> *As the years go by there will doubtless be many, many, many more occasions when I put my clumsy big foot in it. When you chide me for being an overbearing idiot, as you inevitably will, because I'll doubtless deserve it.*
> *Know too that, however misguided, it always comes from a good place. As my mother will attest, I am intrinsically prone to be overprotective of those I adore the most. Unfortunately for you, I now include you in that tiny and exclusive circle, and suspect, rather alarmingly, I already adore you the most of all.*

Your own devoted clod for ever,
Luke

P.S. Apologise to your mother for me, for stealing her precious roses again. In my defence, it was

*an emergency. I shall endeavour to find another
plentiful supply forthwith as we both know I shall
inevitably need them.*

It wasn't an outright admission of love. He hadn't
actually used the heady words I love you at all—but
she could read between the lines. 'For ever' and 'adore'
certainly implied a depth of feeling similar to hers. And
as the years go by also suggested they were stuck with
one another for the duration. She had read the missive
at least thirty times this morning already and was quite
convinced there could be no other way to take it.

The sharp rap on the door snapped her out of her
dreamy revelry and she quickly slipped the precious
missive back into her pocket before anyone spotted it.
'I'll get it!' Because it might well be him and she might
well need to fling her arms around his vexing neck and
kiss him. But as she pulled the door open expectantly,
there wasn't a tall, contrite and sinfully handsome
pirate on the front step, only another messenger.

'I've a message for Miss Charity Brookes.' The boy
held a small letter out. 'I've instructions to wait for
her reply.'

Intrigued, she rushed it to her sister and then stood
over her as she read it. Never usually speechless, Charity blinked back at her dumbfounded and passed it to
Hope to read aloud to their parents.

'It is from Mr Kemble at the Theatre Royal.' She
scanned for the pertinent details. 'After Charity's *virtuosa* performance on the last night of *Così fan Tutte*,
he has decided he must have her for the role of Susanna
in *The Marriage of Figaro* in the new year!'

'An audition?' Her mother's jaw fell open as she hurried over to read it for herself.

'No, Mama—his letter is quite specific. See…' She underscored the pertinent sentence with her fingers, checking it for herself too as she repeated it slowly. "I cannot think of a more perfect fit for the Countess's maid Susanna than you, Miss Charity, and would therefore like to offer you the role." He goes on to say that nobody else has been cast yet but that his mind is quite made up!'

Her mother snatched the letter to show their father, who had also stood. 'Oh, my goodness! Oh, my goodness! It is one of the leading roles in *Figaro* and Susanna has four arias! Four, Augustus! More than any of the other characters.'

'Mr Kemble has asked the messenger to await your response, Charity.'

Her sister nodded blankly.

'Shall I tell him you will think upon it?'

'Of course not!' Her mother dashed over and shook Charity by the shoulders. 'You have to say yes! This is an enormous role… Mr Kemble does you a tremendous honour in offering it to you. Only a fool wouldn't bite his hand off for the opportunity.'

Tears swam in Charity's eyes as she sucked in several calming breaths, then she screamed as she sprang up to hug their mother, then Hope, jumping up and down and beaming from ear to ear. 'Tell him yes! Of course it is a yes!' Then she stopped and clutched her stomach. 'Oh, good gracious I can barely breathe!'

Her father left them squealing and paid the messenger, then hugged Charity tight as he grinned at Hope. 'Well done, dearest. What a day this is turning out to be, ay?'

'Ay indeed! We are blessed, Augustus!' Her mother was beaming from ear to ear. 'A singer, an author and an artist! What did we do to deserve such talented daughters?' She hugged Hope again for the twentieth time and then did the same to Charity. 'I declare not another family in Christendom can boast of three more accomplished, beautiful and brilliant young ladies than my Faith, Hope and Charity.'

'We are blessed indeed,' said her father with a subtle roll of his eyes towards his daughters because she had been saying much the same since last night when Hope had originally told them her news.

'It is bound to make you both more eligible.' It never took their mother long to remind them that they still weren't married. For Roberta Brookes, a happy marriage topped all other achievements by a country mile. 'Accomplished ladies are a much more attractive proposition to the opposite sex.'

Now it was her turn to roll her eyes at her mother. 'Good grief I hope not as I have quite enough propositions from them already, and most of them are quite scandalous.'

'When I said eligible, I meant for marriage, not for T-H-A-T.' Being a complete prude, her mother even managed to conjure up a blush for the innocuous word she couldn't bring herself to say. 'Why did you have to lower the tone?'

'Because you brought up the prospect of men, Mama, when you know Hope is allergic to them.' Charity blinked at her innocently, still beaming at her own unexpected good fortune. 'With perhaps just one notable exception.'

'I'd be happy with just one,' said her mother in her most exasperated tone, 'as I would hate for her to condemn herself to a life of spinsterhood. Of all my daughters, your standoffish sister has always been the one who worries me the most.'

'Would we call her standoffish?' Charity was clearly back to her old self again. 'I've always thought waspish was a better adjective.'

'Or just plain rude?'

Hope glared at her father for joining in. 'I am here, you know.' Then she grinned. She couldn't help it. The happiness was fizzing inside her. 'Not that I shall allow any of you to spoil my good mood today. Not when my annoying baby sister is going to be the toast of Covent Garden and I am going to be in Hatchard's.' And a certain exception had let slip that he adored her.

In honour of the occasion, her mother called for more tea and some of their cook's delicious queen cakes even though they would likely spoil luncheon, and were in the midst of eating them when there was a knock on the front door, and moments later, Maria was shown in with Clowance with Luke a few steps behind her.

'I hear congratulations are in order?'

'They are indeed!' Hope's mother preened. 'Both of my brilliant daughters are celebrating! Hope is finally going to have her work published and we have just this second learned Charity is to be a lead in my absolute favourite Mozart opera. Isn't that marvellous?'

'I adore the opera!' Clowance beamed at Charity. 'In case you missed it, that was my subtle way of hinting at a free ticket.'

'You shall all come to opening night!' Charity spun a giddy circle. 'Wouldn't it be wonderful if our debuts collide, Hope? You on the shelves and me on the stage!'

'I couldn't be more thrilled for you, Hope, as *Phantasma* is a truly outstanding book.' Maria took both her hands smiling, then winked. 'Or should I say H. B. Rooke? What a clever *nom de plume* that is.'

'Oh, that was yesterday's news.' Her mother gestured for them all to sit with one hand while simultaneously using the other to signal for more teacups and another fresh pot of Darjeeling. 'It is all changed for Hope this morning, now that the publisher has seen the folly in his insistence she have a pen name.'

'Does that mean that the androgynous H. B. Rooke is dead?' Luke managed to look both contrite and delighted when he smiled at her, and was obviously still wondering if his apology had been accepted or if she was going to smash the roses he had stolen out of her mother's garden unceremoniously over his head.

She put him out of his misery with a begrudging half-smile over the rim of her cup. 'Dead and buried, the poor thing. Shot in the paddock before the race started.'

'Good… *Good*. I am glad that Crocker fellow finally saw reason.'

'He did. And all on his own too.' She couldn't resist one dig while Maria was congratulating her sister. 'And his name is still *Cooper*, Luke, exactly as it's always been.'

He slapped his forehead as he sat beside her on the sofa. 'Cooper! Yes…' Then his eyes locked with hers and they were filled with apology. 'What an idiot I am… I do hope you will forgive me for it.' It was clear he was talking about yesterday.

'I find your idiocy endearing. Annoying of course, but part of your charm.' While nobody was looking she hooked her little finger through his. 'But I dare say I shall knock it out of you…eventually.'

'Oh, good heavens above!' They hastily jumped apart

at her mother's shriek. 'I have to write to Faith immediately!'

'Please don't! Hope and I will see her in a week.'
Charity's plea suddenly reminded her about their imminent visit to Bath. A whole month without Luke
stretched before her. 'I want to see her face when she
hears our news! Don't you, Hope?'

'Yes.' Her eyes lifted to his and saw that the same
realisation had dawned. 'Of course I do.' As much as
she was desperate to see her older sister, leaving him
would be unbearable.

'I hear absence makes the heart grow fonder.' His
whisper was for her ears only. 'And there is nothing to
stop me taking a detour to Bath if I can find some time
to go back to Cornwall.'

Chapter Eighteen

There are few events in the social calendar, Gentle Reader, that are as fruitful for purveyors of the finest gossip than any entertainment organised by the Countess of Renshaw. We wait with fevered anticipation for tonight's scandalous titbits, and will have reliable ears posted everywhere to be sure nothing salacious escapes us...

Whispers from Behind the Fan
July 1814

Five days later, and Hope was in the highest of dudgeons thanks to the useless fichu which adamantly refused to stay put, no matter how much she stuffed the edges into her neckline. As much as she hated to make Charity right about anything, she was starting to realise the red gown she had hastily donned for the Renshaws' Summer Ball on the spur of the moment, was altogether the wrong sort of gown to adapt. The tightly fitted bodice, which sat daringly off her shoulders, was too low and the delicate watered silk was just too slippery.

Yet as much as she knew the frothy addition she had added really didn't suit the austere cut of the garment, exactly as her maid had said, giving up on it was giving her palpitations. Because apparently Faith's infamous scarlet gown, as her youngest sibling had dubbed it owing to it being the very dress that she had first twirled breathless with the man who went on to be her husband, which had looked so bold and elegant on her slimmer sister, was doomed to be an outrageous scandal on her.

From her hiding place behind a potted palm, she stared down at the good four inches of robust cleavage standing much too proud out of the top of it, and cursed herself for being so stupid as to don the dratted thing in the first place.

She was going to wring her meddling sister's neck for suggesting it and their maid Lily for promptly having it pressed and laid out on her bed to tempt her.

Instead of feeling bold and beautiful for Luke tonight to give him a dazzling lasting memory of her before she left him for a month, and feeling confident about her new status as an official author under contract to the best publishing house in the land, she was now severely doubting her flawed logic. As well as feeling hideously self-conscious because she had left herself wide open to the predatory stares of the very gentlemen she abhorred while the one she had specifically worn it to entice was nowhere to be found.

The last she had seen of Luke, he had been twirling breathless with Charity who had purposely commandeered him almost as soon as he had stepped foot in the ballroom. It was obvious she had grabbed him simply to goad her, knowing full well Hope never danced as a point of principle. Which left Hope to fend off Lord Harlington and then Lord Ealing in quick succession before her wretched fichu had given up the ghost and deserted her too.

She was about to attempt one last try at repairing it, when she spotted Luke's mother hurtling towards the French doors, her face quite ashen and her eyes wild, yet no sign of the ever-present Clowance anywhere.

Fearing for her, and mindful that Luke was concerned that she was throwing herself too quickly back into society on his behalf than she could cope with, Hope hurried out of the French doors behind her. This early in the evening, the torchlit terrace was still empty, but Maria had made a dash for the dark lawn beyond and was several yards down the path when she called her.

'Maria! Is everything all right?'

The older woman stopped short but didn't turn around immediately, seemingly doing her level best to calm herself before she did. 'I thought I might take a turn around the garden. I needed some fresh air. It is so warm in there.' Tiny beads of perspiration dewed her upper lip as she smiled and there was an agitation about her which Hope had not seen in the three weeks she had been in the capital.

'I am not surprised. It is such a crush. I swear half of London is currently crammed in that small ballroom. I wouldn't mind a turn about the garden myself if you would appreciate the company?'

Maria hesitated as she fought for composure, then nodded. 'Your company would be nice…thank you.'

They set off deeper into the garden at a more sedate pace, Maria taking measured, slow breaths as she did so and Hope pretending not to notice to spare the woman her dignity. After several minutes, she was visibly calmer and back to her normal colour.

'I am assuming my son has confided in you all my troubles?'

She schooled her features to not give him away. 'Troubles?'

'Oh, come now, my dear, I know that he has told you because my son is quite besotted with you and he is as honest as the day is long. He would consider himself disingenuous in pursuing his affections if he concealed the sorry truth from you, and quite rightly too. If you are marching headlong into marriage, which I can plainly see you both are, it is only fair you know what you are walking into. If he hasn't, I will.' Dark eyes, so like her son's, dared her to deny it. 'For you have a right to know, even though I would rather nobody ever knew the terrible truth at all and it shames me to have to admit to it.'

'He mentioned you had been ill.'

'I was more than ill, Hope. I was mad. Twice apparently. Though I am certain one of those was not entirely of my own doing, so I try to be kind to myself about that one.' Maria was staring intently, carefully watching Hope's reaction and obviously dreading it at the same time. 'Though I am not any longer, thank the lord. At least I do not feel mad. I suppose that could be more delusion on my part than actuality, as heaven only knows I have been prone to delusions a time or two, but I don't think it is. At least it doesn't *feel* like it is.' She shrugged and smiled without humour. 'This little episode of panic notwithstanding, of course, which I hope you will not judge me for.'

'You need feel no shame nor fear nor judgement from me.'

'But I do, Hope. I fear your pity, because I would hate for you to view me as a lesser, more feeble person because of my past and because sometimes certain situations temporarily overwhelm me.'

Maria squared her shoulders bravely, humbling Hope with her honesty and her trust. 'But it *is* temporary. I become overanxious occasionally, especially in confined or unfamiliar places as I did just then—but it passes, as you can see.'

'I can see, and to be brutally honest with you, Maria, had Luke not confided in me, I would never have guessed you had been ill. He led me to believe you were much more fragile than you are.'

'That is because he is unnecessarily, and dare I say it, annoyingly overprotective and terrified I will lose my wits again. He sees every little panic as evidence of my inevitable decline, the wretch, so I try to hide it from him. Hence I am here and not in there, as he will frogmarch me home and wrap me in a blanket, and treat me like an invalid again.'

'He is annoyingly overprotective.' Which as irritating traits went wasn't so terrible.

'And you won't tell him you saw me in a state?'

'I can think of no earthly reason why he needs to know.'

Maria smiled. 'Thank you. It'll only send him into a panic when even my physician says that there is a stark difference between occasional anxiety and certifiable insanity.'

'A crowded ballroom can be daunting at the best of times, especially if you are not used to it or fear the judgement of others.'

'Alas much as I fear them judging me, it is Luke I would prefer to protect. I should hate for my past to taint his future or make his new life here any more difficult than it needs to be. I so wish I could stop him worrying about me having a relapse as I have absolutely no intention of having another one again.'

Hope reached out to squeeze her hand. 'From what Luke has told me, you wouldn't have had a relapse if his callous brother hadn't had you committed in the first place. He said you were quite well when they took you away and had been for years.'

Maria's smile was filled with regret. 'I was well. I am glad he remembered that...' She stared down at her hands. 'We do not tend to talk about it...at least not as openly as you and I are talking about it now. I know that he worries about my mental state and any mention of it distresses him because he felt so impotent about it all when they took me away. And I never bring it up because I hate seeing him distressed. It's silly really, I suppose, as one cannot erase the past, but I so wish I could properly apologise to him for it. I feel it sits between us—the great unsaid—always hovering in the air but never cleared.'

Hope squeezed her arm. 'You have nothing to apologise for. You were the victim of Cassius. He is entirely to blame.'

'For Mill House and what happened there, yes. Undoubtedly. I know without a shadow of a doubt that dreadful place drove me mad, and on purpose too. But when after Luke liberated me from that cesspit and worked his fingers to the bone getting me the very best care and treatments to make me well again, I came to understand what had sent me mad in the first place and I wish I could apologise to him for it all in a way that doesn't make him feel responsible for that too.' Tears were swimming in her eyes now. 'For I blamed him for it for years and was a dreadful mother to him as a result.'

'Why would you blame Luke for what happened?'

Maria stared at her feet. 'Because it was having him

that sent me mad, Hope. Insanity of childbirth my physician calls it…' Her expression turned wistful. 'I was so looking forward to becoming a mother. Of having something to love and nurture but…' She roughly dabbed her tears away with the corner of her shawl. 'The moment I had my baby I lost my mind. There was no joy, none of the overwhelming love and instant bond I was promised by every woman who had experienced childbirth. Only a deep seated and toxic sadness which ate away at my brain and as a result of it, I neglected to love my sweet, kind and innocent boy for years, allowing the servants to bring him up while I wallowed in my own pit of despair and leaving him to run wild.'

'You weren't well, Maria.' And her heart bled for them both. 'Luke doesn't blame you for any of that, and I doubt he even realises you felt those things.'

'That is because Luke has always been a rescuer at heart who flatly refuses to accept the fact that he cannot change things. He'll work tirelessly until he has found a way around the problem, or over it or under it, and he'll eventually fix it because he cannot bear to see anyone distressed.'

'He is a good man.' One who, ironically, filled her pessimistic heart with hope.

'He was still very young when he found a way to fix me which all my husband's expensive physicians failed to find. Somebody, and it shames me that I have no idea who, taught him to read, and he started reading to me. Book after book after book until all those pages built a bridge between us and dragged me back. He did that again when he rescued me from Mill House too.'

'He never told me that.'

Maria sighed as she smiled. 'He loves you.' As much as that warmed her, Hope had no idea how to respond to that, and settled for a slightly dismissive shrug because it didn't feel right discussing those things with his mother when they hadn't talked about it first. 'It isn't catching you know…my madness…in case that is why you are reticent about committing to him.'

Hope paused and blinked, shocked that the woman would even say such a thing. 'The notion hadn't even crossed my mind.'

'I am relieved to hear it and confess I have been working on that long speech to explain it all to you in case my condition was the thing which was holding you back.' Maria threaded her arm through hers. 'But if it isn't that, then what is it? As I confess I cannot fathom why you are both so keen to pretend you are not head over heels for one another when any fool with eyes in their head can plainly see that you are. Your mother and I are baffled by it.'

And there Hope had misguidedly thought she had been hiding her true feelings so well from her nearest and dearest. Clearly not if Maria and her mother had discussed it, doubtless over one of their many daily cups of tea. 'She hasn't mentioned it.' Which now she considered it, was a trifle odd as her dear mama had been trying to get Hope to find herself a nice gentleman for years and Charity had not been subtle.

'We agreed not to, my dear, as your mother said any interference would likely make you dig your stubborn heels in further and Luke flatly refuses to talk about it either, even though he is not usually so backwards about coming forward. To be frank, all this tight-lipped secrecy is most unlike him when he is normally one for jumping in with both feet once he has made up his mind.'

Hope stared at her hands while she weighed up how

to answer such an obviously pointed and probing question, then decided that after Maria's stark honesty about her illness, she owed her the same. 'It is my fault... I have never been good with trusting men. So many of them have proved to be such predictable disappointments, I am wary of jumping in with both feet now in case...'

'My son disappoints you too?'

She nodded. 'I suppose you think that is unfair of me.'

Maria stared at her levelly. 'I *know* it is unfair of you as he has done nothing to deserve it.' She smiled to soften the admonishment. 'But I understand more than anyone how hard it can be to trust, especially if your trust has been shattered by others. However, if I might be annoyingly philosophical and wise for a moment, I would ask you to look at it all another way. A way my physician helped me to separate my fears from reality. Instead of standing still, paralysed by fear and waiting for the worst to happen, try striding forward to embrace it. You'll have no control over it otherwise.' Then she slanted her a knowing glance. 'And, let's face it, Hope, you'll never stride anywhere if you remain rooted to your balcony, staring at him longingly across those pesky railings while he stares longingly back at you.'

Her smile confirmed that their secret courtship, which Hope had been at great pains to keep private, wasn't the least bit private at all. 'Do you love him?'

Yes. So completely it petrifies me.

'I might.'

'Are you going to marry him?'

'He hasn't asked.'

'He will.' Then Maria grinned a lopsided grin exactly like her son's. 'As I doubt the three dozen rose bushes he's already ordered to be planted at Tregally this month are for me. All yellow—quite a specific order don't you think? When I can assure you, he has never taken the slightest interest in gardening before.'

Chapter Nineteen

Where the blazes was Hope?

Luke stalked around the ballroom again searching for her, failing to understand how a statuesque woman draped in seductive scarlet silk and with such vibrant red hair could remain hidden for so long. He hadn't seen hide nor shimmering copper hair of her for over an hour. She wasn't with her parents, he had checked. She wasn't with her sister either, because Charity was dancing and Hope never danced—even with him—and had given him strict instructions not to ask her because dancing inevitably led to more speculation and they were the victims of quite enough of that already.

That edict had been issued between the strict instructions not to spend more than ten minutes with her all evening in case it led to more speculation in the gossip columns, and to make sure there was at least twenty feet of space between them at all other times—as if that would make the slightest difference. Nor was he supposed to compliment her anywhere where they could be overheard, which basically meant she bristled if he dared say anything charming outside of the balcony.

Then there was the bizarre rule about not looking

at her longingly, which was frankly impossible when she was the most beautiful woman in any room and his eyes couldn't stop drinking her in at the best of times. How she thought he would be able to stop something which was already ingrained in habit, and when she was wearing that seductive red gown to boot, he couldn't fathom. But again, she wasn't ready to make their relationship public yet—even to their own families—because it was still early days.

Early days be damned! As far as he was concerned, hiding it was dafter when they had no earthly reason to hide it at all and he personally couldn't care less who knew they were a couple. However, Hope still had silly notions about him having second thoughts about exactly what he wanted from her. He understood she was reluctant to throw all caution to the wind until she was sure he wasn't simply obsessed with her physical attributes. So he had humoured her and begrudgingly gone along with it all. Trying to do his best to reassure her of his honourable intentions even though he was desperate for her to lead him astray and indulge some of the dishonourable ones too.

If anything—and he should probably tell her this if he ever found her—with all the admiring male glances which she attracted like bees to honey her life would undoubtedly be much simpler with a big brute like him on her arm. She'd feel happier in her positively sinful body and he'd be happier simply because everyone would know that she was his so that he wouldn't have to keep rescuing her from those panting dogs in the first place. Two birds with one stone and undoubtedly the most sensible solution.

Instinctively his eyes narrowed as he frantically searched for Lord Harlington and Lord Ealing as a new worry clouded his mind. What if she had taken refuge from those scoundrels in the garden and then been waylaid there by one who refused to take no for an answer? His pace quickened as he rushed towards the French doors before he instantly skidded to a stop and almost groaned out loud.

'Hello, Lucius.' Abigail looked suitably tragic stood all alone and blocking his exit. 'Are you still angry at me?'

Yes! Of course he was. She had grievously insulted the woman of his dreams and rubbished her entire family. 'Can we *not* talk about this now?' Not when Hope might well be at the mercy of another drooling scoundrel who did not understand what the word no meant!

'I never intended to upset you... I was trying to protect you, Lucius.'

'No, Abigail, you were trying to protect yourself. Heaven forbid your precious reputation be tarnished in any way by my scandals.'

'I will make no apologies for trying to protect you from making a grave mistake but I do not want us to fall out over it. Especially as so much of my life is still too miserable for words.'

Code, no doubt, that she only wanted to heal this latest breach because she still didn't have the deeds to the Mayfair house clutched in her grabbing claws. 'I'll chase the solicitor again in the morning!'

'The longer it all drags on, the more anxious I feel. And with you and me not speaking, I have been so...' Luke instantly stopped listening when Hope and his mother tumbled through the French doors laughing.

'There you are!' The relief that she was not being mauled by dogs was palpable. 'I have been looking for you everywhere.'

'You see, dear, I told you he was besotted.' His mother was wearing her most meddlesome expression as she nudged Hope, but Hope's expression had hardened at the sight of Abigail.

'My lady.' She didn't curtsy either, but instead dragged a layer of frost into the alcove which effectively froze everything, including his mother who was also bristling simply because Hope was.

'Miss Brookes.' Abigail's eyes swept Hope's bold gown with more than her usual customary disdain. 'Scarlet is most definitely your colour.' Then her eyes flicked to his mother and all hint of disapproval disappeared as she dipped into a deep curtsy herself. 'My lady…it is an honour to finally meet you.'

As Hope and his sister-in-law already seemed to be properly acquainted, and clearly hated one another, politeness dictated he should say something to relieve the awkwardness. 'Mother, this is Lady Abigail Thundersley, the Marchioness of Thundersley… Abigail, this is my mother Lady Maria Thundersley, the Dowager Marchioness of Thundersley.'

His usually friendly and talkative mother barely inclined her head and, for the first time in her life, never uttered a single word.

After several truly excruciating seconds of complete silence, an obviously uncomfortable Abigail slid her hand through his arm. 'I was about to see if I could convince dear Lucius to dance with me as I haven't waltzed in for ever.'

'Unfortunately, he promised it to me.' Hope was daring him to contradict her, perhaps not realising she was actually the cavalry and he was so relieved he could kiss her for it. 'I presume that was why you were searching for me, Luke?'

'That it was.'

'Then you had best get to it as it's starting.' His mother had apparently found her voice, and with it, she sailed off into the crowd.

In case he was tempted to linger, which he really wasn't, Hope's arm now claimed his proprietorially. 'And if you will excuse us too.' Without any further ado she led him to the floor.

She waited until they were in the very centre of it before she dipped into a graceful curtsy, her beautiful eyes never once leaving his as she held out her hand. It was only then that he noticed her silly fichu was gone and the acres of creamy, feminine skin now exposed instantly made his mouth dry. As she moved into his arms, there was something interesting swirling in her green eyes as they started to move, and he got the distinct impression, whatever it was, it had little to do with proving her point to Abigail.

'I thought you wanted me to maintain a respectable distance from you at all times.'

'It is a lady's prerogative to change her mind.'

'Even though tongues will wag?'

'There is no point closing the stable door after the horse has bolted.' She shrugged, her smile as affectionate as the ones she bestowed when they were all alone. 'I have just discovered your mother knows about us. And by *know*, I mean she is aware we have adjoining balconies and that our relationship isn't exactly platonic.'

'Well, I certainly didn't tell her.' Even though frequently of late, he had wanted to shout about it to everyone.

'My mother knows too, though probably not about the balcony as you are still breathing and I am not in a nunnery. And if she knows then my father knows because my mother tells him everything. And Charity has known since the outset, including the kiss by the fountain because she used blackmail to prise it out of me—although I never told her about you being naked that time—though I wouldn't put it past her to know we meet out on the balcony too because once she has an idea in her head, she's like a dog with a bone. And if Charity knows, then you can be sure she has made sure that Faith knows too.' She sighed then and stared out at the sea of people who were doing their best not to make it obvious they were watching them with interest. 'Look at them. They all know.' She jerked her head in their direction. 'The newspapers know. Apparently everyone knows about us.'

'I know.' Luke tried not to look too smug because he knew that vexed her, but he couldn't help a bit leaking out and this earned him a haughty glare. 'I think, at this stage, we are the worst kept secret in London.'

'Evidently.' She sighed as she smiled. 'Therefore, you will be delighted to also know that I have decided to embrace the public exposure by making our courtship completely official with a definitive statement which cannot be misconstrued. Hence this waltz. When everybody knows I rarely dance, and I have certainly never danced this in public. Consider yourself honoured, Lord Trouble.'

He did. The only way Hope would take such a big step was if she trusted him completely. 'Does this mean I can publicly tell you that you have never looked more ravishing?'

'It does.' Her arm snaked tighter around his shoulder, bringing her delectable body scant inches from his and scandalously closer than propriety allowed. 'Furthermore, if you manage to finish this waltz without once stomping on my toes with your big, cloddish Cornish feet, I might even allow you to ravish me by the fountain afterwards. And with no fear of my pushing you in it either.'

That hadn't been an empty promise. As soon as the dance was done, they crept out into the garden, and indulged in the most splendid mutual ravishing which Luke was still reeling from hours afterwards. There was no chance of all that lust abating any time soon either, as the moment she emerged on the balcony in that seductive red gown, every drop of blood he possessed rushed to his groin and still seemed to have no desire to leave it an hour in.

'I wish I wasn't going to Bath.'

'We still have another whole day left.' Only the one. Which was likely why they were both still out here procrastinating when it was long past their usual bedtime.

She huffed, sadness written all over her lovely face. 'And I have to spend half of it with Mr Cooper.' He was flattered that her dreams didn't mean more than him.

'That will only take a couple of hours and you'll be mine from noon. How about I meet you then at Gunter's and I'll treat you to one of those dreadful purple ice creams you like?' She nodded, still looking sad and he couldn't bear it. 'And in a few weeks, I will stop by Bath with my mother to see you and perhaps you and your sisters could accompany us to Tregally. I am sure you would appreciate a change of scenery then.' He knew already that a contrived and brief visit to Bath wouldn't be enough to stem his longing.

'Even so... I shall miss you.' She was leaning against the wall so she could look up at the stars. There was something different about her tonight. An easiness about their relationship and a new confidence in her body which suited her immensely.

'Not as much as I shall miss you.'

Still staring out at nothing, Hope sighed. 'If I ask you an intensely personal question, Luke, will you answer it honestly?'

'I might.'

She slanted him a peeved glance. 'Then I shan't bother asking it.'

'All right—I'll answer honestly.'

'Promise?'

He drew a cross over his heart with his index finger, feeling it quicken as it did so because something, he had no clue what, seemed to have shifted and even the air around them was filled with expectation.

'Why have you ordered three dozen yellow rose bushes for Tregally?'

He was going to strangle his mother for her meddling, when Hope wasn't one to be rushed into anything, especially if nudged. 'Because they are your favourite.'

'But why plant them in your house in Cornwall when I am here?'

She was staring at him now, part knowing, but with enough doubt he understood she needed to hear the truth to fully trust the enormity of it. 'I suppose, because I was rather hoping it might be *our* house in Cornwall some day.'

She was quiet for a moment, her expression thoughtful. 'When do you envisage some day to be?'

His stupid heart was now threatening to beat out of his chest. He hadn't expected to be having this sort of conversation now. He had assumed, that like everything about their romance, it would edge forward incrementally. She had only just granted him his first

dance and by default acknowledged publicly that there
was a relationship between them. In his head, he had
set a reasonable target for next spring to make things
more official. When he had whittled away all her doubts
and sorted out exactly what he was going to do here. 'I
suppose that depends upon you and how far away you
need some day to be before you are prepared to take a
chance on me.' Which was clearly at a potentially much
faster speed than he had anticipated.

Perhaps too fast?

His already racing pulse ratcheted up a bit more.

'And if I didn't need it to be that far?'

Where he expected panic came relief. It washed
through him like the Writtles' infamous champagne,
leaving him dizzy and grinning. 'Then I am game if you
are and I'd happily march you up the aisle tomorrow.'

Still resolutely staring out into the night, she slowly
smiled before she turned to him. 'You'd have to ask
first.'

'I thought I just did.'

'Not properly.'

'When do we ever do things properly, Hope?'

'Still...' She folded her arms, which did wonderous
things to her cleavage, and tapped her foot impatiently.

'Oh, for goodness sake!' He couldn't help but laugh
as he dropped to one knee. 'Hope—will you do me the
honour...'

'Wait!' She was giggling too, then she hoisted up
her skirts and flung one shapely leg over the railing.
'There absolutely cannot be a balcony between us. Not
for something this momentous.'

Luke scrabbled to his feet to help her and she practically fell on him on the other side as she leapt across the
three-foot gap more frantically than intrepidly, clinging

to him in obvious relief as he caught her and assisted her over the second railings. Instantly his eyes dropped to her lips but as he dipped his head to taste them, she shoved him out of the way. 'Back down on your knees if you please, Lord Trouble. If it is the last thing I ever manage to do, I shall make you do at least one thing properly in this courtship.'

With as much solemnity as he could muster, and with both of them still laughing at the utter, wonderful absurdity of it all, he did as she commanded and took her hand. 'Hope…' He frowned, racking his brains for any recollection, then shook his head. 'Do you have a second name?'

'It's Prudence.'

'Of course it is.' He couldn't help but roar at that. With her overly cautious nature it somehow seemed more fitting. 'Very well… Hope *Prudence* Brookes, would you do me the great honour of consenting to be my wife?'

For a split second she strapped on her haughty bravado, examining her nails while doing her best to stifle the sparkling sunshine in her eyes. 'I might.'

'Might?' He was all done kneeling and tugged her into his arms to nuzzle the sensitive spot at the base of her ear which always made her sigh. 'What you mean is yes, Luke. Of course I'll marry you. You are the man of my dreams. My heart beats for you and my body yearns for you. Ravish me again this instant.'

She arched to give him access and looped her arms around his neck. 'You're incorrigible.'

But she was most definitely sighing as his lips found the right place. 'That I am, but I suspect you'll still marry me anyway.'

Chapter Twenty

There was something about the way Luke kissed her which always completely scrabbled her wits, and this one was no exception. He started with her neck, his big hands exploring the curve of her waist and hips, only moving to her mouth when she had shamelessly splayed herself against him to prevent him prolonging the agony further.

Except this time, as his lips whispered over hers, something felt very different.

She felt very different.

It might have been his proposal. It might have been the heady knowledge that he adored her enough to plant not one, but two separate beds of yellow roses for her. It might also have been the romance of the waltz and the sublime intimacy of the beautiful starlit night around them now, or her imminent trip to Bath which made everything feel so poignant. But whatever it was, she was prepared to take Maria's advice and stride boldly towards it for a change, rather than shy away from it, paralysed by fear. She had done too much of that with him and he deserved better. He had always been her friend first and foremost. Her ally and her confident.

Soon, he would be her husband too and they would have exactly the sort of marriage she had always dreamed of. One of two equals and mutual respect.

Except with Luke there would also be passion. An aspect of a partnership which she had underestimated, not understanding that a man's desire could be a beautiful and liberating thing instead of a violation. She was excited by the rigid press of his hardness against her belly. Curious about it and the next stage of their relationship. The intimacy of living with a man. Being with a man. Waking up next to him each morning. Going to bed with him at night. Seeing his naked body again—but being able to touch it and explore it. Succumb to it. Both friends and lovers—husband and wife.

When the tone of the kiss inevitably turned carnal as the mutual lust between them quickly burned too hot and once again became unbearable, it was Luke, as usual, who pulled away, trying to rescue them both before the sublime pull of it banished all good sense.

He held her at arm's length, his breathing gloriously erratic and his intense gaze darkened by desire, and she realised that, as usual too, he was giving her all the power. For Luke, his own needs and wants always came secondary to hers, and likely always would. She knew that now without a shadow of a doubt. There was no ulterior motive. No hidden agenda. To him she was more than a conquest. He adored her.

All of her. Body and soul.

Wanted to marry her and would probably spend the rest of his life doing everything in his power simply to try and please her, and doubtless making the odd hash of it because he adored her most of all.

With him by her side, it was hard to feel pessimistic. Luke was all optimism and solutions rather than disappointments and defeat. The light to her shade and the love of her life.

She stared deep into his eyes, saw the emotion as well as the desire swirling in them, and knew the depth of his feelings mirrored hers. As she cupped his cheek, she smiled. His mother was right—what was she waiting for?

In less than thirty-six hours she was going away and wouldn't see him for an eternity. Only a fool would waste a moment of that.

Instead of allowing him to be the noble gentleman and the eternal rescuer, the natural sensual and feminine part of her which she always tried to suppress came to the fore. She traced her fingers lovingly down his cheek, then boldly traced the pad of one around his lips, biting her own because they ached for him so much. His eyes dropped to them and heated, and simply because she suddenly felt all powerful and wantonly, sinfully wicked, she gave in to the urge to undo his cravat slowly unwinding it from his neck.

'Are you trying to kill me, woman?' His breath hitched as her lips nuzzled his jaw and the muscles in his chest bunched beneath his clothing as she ran her palms over them. 'There is only so much restraint I can muster.'

She answered his question with a kiss so decadent and thorough, they were both panting by the end of it.

By then she had undone each and every button on his waistcoat, and her greedy hands had not only untucked the tails of his shirt from his trousers but had burrowed beneath it to feel the heat of his skin. Skin she hadn't been able to forget since the day she had seen it all exposed and soaking wet on this very balcony. However, this time his nipples were puckered with desire and not the cold, and his heartbeat beneath her palms was like a rapid hammer against his ribs. His expression wasn't the least bit cocky and smug. It was wary. Questioning. Hopeful.

She unsettled him.

Overwhelmed him—and that knowledge was intoxicating.

The infamous red gown now felt too tight. Too much of a barrier between her needy body and his. Hope craved his touch, ached for it. Yet so far, his hands had remained too respectful and would remain so unless she invited him to be otherwise.

'I wore this dress for you, Luke.' She didn't recognise her voice. It was sultry. Seductive. She kissed him again. Used her teeth to nibble on his bottom lip, wanted to explore how far she could push him before he cracked. 'Do you like it?'

'Yes.'

His voice was gruff. Slightly strangled because he was holding himself back. So she did the only thing she could think of to set him free while enslaving him further. She tugged him by the hand into the dimly lit privacy of his bedchamber and then turned her back to him.

'Good...then help me out of it.'

She heard him swallow as he hesitated. Heard his indecision. Could imagine how his nobleness and need to always do the right thing warred with the base urges all men suffered from.

She smiled as she removed a pin from her hair and the fat curl bounced against her shoulder, enjoying leading him into temptation. 'I am inviting you to bed, my Luke...exactly as you requested.'

His fingers were clumsy on the laces, his soft breath

uneven against her neck. Twice he gave in to the urge to press his lips to where her pulse beat but the effort it took to stop at that was palpable. As soon as the bodice was loose he stepped several feet back. Rescuing her again in case she had a change of heart and she loved him all the more for that selfless gesture.

As he watched her, she slid the garment from her shoulders until gravity took it to puddle on the floor around her feet. Only then did she turn around, suddenly feeling every inch the sultry vixen or Aphrodite she had so often been called. Only this time, she wanted to be those things, expressly for him. She had never stood quite so confidently in only her undergarments before, usually loathing the sight of her cumbersome breasts trying to break free over the top of her stays. But Luke's eyes were on fire as he took it all in and tried and failed to keep his gaze fixed on her face.

Yet his lust-filled stare didn't feel the least bit like a violation, more like a benediction, because he wanted all of her.

For ever.

When she walked towards him this time, he didn't hesitate at all. He hauled her into his arms and as he poured his heart into the kiss, he allowed his hands to wander, filling them with her still-bound breasts while the stark, impressive evidence of his desire pressed insistent and proud against her.

In a frenzy of lips, tongues and teeth, they stumbled backwards on to the bed. His fingers found every other pin in her hair until it tumbled wildly around her shoulders. Hers tugged his shirt up his body and over his head before they headed to his waistband and she undid that too, pausing only long enough so her stays could be tossed to the floor and she could tug the tight fabric from his hips. Then, as she sat back on her heels as his manhood sprang free, her nerves finally got the better of her.

They must have shown in her expression, because tenderness instantly replaced Luke's fervour. 'I won't hurt you, Hope. I couldn't...' He cupped her cheek, looking every bit as overawed as she. 'I love you.'

'I know.' It wasn't that which had brought her up short. 'I love you too, Luke...so very much.' So much, it rocked her to her core. 'And I am not scared.' Not of that at least. But now that he was naked—at her instigation—he would expect her to be the same, and she wasn't sure she was brave enough, and certainly wasn't confident enough, to show him everything as brazenly as he.

To cover it, she leaned over him to kiss him again, intent on distracting him from the fear he had seen in her eyes, but as she reached for the lamp to snuff it out, he caught her wrist. 'It hardly strikes me as fair that you get to see me, but I am denied the pleasure of seeing you.' From beneath her, two dark and much too clever eyes seemed to bore into her soul as his hands smoothed the last layer of her chemise from her shoulders, then he smiled when she clutched it tight to her chest.

'And there I was thinking you were fearless.'

'Frankly, there is just too much of me to be fearless.' She didn't have the compact and neat figures of her peers.

'Thank goodness.' He was smiling. Amused by her sudden prudishness. Above her hands, he traced the top of her breasts with his finger. 'Don't judge me, but it is one of the things I have always liked about you.'

'And the thing about myself I most dislike.'

'I know...but for all the wrong reasons. You are the

most beautiful woman I have ever seen, blessed with the most sinful and tempting body.' He wound a finger in one of the curls that rested against her nipple, purposely grazing it as he did so. 'And I am going to need to kiss it all if I'm going to make love to you properly.' Looking her dead in the eye, he grinned and tugged the fabric some more. 'Or is it your plan to keep your breasts hidden until death do us part, because I can tell you now that isn't going to happen as I'll hatch a cunning plan to get my wicked way soon enough. I am resourceful like that.'

He was and when he put it like that, her reluctance to bare all now did sound a bit daft. 'I have fantasised about this moment for months, Hope, but I am happy to wait a few more to consummate our love if you think it might improve your self-confidence.'

Then to vex her, he folded his hands under his head, his cocky, lopsided grin letting her know in no uncertain terms that he knew she couldn't go another hour, let alone another month without feeling him inside her.

She let the flimsy garment fall and he almost groaned aloud as a painful bolt of lust ricocheted through him. Instead, he sighed as his eyes drank her in. Her breasts were full and round and perfect, capped with dusky nipples which he was desperate to taste. The trim waist flared over the generous hips he loved, and as she primly knelt on the mattress awaiting his judgement, only the top of the red curls which nestled between her pale thighs were visible.

'The fantasy was outstanding...but you are better, Hope. So much better than I could have imagined.'

When he could stand it no longer, and had to touch, he did so with reverence, knowing he was indeed the luckiest man in the world but that she wouldn't believe him if he said that. 'Look what you do to me.' He took her hand and wrapped it around his erection. Then caressed one of her sensitive puckered nipples so that she could feel his body twitch and pulse with need. 'What on earth makes you think that you do not please me? I am overwhelmed, Hope. A lost cause. All yours to do with as you please.'

It was pure torture watching her hand explore the shape of him, and he had to close his eyes because the pleasure was so intense. Because he had to, Luke kissed her lips again, dragging her on to his lap so that skin touched skin. Her breasts filled his hands, the saucy tips pebbling as his thumbs gently traced them. Only when he felt her sigh into his mouth did he lower them both to the mattress so that he could carry out his promise.

He trailed his lips over her shoulders first, then down her arms. Kissed every finger before he moved to her stomach, and down her legs, then took his own sweet time retracing the route, waiting until she was moaning, impatient, before he finally allowed himself to taste her breasts.

She groaned when he finally sucked her nipple into his mouth, and seemed delightfully surprised it brought her pleasure too, until the quest for pleasure took over and she anchored his head there with her hands. Sensing she needed more, he allowed his fingers to wend a lazy trail to the seductive triangle of curls, her hips instinctively rising to meet them.

She trembled at his first touch. Her body soft. Already wet and ripe. As he stroked her and that tight bunch of nerve endings awoke, she struggled and writhed, murmuring nonsense as encouragement until she forgot to be embarrassed about her beautiful, lush and overtly feminine body and thrust her breasts towards his mouth demanding they be worshipped too.

In mere moments, she was on the cusp, her muscles tense and her hips straining against his touch. He had never seen anything so alluringly erotic in his life as Hope in the throes of ecstasy. And she was his.

All his.

'Don't stop, Luke…please don't stop.'

'I won't, love.' Her eyes fluttered closed, and as her hips bucked he gathered her close and kissed her as she came apart in his arms, capturing her cries in his mouth as she violently shuddered her release and collapsed boneless against him.

Only then did he roll above her, moved beyond recognition by the gift she had bestowed upon him, yet still desperate for everything and needing to know her completely. As he kissed her, she stretched her limbs contentedly, opening her long legs in welcome and sighed as she kissed him back.

He tried to take things slowly, but his body was possessed and desperate to be in hers.

He tried to bring her to the cusp of oblivion again before he intruded, but his gloriously wanton and voluptuous new fiancée was having none of it. She reached between their bodies to stroke him too, smiling triumphantly at the profound effect her touch had on him, then when he could obviously bear no more, guided him to her entrance. Inviting him in. Those siren's hips again rising to meet him until he couldn't wait a second longer. It took every ounce of strength he had not to plunge mindlessly into her wet heat, to gently inch himself inside, only to stop short when he reached the barrier of her virginity and the barrage of intense, possessive emotions which assaulted him as he did.

He would be her first and her last. Her one and only. No one would ever know her as completely and intimately. He was humbled and elated, and so filled with love it felt as though his heart might burst.

They held each other tight as he pushed past and slowly began to move. Tentatively at first so she could get used to the size and shape of him, but as passion began to build again, she soon dictated the rhythm, enthusiastically meeting him thrust for thrust. As the walls of her body caressed him from root to tip, those long legs hooked around his hips and her fingers traced his face, more words of devotion spilled unbidden from his lips. Eyes locked, bodies joined, souls in perfect tempo, the need for words was gone and he lost himself in her entirely and all was unimaginable pleasure and exquisite pain.

Nothing existed except them and that moment. The tangled limbs. The knotted sheets. Breathless, joyous, wonderous oblivion. Total trust. Complete surrender.

A climatic explosion of light and stars and happiness.

All wrapped tight and comforting in love.

Chapter Twenty-One

They didn't waste the final hours of the night on sleep, even though they were both thoroughly sated and exhausted. Instead they talked and made plans. Hope sat propped against a nest of several pillows and Luke staring up at her, his head in her lap and his face mere inches from her shamelessly still-bare bosoms.

Bosoms which she had more affection for now that she knew they could bring her so much pleasure and because he adored them so very much.

'I think it makes sense to offload the bulk of your shares. Especially as owning them in the first place causes you undue worry.' He had just outlined his plan to simplify his estate to make running it more manageable.

'It's not worry, exactly…more that I much prefer to fully understand it all. Which I can't when all those separate businesses are run by faceless others who own more of a stake in the outcome than I do.'

'You need to be in control.' She understood that about him know. Luke had to be master of his own destiny because for so many years he had been at the mercy of others. 'I cannot say I blame you. What will you do with the equity? Or will it sit in the bank with all the rest of the money?' Another thing he wasn't easy with. He had worked hard to be financially comfortable and independent, but to be now so rich that money was no object didn't sit right with him. 'Unless you intend to become philanthropic.'

'I've thought of that and it goes without saying that some institutions should benefit from it. Like Dr Long Fox and Brislington House. I would trust him implicitly after he helped my mother. But others that I know precious little about and have no relationship with...' He idly tugged one of her curls as he frowned. 'Again—the lack of control would keep me awake at night. How do I ensure my charitable gift gets used in the right way and goes to the right people?' He rolled his big body so that he could face her, propping himself up on one elbow, as unashamedly naked as the day he was born, rumpled from their lovemaking and as sinfully handsome as she had ever seen him. 'I've been thinking about duplicating his ideas and those of others like him, and perhaps setting up my own hospitals around the country and here in the capital. I keep reading about the horror stories of the York Asylum and Bedlam, so similar to the atrocities of Mill House, and feel obligated to rectify them in some small way. If I cannot shut them down, at least I would like to offer an alternative. I certainly have the money and with all the property in my portfolio, there has to be some place suitable to make a start. What do you think?'

That she had picked the very best man in the world to fall head over heels in love with. 'I think, as a marquess who now has a voice in Parliament and bizarrely seems to be earning the respect of everyone despite your annoying roguishness, you could do both. Open hospitals and use your dazzling Duff charm to align others to your cause to change the law. I suspect you'd have a lot of support for it. There have been rumblings of concern for years.'

His expression was thoughtful as he let that sink in. 'I never thought of that but it's a good idea. There is no earthly reason why I couldn't do both. It would be good to put this damn title to use too.'

'Then here's another idea to consider—involve your mother. For who better to spearhead your crusade than one who has suffered it?'

'Oh, I couldn't do that.' He didn't bother giving that a second's thought. 'She isn't strong enough.' He tapped his forehead. 'Too much stress might cause a relapse.'

Overprotective to the bitter end. 'I think she might surprise you.' She had certainly surprised Hope.

'She's been through too much.'

'I know she has. We had a long chat about it all last night in the garden.' She wouldn't mention Maria's brief moment of panic. A promise was a promise after all, even if it meant keeping it from Luke. 'She told me everything and has quite an interesting perspective of it all now that she is out the other side. She even suggested I should write a novel based on the way the supposed lunatics are treated. You should talk to her about it too. At least gauge her opinions on the idea before you run ahead in your own well-intentioned, over-protective and cloddish Cornish way. To do this properly, to do your brilliant future hospitals justice, you need to be able to see both sides of the coin.'

His eyes narrowed playfully. 'Is this what I have to look forward to? A lifetime of nagging, logic and sensible ideas which stop me from making a ham-fisted hash of things.'

'Among other things.' She kissed him and sighed as it inevitably made her want more. 'I'd better go. The sun is coming up. My mother will kill us both if she discovers I'm missing.'

'Or we could make a mad dash for Gretna Green instead? I could have my wicked way with you all the way there and all the way back...'

'Tempting—but I fear my mother will definitely murder us then. She's waited twenty-three years to see me married, and, after Faith, adores being the mother of the bride. If she doesn't get to crow about it from the rooftops, there will be hell to pay so best to stick to our original plan of September.'

He watched her stuff herself into her dress, an odd experience when she had never done anything like that in front of a man before, and helped her roll undergarments into her stays. He would have followed her stark naked out on the balcony too if she hadn't insisted he put something on in case one of the other residents of Bloomsbury happened to see him. And because he had a flimsy relationship with propriety at the best of times, he insisted on giving her a searing kiss before he helped her back to her own. As he handed her the bundle of unmentionables, his eyes raked her possessively one last time.

'Will you lie with me tonight?'

'I might.'

'That's a resounding yes then because you, madam, cannot keep your hands off me. And who can blame you? I am irresistible and quite the catch.' The cocky, lopsided grin was back with a vengeance.

'*Talk* to your mother, Luke. The pair of you never talk about her illness and I think she really wants to.'

Then she blew him a kiss. 'I'll see you at Gunter's, and if you aren't vexing for once, I'll let you distract me in the park afterwards.'

Hope skipped breakfast with her family. Not because she wasn't starving—because after the long and eventful night with Luke she was famished—but because she didn't trust herself to behave normally around them. She needed a few hours to digest everything before she risked conversing with them in case they instantly spotted the change in her, knew she had been thoroughly deflowered and was totally delighted to have been so. Parts of her still throbbed from their joining, an unsettling and constant reminder of the level of intimacy they had indulged in. Because of her body's eagerness to experience it again, her cumbersome bosoms, in particular, were heavy and expectant and there was an unmistakable need between her legs which would likely send her quite mad herself if it wasn't dealt with soon. Their passionate lovemaking had all been so enlightening, satisfying and freeing, she practically floated to Paternoster Row, grinning like an idiot yet still feeling slightly guilty that she had twisted Luke's arm into a proposal.

In all good conscience, she would have to talk to him about that before they announced the news to their families later. Just to be certain he did want to marry this September and not wait a little longer until they knew each other better.

She handed over the signed contract which her new fiancé had gone over with a fine-tooth comb, then settled down for a long but interesting meeting with her new publisher where he appraised her of all his plans.

He wanted to release *Phantasma* in January. The logic behind this was that people preferred to read ghost stories in the depth of winter, when the joy of Christmas was done and several more months of depressing cold weather stretched before them. As that made perfect sense to Hope, she trusted Mr Cooper to know the business aspect of the book market far better than she ever could.

He also had a revolutionary plan to release the first chapter to one of the newspapers on the publication day to generate excitement, assuring her that once they had read the opening scene, they would need to know who the Phantom was. The timing, he added, would be doubly advantageous as it would coincide with Charity's debut in *The Marriage of Figaro* and the wave of publicity which was bound to accompany both daughters of England's premier portraitist and his famous soprano wife was something money couldn't buy.

His rapid about-turn about her using the name Brookes all now made sense. As much as they all frequently lamented the gossip columns' obsession with them, she now understood why her parents said it was both a blessing and a curse. For once, the family notoriety would work in her favour and it was about time too.

As the meeting came to a close he beamed at her across the table. 'I suppose the only thing left to discuss is the exact name you want on the binding.'

'I thought we had agreed on that?'

'Indeed we have, my dear, but I have heard that by then you might not even be a Brookes at all.' He smiled knowingly. 'Obviously, you can of course, have Hope Brookes stamped in gold leaf on the binding and for obvious reasons I should like to keep the Brookes at all costs.' In view of his initial reluctance, the irony of that statement was not lost on her. 'But you could add a hyphen and the Duff.'

Hope Brookes-*Duff.*

She let that sink in for a moment and decided she liked it. They would have been married a good three months by then and it seemed fitting to acknowledge their union in that way. Luke was her biggest fan, in so many ways and she had him to thank for pushing her into submitting her novel. 'I think I would prefer Hope Brookes-Duff.'

'Then that is what it shall be.' He stuck out his hand and shook hers. 'Welcome to the fold and my hearty congratulations on your engagement. You've got yourself a good man there. Smart and charming.'

She did and smiled proudly as Mr Cooper led her to the door, until the ramifications of what they had been talking about suddenly struck home. 'How did you know we were engaged?' Because she certainly hadn't been until the small hours of the morning and she hadn't even told her own family the news yet. The pair of them were going to announce it tonight at dinner. Or so she thought.

'Well...er... I...' His eyes were blinking rapidly. 'I think I read it in the newspaper.' He was clearly lying.

'Mr Cooper—have you, by any chance, met my fiancé?' How else would he know that Luke was both smart and charming?

'I...er...obviously we recently met at some function or another. I forget where.' He waved his hand dismissing it, a hint of panic in his eyes. 'You can tell a great deal about a chap from one meeting and your Luke...' He clamped his jaws shut as her eyes narrowed, clearly realising he had just dug himself into an enormous hole.

Just call me Luke!

The sneaky scoundrel had obviously gone behind her back despite her explicit instructions to steer well clear. 'Did you happen to meet him last Tuesday, Mr Cooper?' The morning when she received Mr Cooper's missive appraising her of his change of heart straight after the night of the roses and Luke's pretty apology. Then blithely and convincingly congratulated her on Mr Crocker seeing sense.

Crocker!

The devious, conniving, overbearing… 'He came here, didn't he?' And she was going to wring his neck when she got her hands on him. Decorate him in violet ice cream in the middle of Gunter's while she gave him a piece of her mind. 'He put pressure on you to allow me to use my real name instead of a pseudonym.'

'Er…not exactly.' Mr Cooper retrieved his handkerchief and used it to nervously mop his brow. 'I've stupidly put myself in an impossible position because I promised him faithfully I wouldn't mention it.'

This time, her tone was stern. 'Did Luke bully you into using my name?'

'Of course not! I am not a man to be bullied, even by a shareholder.'

'A shareholder!' This was going from bad to worse. All this time Luke had had shares in Cooper and Son and not said a damn word about it! Now, all her doubts about her ability as a writer sprang to the fore, making her question why the publisher had wanted her book in the first place. Was this all Luke's doing? In his well-meant and over-protective interference to make her dream come true, was he unintentionally setting her up for a fall?

Mr Cooper winced, then huffed, defeated. The game was up and he knew it. 'To be fair to him, he had no idea he owned shares until last Tuesday, and simply came here to introduce himself.' There was no *simply* with Luke. The wretch had done it all deliberately. 'And then we got chatting and he mentioned he had read your book and we had a long discussion about the sublime complexity and page-turning qualities of your plot, Miss Brookes.' It galled that those compliments stroked her ego even though she was still righteously furious at Luke for his interference. 'Then he was the one who suggested January as the perfect release date as he and his mother always read macabre stories to while away the long winter nights in Cornwall...' All so totally Luke. 'And then he happened to mention how clever it was of me to have signed you when the name Brookes and publicity went hand in hand. Especially after all the recent splendid coverage of your mother's performance in *Così fan Tutte* and your sister's recent success in the art world and I realised I was missing a trick in not using your real name...'

Of course he hadn't intimidated her publisher. Luke had charmed him. Utterly dazzled Mr Cooper into re-evaluating his own rigid stance until he considered it his own idea in the first place.

How annoyingly clever of him.

'Then news of your youngest sister's success leaked out and it seemed as if the planets were aligned. It was only at the end of our conversation that he mentioned he was biased about your literary genius and that you were going to be his wife.' A full week before she had pushed him into asking her to marry him.

That gloriously inescapable fact seemed to banish all the anger.

He was intending to ask. Always had been. She hadn't twisted the dratted man's arm at all. Perhaps she wouldn't strangle him, but the jury was still out over the ice cream.

Hope hailed a hackney to take her to Gunter's, where she impatiently waited an hour for him to arrive. When he didn't, in a panic and imagining all sorts of hideous reasons to explain it, she hired another one to take her home where she was met by a white-faced Charity and her mother, who rushed towards her the moment she put one foot through the front door.

'What's happened?' Because clearly something hideous and catastrophic had. But of all her panicked and hideous imaginings, nothing could have possibly ever prepared her for the catastrophe which had.

Chapter Twenty-Two

*There is always a scandal at the Renshaw Ball,
but I am all astonishment at what must surely be
the biggest of them all. For the reclusive Dowager
Marchioness of T. apparently never eschewed
society at all—she was instead an inmate in a
private madhouse for lunatics in Wiltshire! And
if that bombshell wasn't shocking enough to have
you reaching for your smelling salts, Gentle
Reader, then the accounts of how her insanity
rendered her both witless and incoherent will! For
I have it upon the most intimate authority from
a lady close to the besotted Marquess that his
mother's physicians had to restrain her repeatedly
over the years simply to prevent the deranged and
deluded Dowager from hanging herself by the
neck from the rafters of her cell...*

Whispers from Behind the Fan
August 1814

Five days on and Luke still couldn't think of Hope's
betrayal without wanting to smash something with his
fists. Even if she hadn't betrayed him outright, because

he couldn't believe she was that cruel and callous to have gone to the newspapers herself, she had betrayed his confidence somewhere and that was unforgivable.

Thanks to her indiscretion, perhaps tattling to her flighty sister Charity or the unsubtle Roberta who adored gossip because she liked to be the first to spread it, she had completely ruined his poor mother's life. All those years of suffering, then the years of slow recovery, all his painstaking work to keep it all a secret to protect her were all now for nought. One careless conversation and it had all come crashing around their ears. The awful truth was out, and the impending relapse was as inevitable as his heartbreak and he couldn't bear the thought of it.

Or her.

His own stupid fault for trusting Hope in the first place, he supposed, when he was usually so cautious about letting anyone in. It was, no doubt, brought about by the profound effect she had always had on him. But then again, he should have known better, as she had a profound effect over all men so he should have steered well clear. Instead, he had uncharacteristically thrown all caution to the wind and had been thoroughly seduced by the siren from the outset, and cross-eyed with lust, he had left his mother exposed. What had he been thinking to bare his soul to a woman from a family who made a near weekly appearance in the scandal sheets?

He never should have dragged his mother to London and he certainly never should have allowed himself to fall in love. Two hideous and gross errors of judgement which would have far-reaching and horrific consequences. All he could do now that he had returned her to the sanctuary of Tregally at breakneck speed, was wait for the inevitable fallout and deal with it as best he could.

To that end, he had sent a message to Dr Long Fox the moment they had arrived home late last night, informing him he would need to receive his mother at Brislington House as soon as there were obvious signs her health had begun to deteriorate.

His mother had put a brave face on it all though the long journey—but that mask would crumble soon enough. Bitter experience told him it was a matter of when, not if, and he had to be prepared. Perhaps for another long haul. In the meantime, all he could do was wait, quickly offload as many of his responsibilities in London as he legally could, and batten down the hatches again to prevent exposing her to more danger. It wasn't much of a plan but, frankly, the best plan he could make in such a hurry.

If only it didn't all hurt so blasted much.

If he could focus only on his mother and forget Hope, then he wouldn't feel quite so out of control. However, his emotions were all over the place, clouding his mind while his heart bled buckets inside his chest.

He rested his forehead on the leaded glass of his study window and listlessly stared out at the stars.

What a hideous, but totally avoidable, mess.

'Couldn't sleep?' His mother's voice behind made him jump and he instantly squared his shoulders, not wanting her to see that he was broken too when she needed all his strength now more than ever.

'I have too much to do.' She was pale. Dark shadows ringed her eyes, making her look older than her fifty years. 'I still need to write to my managers and my solicitor before I can go to bed but you should try to get some rest. Shall I fetch you some hot milk?' Five days on and the crushing guilt meant he still couldn't be in his mother's company for more than a minute or two at a time. This time he couldn't blame his uninterested father or his callous brother for threatening her mind. Ultimately, this mess was all his fault.

He was a blasted idiot!

Idiot!

And he should have known better.

'I'd much rather some company.'

'I'll go wake Clowance.' The nursemaid would know what to do. If anything, out of the three of them, Clowance was calmly taking it all in her stride.

'Is it your plan to avoid me for ever, Luke? We've hardly swapped ten words since we left Bloomsbury. Please talk to me.' She stroked his arm. 'I can see you're hurting.'

Of course he was hurting. He was in hell. 'I should never have subjected you to London.' Some of the guilt leaked out before he could stop it and he burdened her with his pain. 'I keep thinking that if I'd have left you here or simply left the solicitor to deal with my unwanted inheritance and stayed here in the first place, none of this would have happened. I'm so sorry.'

'I told you to go to London, as I recall, to have a grand adventure and then I pushed you into visiting because I wanted one too.'

'Still—I should have mitigated against all this. I should have anticipated it.'

'Why? Because I am your sole responsibility, put on this earth purely so that you could nobly protect me?' She shook her head. 'I never had you so that you could be my parent, Luke. That is not the way our relationship should be, and I hate the fact you feel so beholden and responsible when none of what happened was ever your fault.'

'*This* is my fault.'

'Of course it isn't.' She rubbed his back and stared out into the darkness too. 'It's funny… I've dreaded this moment for years. Dreaded being exposed. Dreaded peoples' judgement of me and their judgement of you. Dreaded how I would cope with the shame of it all—dreaded *if* I could cope with the shame of it all. Now that it's finally here, I have to say it's all a strange anticlimax.' Typically, she was minimising the impact to spare his feelings.

'It is perfectly understandable that you feel devastated and lost. You have no need to hide it.'

'I do feel devastated.' She frowned, tilting her head to stare at him. 'But for you—not for me. You are putting me before everything again when I had finally hoped you were putting yourself first. You were so happy in Bloomsbury, my angel. Much happier than I have ever seen you.'

'We'll be happy again.' He would do whatever it took to find his mother's smile. 'I promise you it will all pass. We'll get through this together and in a few months what happened in London will be another part of the distant past.'

She shook her head. 'Do you seriously think you will get over her in a few months?'

'This isn't about me.'

'No…of course not. Heaven forbid you do something for yourself for a change. Prioritise your own life and your own happiness.' For some reason she was angry at him. 'Not when you have to watch me like a hawk for any sign I might lose my mind again! Clowance told me you've contacted the physician in anticipation of my next bout of insanity. She also told me you'd told her to watch me in case I start to behave irrationally.' She prodded him hard in the bicep. 'Your lack of faith is beyond insulting, Luke! And for the record, if anyone is being irrational right now it is you.'

'Clowance shouldn't...' She stayed him with her hand.

'Firstly, Clowance is my friend first and foremost nowadays, so she jolly well should have, and secondly, she trusts me enough to know that this will not break me, Luke. Do you hear me?' She grabbed him by the shoulders and shook him. 'This will *not* break me! If anything, I am relieved it is all out in the open because I now no longer have to dread being exposed. Why should I care who knows what happened at Mill House? That place is an outrage which needs exposing and what happened to me there is what sent me mad the second time. That Cassius could do that to me out of revenge, legally and with no recourse, makes an ass out of the law. People have the right to know that.

'The more I think upon it, the more I think I should have stayed put and talked to the newspapers myself, put forward my side of the story and the side of all the other poor wretches wrongfully incarcerated in similar hellholes still suffering all the abuse. Or better still allowed Hope to use her talent with words to tell the world what is happening to people up and down the country. I would have preferred to have told the truth with my head held high and proved to them that I am as sane as anyone, rather than running away with you like a coward and proving their suspicions to the contrary!'

'Protecting you isn't cowardly!' And he resented the implication. 'It is a responsibility I have always taken seriously, even if that is detrimental to my own happiness.'

Instantly her face changed to one of pity and she stroked his arm again. 'If you love her, don't you think you should have given her the benefit of the doubt and at least waited for her explanation? I cannot imagine Hope would ever go to the newspapers. You only have to read her book to see that she is principled and has a strong social conscience. And she loves you so very much, I cannot think what she stood to gain to jeopardise it all?'

'An explanation wouldn't have changed the facts, Mother.' Not that he could have borne looking at her when he had to bid her goodbye. His overwhelming love for her would have made him waver when he needed to be resolute and his intense feelings would have clouded his judgement and stopped him from doing what his mother needed. 'Whether she went directly to them herself, or she told someone who did, the fact remains she betrayed my confidence and yours when we entrusted her with the truth. Whichever way I try to dress that up—and believe me I have tried—that betrayal is unforgivable.'

'But it makes no sense, Luke. She loves you. A blind man with blinkers on could see as clear as day you were the only one for her. The poor girl must be heartbroken.'

A feeling which was quite mutual. 'Hearts mend.' Or at least he prayed they did as his had truly been bludgeoned to pulp. The bleak and utter hopelessness of that was killing him. All the despair and pain must have showed on his expression because tears filled her eyes. 'Oh, Luke...perhaps...'

Not a conversation he could have without disgracing himself by blubbing like a baby at the cruelty of fate and the feckless woman who had destroyed him. In case he did, he made sure he was stalking towards the door before he risked answering. 'There is no perhaps, Mother. She let me down. I cannot forgive that.' Before the door slammed decisively behind him, his mother couldn't let it lie.

'I let you down for years, Luke—and you forgave me. And we both know I treated you far worse.'

Most of the interminable carriage ride to Bath went past in a blur of abject misery, not helped by the fact Hope had had to take it all alone. At the last minute, Mr Kemble decided he needed Charity to help him choose a fitting Figaro to play opposite her. He wanted a youngish tenor with whom she had chemistry and said he wouldn't be able to gauge that unless she was there to sing and act beside him. Ergo, despite her sister's loud objections and genuine concern, Hope was visiting Faith alone with only their trusty coachman Evan for company. His wife, their maid Lily, and Charity would join them both later once her perfect Figaro was found.

It was probably just as well.

Had her sister been with her she would have been dreadful company, her mood veering dangerously between utterly bereft and so furious her blood was literally boiling, while she tried to comprehend how Luke could have come to the conclusion that the only person who could have passed on the story was her.

Not that he'd had the decency to say as much to her face. Instead, he had hightailed it back to Tregally as soon as the morning paper had been delivered and accused her of the awful crime in a letter which five days on she still couldn't quite believe as he had spewed such venom.

Three words was all he thought she warranted after the night they had spent together. Three words which he had clearly written in a hurry before he thrust the missive at Charity then rode out of Bedford Place moments later. Three paltry words was all it took to completely split her heart in two.

How could you?

Not *Did you?*

Not *Can you think who?*

Not even a wounded *Why did you?*

In his stubborn, stupid, big cloddish Cornish head, she was automatically guilty before he had even considered any other possible explanation and she was still reeling at the staggering speed at which he had come to that conclusion. Almost as if all the promises they had made to each other suddenly meant nothing and neither did she.

The carriage slowed as it turned into a short drive and she spied her sister and Piers waiting at the end of it. Faith was grinning from ear to ear as her husband helped Hope down and hugged her tight. Then she frowned at the distinct lack of Charity.

'Is it just you?'

'Only until Charity is free.' There was no point in delaying the big announcement. 'She's been given one of the lead soprano roles in *The Marriage of Figaro* at Covent Garden. It will open in January.' Hope tried to inject as much excitement into her sister's brilliant achievement as she could as they walked into the house, understanding that Faith needed to hear it properly and Charity deserved the credit too. They were settled in a sunny parlour awaiting tea by the time she finished.

'Why that is marvellous! I am so happy for her!' And by the delighted look on her face, Faith was more than just happy at Charity's success. There was something different about her. A radiance and vitality which she assumed was everything to do with Piers and her new-found happiness with him, and which she might well have glowed with herself less than a week ago when everything about her future had seemed rosy. 'What else have I missed? As much as I have adored honey-mooning all summer, I've missed you all horrendously. I don't think our family have ever been apart for this long before.'

'Well... I got a publisher for my book.' How hollow that all felt now despite the beaming smile she forced. 'Cooper and Son's bought it, so I will finally be in Hatchard's in the New Year. January as well, so that will be quite the month, what with Charity's opening.'

'Oh, Hope!'

Faith jumped up and bounded over, hugging her again, her usually slender waist considerably fuller than normal. 'That is the best news of all! Though I never doubted you could do it. You have always been so driven—I suppose all three of us follow Mama and Papa for that—but I always envied you your single-minded determination and confidence in your own abilities.' Clearly Hope's veil of bravado was supremely convincing if her most similar sibling hadn't spotted all the raging uncertainties swirling beneath the surface.

As she stepped back, a surprisingly stiff summer breeze through the open windows plastered the bold yellow muslin to her eldest sister's body and her hand instinctively went to her stomach as Hope's eyes dropped there. Then she beamed again, her gaze immediately going to her husband and the pair of them shared such a look of overwhelming affection the intensity of it actually hurt. The wave of longing for Luke suddenly so intense her chest ached.

'As you can probably see, Piers and I have some news too.' Faith smoothed her dress tight and the tell-tale shape of her bump was unmistakable.

'You're pregnant!' Another pang of emotion floored her. Not just the overwhelming happiness for her sister, but a deep well of sadness for herself, mourning the sudden loss of something she hadn't realised she wanted but which had been torn away when Luke had left her.

'I am. Very. I've been holding out to tell you all in the flesh, Piers's family too. So please don't write to Mama and Papa about it till we all head back to London at the end of the month. I want to see their faces when they realise they will be grandparents.'

'Our mother will be beside herself.' Hope could picture it already. The fussing, the fawning. The proud shouting from the rooftops. 'She'll be counting the minutes till she can call herself Grandmama and will likely bankrupt Papa with all the shopping she will do. When is the baby due?'

Faith and Piers shared an odd look, before she shrugged and laughed. 'January too. Once again, I fear the Brookes family of Bloomsbury shall have to endure another scandal as nobody is going to believe this little thing will be a good four months premature.' She patted her stomach again, looking so blissfully happy, Hope was filled with envy. 'The world will know we anticipated her vows.'

A habit which was clearly a Brookes family trait, seeing as she had too. Not that she held out any hope that she and Luke would now take any, because she certainly wouldn't beg. And if the stubborn wretch had that little trust in her to have believed her guilt in the first instance, she wanted no part of him.

Perhaps, if she kept telling herself that, she would come to believe it.

'But scandal is our middle name after all.' Faith brushed it away as no matter, obviously no longer caring one whit what the world had to say about her. 'Although according to Charity's frequent and salacious letters, you've been the one causing all the scandal of late, Hope—and with a dissolute marquess no less. The one you allegedly pushed in the fountain at my engagement ball.'

That comment earned her a very knowing look over the rim of Faith's teacup. One which made it plain Charity had told her absolutely everything she knew. 'Our baby sister says he is big and tall, is as handsome as sin and looks like a pirate. She is utterly convinced he is *the one* and that, as unlikely as it seems when one considers that you have always been more cynical than I, Charity is adamant you are hopelessly in love with him. Is she correct?' The familiar teasing tone caused a knot of hurt in Hope's throat that would take all her legendary bravado to hide. 'Are more wedding bells imminent?'

She tried to swallow past it. Tried to smile. But it was then, to her complete horror and shame, that the unsentimental, emotionless and pessimistic middle Brookes sister did something she hadn't done in front of another living soul since the day she turned fifteen. She collapsed against her most level-headed sibling in an emotional and noisy heap, then cried her eyes out for over an hour.

Chapter Twenty-Three

'So let me get this straight...' Alone together in the drawing room after poor Piers had beaten a hasty retreat, Faith passed Hope yet another clean handkerchief to blow her nose in. 'Somebody leaked the story to the newspapers and Luke thinks it was you. You are certain about that?'

She retrieved his tatty final missive from her pocket and passed it to her sister, then cried some more. 'I didn't even deserve the benefit of the doubt. Just a goodbye.'

Faith stared at the note for the longest time, then screwed up her face. 'I see hurt here, Hope—but not goodbye.'

'His leaving was the goodbye. His housekeeper said he packed up everything before they all left and instructed her to close up the house. He isn't coming back.'

Her sister wrapped one arm around her shoulders and tugged her close. 'He's hurting. Men are at their most irrational when they are in pain.'

'He should have at least talked to me. Looked me in the eye to make his egregious accusations.' Given her a chance to make him see sense. 'But Luke always thinks he knows best and then runs on ahead, half-cocked.' Trying to do the right thing to protect those he loved most of all.

'Who else knows about his mother's past? Physicians? Servants? Former associates and acquaintances?'

'I have no idea.' And no clue where to start. She had hammered on the door of the newspaper the same afternoon Luke and his mother left, demanding to know who their source was, and had been kicked out on her ear.

'Did you tell anyone anything? Is it possible you were overheard discussing it?'

'Not with Luke...no. We were...' She stopped herself before she said the words *in my bedroom*, but her sudden wince was all it took to convey that truth to her wily sister.

'Ahh... I *see*.'

'We weren't...' She could feel her cheeks heating. 'At least not then...'

Faith patted her hand and grinned at the confession. 'It's all right, Sister dear. You do not need to explain that to me. Not when I am the one who walked up the aisle apparently at least three months pregnant. With the right man, all propriety flies straight out of the window along with all your inhibitions.' Then her eyes flicked to Hope's stomach. 'Is there a chance you could be...?'

'No!' Maybe. There certainly hadn't seemed any need to take precautions. 'Possibly... I sincerely hope not as that would rather complicate things.' Which were quite complicated enough already. She didn't want him because he felt beholden. 'I suppose somebody could have overhead me and Maria talking about things in the garden—not that we saw anyone.' Hope threw out her hands, exasperated. 'And not that he would believe either, when he is so wedded to his outrage and unfair disappointment in me.'

'Do you love him?'

'I did.' Her attempt at haughty bravado lacked conviction and her shoulders slumped. 'I do.' And likely always would too.

The irreplaceable wretch!

'Do you still want to marry him?'

'Only if he accepts the fact I am entirely innocent.' She wouldn't live with his doubts. That unsatisfactory compromise would be a step too far. 'He should have trusted me. Implicitly.' Like she trusted him.

'He should—but men consumed by love are gloriously irrational, so as the more sensible sex we must afford them the occasional bit of slack. Do you remember Piers's irrational jealousy when he saw me dancing with Edward Tate? When I thought all was done and dusted between us, it was you who intervened. Your sensible advice saved us and because it worked, I shall repeat it back to you. If you believe he is the one, that he is worth the risk and the effort of eternity, then you owe it to both of you to fight for your happiness. It's barely two days' drive from here to the Cornish coast. Why don't we go there now and you can look the idiot in the eyes and make him see sense?'

Proud anger was instantly replaced by fear. 'And if he doesn't?'

'We cross that bridge when we come to it. *If* we come to it.' Faith shrugged, her eyes filled with sympathy as she took her hand. 'But better that than remaining a bystander wedded to her own self-righteous outrage and regretting it for ever.'

Luke was soaked to the skin by the time he got home from his evening ride. Soaked by the violent summer storm which matched his thunderous mood, chilled by the stiff sea breeze which had ruthlessly battered the cliffs like Hope had battered his poor heart, and thoroughly exhausted. A restless, impotent week of practically no sleep wasn't doing anything to help heal his shredded emotions, neither were the endless, mindless rides he now took to clear his head. Two hours on this one and his damn head was still as confused as it had been last week and instead of lessening, the relentless pain in his chest was getting worse.

Which would have been bad enough without all the nagging doubts, which like his nagging mother constantly told him he should have stayed. Should have listened. Should have at least given her—them—a chance before he had slammed that door quite so decisively because he thought he knew best and was hurting so bad he wasn't rational.

Now, it seemed it wasn't his mother's mind that was failing on the back of that hasty decision—but his. He had mislaid it somewhere on the road between Bloomsbury and Tregally when the enormity of what he had lost permeated his soul, and like a virulent cancer, destroying a bit more of it with every passing day.

He stared up at his house as what was left of the day disappeared behind it, not caring that rain still poured down his neck, beneath his collar and down his spine, and seriously considered turning his poor horse around to traipse another directionless route around his grounds again rather than go inside. Because going inside when the lamps were lit inevitably meant staying still and that gave him nothing whatsoever to focus on for the rest of the night but his own misery. Instead, he wearily led his mount to the stables, intending to brush it down himself for something to do until he saw the fancy carriage parked inside it.

Bizarrely, he knew that Hope had arrived in it before he sprinted to the house to find her, and skidded to a sodden stop in his parlour. He knew because his shrivelled, trampled heart started to beat again in his chest and the foolish optimistic voice in his head was praying that she could make it all right long before he saw her sat there with his mother and her older sister. Praying her arrival would miraculously fix things but fearing they likely wouldn't most of all.

Her green eyes were troubled. The shadows under them as deep and as damning as his. 'You're drenched.'

'It's raining.' An explanation which was rendered immediately unnecessary by the sudden flash of lightning beyond the dripping windows and the deep rumble of thunder which quickly followed it.

'It's late and this storm is in for the night.' His mother touched her sister's hand. 'Why don't I show you to your room, Faith?'

The panic was instantaneous. 'They can't stay here.' If things were doomed to remain unresolved, he couldn't bear the thought of her sleeping under the same roof. So close and yet so far. 'They can stay at the inn in Tintagel.'

'You'd send a pregnant woman and your intended twenty miles, along unfamiliar coastal roads in the dark in this weather? Over my dead body, Luke!' Then she prodded him, unaware that the pain of the use of the word intended stung more than any pointed finger could, because he had no idea if she was still his intended or not. Whether she still wanted him or not, or whether he could forgive her or not. 'Hope has travelled two days to get here to speak to you, and you'll hear her out, or so help me I'll murder you myself!' And with that, she left them, taking the silently disapproving sister with her.

'I didn't go to the newspapers, Luke.' Hope stood with more quiet dignity than he could muster. 'And you should have known that without my coming here to say it.'

'But you spoke to someone, Hope, didn't you? You betrayed my confidence and my mother's and made it impossible for us to stay in London.'

The sudden anger swirled in her eyes. 'I spoke to no one. It wasn't my secret to tell. Either someone overheard me talking to Maria in the garden or somebody else knew what happened.'

'You expect me to believe you never confided to one of your sisters?'

'Yes, Luke, I do.' She folded her arms and stared, exasperated. 'Why on earth would I betray your confidence or your mother's when I love you and would never do a thing to harm you?'

'I have no earthly idea.'

'Why would I lie, Luke?' She grabbed his hand. Laced her fingers tight in his. 'After everything…after what we did? I love you! I gave myself to you! Body, heart and soul.' He could hear her tears and they were like torture. 'Why would I ruin that when you are my everything?'

The cruellest words he didn't want to hear.

'I don't know, Hope.' He wanted to believe her. Needed to so much. 'But even if it was an accident, I cannot forgive it.' He extricated his hand as he stepped away, needing the distance. 'The stakes are just too high—the risk too great. If it were just me you had hurt, I could…but it isn't. I have a responsibility to my mother and her recovery. I have to keep her safe no matter.' And he couldn't do that if he couldn't trust every single person around her.

'You hold me entirely to blame for somebody else overhearing?' She looked so wounded. 'Even though I could have had no possible idea that they have done so and your mother volunteered all the information freely? And you have no other candidate who could have betrayed you? None? Not a single other person in your entire thirty years could possibly know some of what happened?'

When he didn't answer, she shook her head, those clever green eyes hardening to flint. 'You are a fraud, Lucius Nathaniel Elijah Duff. A two-faced, lily-livered, disingenuous fraud. How dare you make me fall in love with you and then abandon me at the first hurdle!' She stalked to the door and tugged it open, then jabbed her finger hard in the air. 'And how dare you lecture me on trust and fearlessness when you are incapable of either virtue yourself! What a crushing disappointment of a man you truly are! At least all the others never pretended to be worthy.'

He heard her march down his hall and up his stairs. Heard a door slam while he remained rooted to the spot. His mother bustled in seconds later, looking alarmed and exasperated in equal measure. 'She didn't deny it, then?' She lowered herself to the arm of the chair, stunned. 'I cannot believe it.'

It took all his strength to shake his head. 'She denied it. Claimed she never said a word to another living soul and never would. Suggested someone must have overheard you both discussing it in the garden at the Renshaw ball.'

'Did it occur to you to believe her?' Of course it had. He had wanted to believe her so much he was still sorely tempted to chase after her and beg her to stay for ever. 'As I cannot believe it was done with any malice, even if it was done at all.'

'Whether it was intentional or not makes no matter.'

'If we were overheard it certainly matters, as the way I recall that particular conversation, it was entirely one-sided. I did all the talking and Hope listened, so if they overheard anyone, it was me. Doesn't that make it all my fault and not hers?'

'She fed you the questions.'

She vehemently shook her head. 'I had a speech all worked out. I wanted her to know the whole truth about what happened in case it was my illness which was keeping you both apart. In fact, I told her much more than was printed in the papers. Things I have never even dared to tell you.' She frowned then. 'Things about my first bout of madness which I'd have thought were much more salacious than all the nonsense about them treating me in a spinning chair and bleeding me twice monthly.'

As much as he wanted to believe it, he needed proof. 'Like what?' Because they certainly knew all about the laudanum and the restraints and how nonsensical she had been by the end of those three long years.

'Like the fact that it was birthing you that sent me mad in the first place and that I couldn't bear to look at you at all until you were nearly three years old. I hated you that much.'

'What?' He was reeling. 'You hated me?' How had he not known that?

'I don't hate you any more, dear, so don't look so distraught. I was ill. Dr Long Fox calls it the insanity of childbirth and he believes it is more common a condition than most people realise, although I had a particularly dreadful dose of it. Hope and I talked extensively about it, yet the newspapers made no mention of it. Their report was too obsessed with Mill House, which we barely touched upon at all as I recall, and when we did I am sure I was vague on the details, though the ones they printed were so accurate.'

'Not that accurate! They said you tried to hang yourself.'

'I did, dear. But I certainly never mentioned that shameful secret to Hope any more than I ever did to you. In fact, not even Clowance knew. Some things are just too personal.'

It was his turn to slump in the chair.

Chapter Twenty-Four

If Hope expected him to cool down and quickly see sense, he didn't. As the storm raged outside, and long after an overtired Faith had gone to her bedroom, he remained resolutely downstairs ensconced with Maria.

As miserable as she was by this depressing turn of events when she had hoped the grand gesture would be enough to get through his thick, Cornish skull, she flatly refused to cry herself to sleep. She had shed enough tears over Luke and the tragic truth was, if he couldn't trust her and her love for him, then they really were done and the wretched long journey from Bath in the worst possible weather had all been for nothing. With as much dignity as she could muster, she would leave first thing and never darken the dratted fool's door again. And good riddance to him!

She furiously tossed her brush back in her over-night bag and hauled out her nightgown. Let him wallow in his self-inflicted martyrdom alone for ever. She wouldn't care and she wouldn't miss him. In her temper, she knotted the laces on the back of her dress rather than undo them, forcing her to fight her arms out of the stupid thing done up. Which meant she was in the midst of wrestling the too-tight bodice over her breasts when her door was flung open and he came in uninvited, still dressed in the crumpled damp clothes he had come home in, like a wet dog with his tail between his legs.

'Can we talk?'

Trapped neither in nor out of the dress, she grabbed a pillow to cover herself before she glared at him with haughty disdain. 'I tried that and you refused to listen!'

'I thought we had already established weeks ago that I am a ham-fisted clod with straw for brains. If we hadn't, then I'll reiterate it now.' Defeated, he sat heavily on her mattress. 'I am sorry, Hope. I should have believed you and I certainly should have afforded you the right of rebuttal before I stormed off like a lion with a thorn in his paw, dragging my poor mother with me and behaving like a coward.' Two dark and very miserable eyes peered up at her through a windswept riot of wild hair. 'My only defence, not that it is any way a defence, is I have never been hopelessly in love before, so had no concept of how irrational that state would render me.' He shook his shaggy head, his expression more wretched than she had ever seen it. 'My mother went mad because she gave birth to me.'

Hope nodded, feeling sorry for him for that awful fact. 'She told me.'

'Yet you never told a soul—even me.'

'It wasn't my secret to tell but I did urge her to talk to you about it as she carries a lot of unnecessary guilt for it. For it wasn't her fault. Apparently, many physicians are starting to recognise such melancholy after childbirth as an uncommon side effect.' In the absence of anything else to fill her time between the interminable carriage ride from Bloomsbury to Bath, Hope had done her research.'

'She said she didn't tell me because she didn't want to make me feel any more guilty than I already did for not being there when they took her away to Mill House.'

'And do you feel guilty for that? Even though you know none of it was your fault?'

He sighed and his big shoulders slumped. 'It's like an enormous sack of potatoes which I continually carry on my back and likely, according to my considerably much more rational mother, I use it to justify being an overbearing, self-righteous and controlling idiot.'

'You are all those things sometimes, I cannot deny.' They were part and parcel of his legendary Duff charm.

He nodded. 'I would have picked you roses but the bushes have only just been planted and the damn things are only twigs.' Then she saw tears swimming in those soulful brown eyes and all her residual anger at him melted in one fell swoop. 'She tried to hang herself at Mill House. Twice.' He held up two fingers just in case she couldn't count. 'Because in her confused state thanks to the drugs and the punishments, and because she never knew I tried to visit, she thought I had abandoned her and wanted all the pain to end.'

He swiped a tear away and Hope couldn't stand it any more. She dropped the pillow and wrapped her arms around him. 'None of that was your fault, Luke. You cannot take on the guilt for Cassius's cruelty. You were only eighteen, powerless and all alone. He was the villain of the piece and both you and your mother were his unwitting victims.'

Whether he believed that yet or not, she couldn't tell. Knowing Luke, he'd always blame himself as that was how he was made. A noble rescuer to his core, one who would likely have to pick a thousand roses before she knocked that stubborn habit out of him. 'My mother is adamant she told nobody about those suicide attempts except for Dr Long Fox. Not you, not Clowance and certainly not me, so how the blasted papers got hold of it I have no clue.'

'Somebody else must know.'

'Again, a fact which my annoying, nagging and rational mother has bashed me over the head with. We spent the last hour going through that damning article and she pulled out several pertinent details which I, in my disturbed and heartbroken state, completely missed. Aside from omitting the insanity of childbirth, they knew scant details about her first, real illness and her subsequent treatment here in Cornwall.' He counted them off on his fingers. 'They also apparently knew nothing about her final and most intense bout of treatment at Brislington House, where she initially veered, as you know, between catatonic and nonsensical for a good year after I rescued her. However, they were incredibly knowledgeable about what happened in Mill House—privy to information that I never was. I was barred from the place by Cassius and was never able to receive any reports on my mother.'

'Then the leak has to come from there or it can be traced to it. They must have sent reports to your brother as he paid the bills. Could they have gone to one of your managers? Could one of them, disgruntled by your interference, have leaked those reports to get you off their back? If we have learned one thing about Cassius in these last few months, it was that the man did like to delegate...'

'Delegate!' He slapped his forehead. 'Of course he did. Cassius didn't like to get his hands dirty and delegated all the responsibilities he had no patience for!' He smiled for the first time, but it came without any of his charm and mischief. 'Abigail leaked it! She told me once that she answered *all* his correspondence. Dealt with all the unsavoury issues he created, kept all his secrets and protected his reputation. I'll lay money it was her. Her father lives in Salisbury and Mill House is in Wiltshire so I wouldn't put it past her to have found that awful private madhouse in the first place!'

'But without proof, those are quite serious accusations to put to her...' Hope frowned as something sparked in her own memory. 'Although it would certainly explain her horror when she tried to call and I informed her you had gone expressly to Cornwall to fetch your mother. She was visibly unsettled by the news. More unsettled than she was to learn that we were neighbours when she did her utmost to put me in my place as she staked her claim to you. I do recall feeling that was particularly odd at the time but put her hostility down to my being a Brookes instead of a blue blood. As you probably guessed, we sisters and she have never got on but she knows none of us suffers fools gladly so she usually gives us a wide berth.'

'She wanted to marry me.'

'What?' Hope was appalled.

'But calmed down about that when I promised to gift her the Mayfair house.'

'You wanted to gift that witch one of your most valuable properties? Have you any idea how many of your hospitals that tiny piece of Berkeley Square alone could fund?'

He smiled and took her hand. 'And perhaps that is exactly why she exposed my mother's scandal and did her manipulative utmost to make it look like you were the culprit. She sees you as a threat, Hope. My clever, level-headed second pair of eyes who might have thwarted her if we married at the speed at which all the gossip columns suggested.'

'You'll still need proof to clip her spiteful wings.' The thought of it all made Hope's blood boil.

'I'll get it. My solicitor holds all the accounts and he'll have kept all the correspondence pertaining to them. He's annoyingly thorough about paperwork. But in the meantime...' He cupped her cheek and stared deep into her eyes. 'Are we all right, Hope? As I have no idea how I am supposed to navigate my strange new world without you by my side to stop me from thinking I always know best, when clearly I know nothing.'

'You knew how to get Mr Cooper to see sense and how to convince him it had all been his idea in the first place.'

'Ah...you know about that, do you?'

She took his hands, revelling in their warmth and strength and well-meant stubbornness. 'Can we make a pact you and I? No matter what it is and no matter what else we have promised to others, can we solemnly pledge never to keep any more secrets between us, Luke?'

'I'll agree on one condition.'

'Which is?'

He kissed her and smiled wolfishly against her mouth. 'That you allow me to unlace this stupid dress you're trapped in while you strip me out of these cold wet clothes before I catch my death.' He didn't wait for an answer as his fingers went straight to the task. 'Besides, I'm pretty sure there are a few spots I haven't kissed, so I shall need to remedy that now or I won't sleep. And because I have a lot of flesh to cover and a thorough job will likely take me several hours, you'd best get naked immediately, Hope, so I can properly make amends for being such a straw-brained clod.'

'You're incorrigible.'

'That I am—but you love me for it.' His lips nuzzled the most sensitive spot of her neck and she knew she was already lost.

She sighed and surrendered to the pleasure.

'That I do, Lord Trouble.'

With all her full-to-bursting but no longer pessimistic heart.

What a week it has been, Dear Reader, and it is still only Tuesday! Yesterday Mayfair witnessed not one but two separate bouts of fisticuffs. The first occurred in Hatchard's, when two tenacious matrons came to blows over the last copy of Phantasma *left on the shelves. Mr Hatchard himself couldn't separate the two, and despite assuring them that more copies of the lauded new novel by Hope Brookes-Duff would arrive on the morrow, a constable had to be called to bring order and peace to Piccadilly!*

But then the poor chap was called again, to Berkeley Square, to assist in the eviction of the disgraced A., Marchioness of T., who had to be practically peeled from the railings while her belongings were unceremoniously loaded on to a cart by her burly brother-in-law.

Rumours abound that he, along with his indomitable mother, intends to turn the luxurious mansion into a hospital for the insane despite uproar from their well-heeled neighbours.

And, if that wasn't enough scandal from that entertaining family, while they all celebrated tonight's eagerly anticipated opening of soprano Miss C. of Bloomsbury in the Theatre Royal's The Marriage of Figaro *at Vauxhall Gardens later last night, the Viscountess E., sister to the Marchioness of T. and the above-mentioned Miss C., went into labour. We are delighted to hear that the first grandchild of the B. family from Bloomsbury is doing well and that the proud father is already quite besotted with his little girl.*

However, the persistent rumour that Miss C. of Bloomsbury has vowed to compete with her talented elder sisters by topping them both with the grand and lofty title of Duchess has yet to be corroborated...

Whispers from Behind the Fan
January 1815

* * * * *

*If you enjoyed this story, be sure to read
the first book in Virginia Heath's
The Talk of the Beau Monde miniseries*

The Viscount's Unconventional Lady

*And whilst you're waiting for the next book,
why not check out her other great reads*

Lilian and the Irresistible Duke
Redeeming the Reclusive Earl
"Invitation to the Duke's Ball"
in Christmas Cinderellas

*And look out for the next book in
The Talk of the Beau Monde miniseries,
coming soon!*